☑ W9-CAV-307

THE CROCODILE'S KILL

EAST TIMOR CRIME SERIES Nº1

Chris McGillion

coffeetownpress

Kenmore, WA

Coffeetown Press books published by Epicenter Press

Epicenter Press
6524 NE 181st St. Suite 2
Kenmore, WA 98028.
www.Epicenterpress.com
www.Coffeetownpress.com
www.Camelpress.com

For more information go to: www.Epicenterpress.com

All rights reserved. No part of this book may be reproduced or transmitted in any form or by any means, electronic or mchanical, including photocopying, recording, or any information storage and retrieval system, without permission in writing from the publisher.

This is a work of fiction. All characters, events and village names are the product of the author's imagination.

The Crocodile's Kill
Copyright © 2022 by Chris McGillion

ISBN: 9781942078753 (trade paper)
ISBN: 9781942078760 (ebook)

Printed in the United States of America

Dedication

To Spooks

Acknowledgments

My thanks to Michael Jackson (Emeritus Professor, University of Sydney) for igniting my passion for crime novels, Raymond Harding and Bill Blaikie for generous and excellent editorial advice, Spiro Zavos for teaching me how to write in order to be read, Rick Jacobsen as a sounding board for plot ideas, Damian Grace for unflinching if questionable confidence in my abilities, my Tetun language teacher and adviser on things Timorese Domingas Gama Soares, Kavita Bedford for travelling the same road in tandem and with encouragement, and last, but not least, my wife Cathryn for tolerating the self-absorption that engulfs me when I'm writing.

Prologue

*T*he forest bordering the main plot where the young man grew food for his household was inhabited by the spirits of the dead. If anyone ventured into the forest without permission the spirits would be angered, and the trespasser could invite their revenge. But there was no way to eke out a living in this rugged and remote part of East Timor other than by subsistence farming and when the man was married and had another mouth to feed, he prepared a second plot inside the forest for there was no other land available for him to farm. The plot he chose was just inside the land reserved for the spirits and he convinced himself they wouldn't mind. Besides, he wore a small stone talisman the sorcerer he'd bartered it from said would protect the wearer from harm.

He was weeding the new garden now with a hoe he had fashioned from scrap metal and a pole. It was hot and he was sweating. He stopped to stretch his back and wipe his brow and when he did the silence and the stillness distracted him. The wind had dropped, the trees hung limp in the afternoon heat, and there were no birds to be seen or heard. The dogs were asleep, and the piglet was lying in its enclosure. His wife had walked down the dusty track to the kiosk for cooking oil, hence there was no swoosh of her broom as she swept the yard or banging of pots as she prepared the evening meal. Everything was quiet, totally quiet, and for a moment he sensed that the world around him had sucked in all the sound, all the movement, all the air and was holding its breath before releasing it in a gale.

That's when they jumped him. They came out of the trees and long grass in the further reaches of the forest. They punched him to the ground then kicked him and hit him with whatever they could lay their hands on—rocks, sticks, his own hoe—until he lay unconscious. They tied him to a makeshift cross made of freshly cut bamboo poles they had brought with them and dragged him to the front of his hut. Four of the men pitched him up against a large sandalwood tree in full view of the dirt road that fronted the hut. One used a sharp knife to inflict the stigmata into his hands, feet, and side. Those wounds would drain him of his supernatural powers and impose the white magic of Jesus over the black magic that had taken hold of his soul. Another man took a plastic lighter from his pocket and struck it against dried leaves on a branch he had found in the yard. He threw the branch onto the parched thatch of the hut and the roof burst into flames. He lit another branch and threw it through the open door to ensure the hut and all its contents would be razed to the ground. The last of the men cut the throat of the piglet that had started squealing at the mayhem and heaved the carcass into the pyre.

The first the young man's wife knew something was wrong was when she heard the dogs barking, looked up and noticed smoke curling up above the trees as she walked back home. It was too much smoke, too thick, and too dark to come from anywhere but their hut. In her panic she thought it must have started from the stove in the lean-to she used for cooking but as she began to run, she thought again. Perhaps her husband had laid down on the mat on the dirt floor of their hut and fallen asleep with a cigarette in his fingers. She cursed him for that but as she drew nearer caught the smell of burning flesh and screamed. She dropped the cooking oil and ran toward the hut but when she reached the yard, she saw her husband hanging against the tree. She stopped, blessed herself, and collapsed in the dirt at his feet.

The dogs were barking furiously now as they ran back and forth in front of the burning hut. Neighbours further down the road had also seen the smoke and heard the dogs and some, though only a few, had come running. Two of them cut the young man down, his body naked and bloodied, while another watched the hut collapse as its wooden frame turned to black cinder and then to ash. Inside the doorway lay the piglet that its owner had been keeping to mark the *anniversary of his wife's mother's death. Fat sizzled from the sides of its bloated body. None of the neighbours had a vehicle but one went for help. By the time the local priest had driven up and they'd taken the injured man to the clinic, he was dead.*

In the sacred meeting house where the assailants had been given permission for the attack they now regrouped. They were sullen. They knew they would have to wash the blood off their hands and off the knife, but that could wait. One or two were shaking with remorse as the gravity of what they had done sunk in. They passed a container of palm wine around to settle themselves. None made eye contact with another.

"We should have cut off his head and put it on a pole as well," said one of the harsher men after a while.

"We did enough," grunted an elder and the group fell silent once more.

The marriage between the young man and his wife had been an arranged one, as many are in the rural districts of East Timor. He had been good to his wife but not in the way a husband should be. His sexual preference meant that his wife had borne no children even after three years of marriage and that seemed odd to the villagers. He had also aroused suspicion when he was spotted skulking through the village at night for what reason no one could tell. After a baby disappeared in the area and a rumour had developed that a demon must be involved, even more attention turned to him. He had been liked well enough, but he had also been a little odd and among people for whom conformity meant security that had been enough to seal his fate.

No one would be held accountable for the young man's death. It would be seen as reasonable, even necessary under the circumstances. And because he was regarded as a demon he would be buried outside the village in an unmarked grave and his wife would have to move elsewhere with whatever possessions she could salvage. After all, anyone associated with a demon could themselves turn evil, threaten the village, and thus become a target for vigilantes. That is why one of the men involved in the attack had wielded a rock with particular ferocity. He wanted to be regarded as a zealous defender of his community rather than have anyone suspect he was cowardly or effete—much less the kind of man who would take another as a lover.

Chapter 1

The building was a disused mechanic's workshop in an abandoned industrial block on the outskirts of Flagstaff. The door at the front was grated and hard to breach. The one at the back, set aside for entry to living quarters, was old and rotting around the frame and would yield to a solid blow. A grubby white van was parked in the yard behind the workshop by the back steps. He'd left the gate into the yard unlocked in a hurry to get inside and do whatever it was he was going to do to the girl.

The thought was torturing FBI Agent Sara Carter.

"What the fuck is keeping them?" she said and punched the steering wheel.

"It's only been a few minutes, Sara. They'll be here," said her partner, Frank Rozzetti.

"I don't like people calling me Sara," she said. "I told you that."

"Sorry, sorry, I know," said Rozzetti trying to mollify her tetchiness. "I forgot."

Flush against the workshop on its right was a two-storey brick warehouse. The only way in was by a front roller door which was padlocked. On the opposite side of the workshop was an alley across from a disused junkyard protected by a high mesh fence. He was theirs for the taking, she knew that, because even if he made a run for it, he'd remain in clear sight and they could take him easily.

"Come on," she grumbled. "Come on!"

They were parked in an unmarked sedan on the corner where the far end of the alley met a road. An Arizona State police cruiser was concealed two blocks away and the two officers from it sat silent in the back of the FBI agents' car. All that was missing was the other FBI unit to cover the front of the workshop.

"Come on, goddamit," Carter hissed again.

"I know this means a lot to you but you'll screw it up if you let the past get under your skin," Rozzetti said. "You could put the girl at risk and—"

Just then Rozzetti's radio earpiece came to life and he covered it with his hand to listen.

"Holy shit," he said and turned to Carter. "They've collided with a garbage truck and Tanner's knocked out cold. Rainey's with him. He's called in another unit. Five minutes, tops."

Carter was thinking of the van, the unlocked gate, the likely horror unfolding inside.

"I'm not waiting," she declared. She turned to the two uniformed police officers. "New plan. You two cover the front. We'll go in the back. Leave the battering ram. Move!" She was out of the driver's door as the troopers started up the alley. "Break down the door," she barked at Rozzetti. "I'm in first."

He grabbed the battering ram and zigzagged toward the rear door of the workshop using the van as a blind. Carter shadowed him, sidearm drawn.

"Now!" she cried.

Rozzetti mounted the few steps, swung the battering ram at the lock and the door flew open and bounced back off an inside wall.

"FBI!" Carter shouted.

Kitchen area: empty. Bathroom to the side: empty.

She slid through to the next room, her back hard against the wall. Rozzetti was close behind, scanning alcoves, cupboards, furniture.

The girl was on a mattress in the corner. Ajei Billy, from just south of Tuba City. Pretty Navajo girl. Twelve years old. Abducted from a bus stop on her way to school. Her hands were tied to a duct behind her head. She was naked, skirt, blouse and underwear scattered across the floor with her sneakers. Carter registered the welt developing under the girl's left eye, the bruises on her arms and wrists, the blood on the inside of her thighs. Ajei was panting through her nose, tape covering her mouth.

The terror in the girl's eyes ignited rage in Carter. "It's okay. I'm a police officer," she said trying to temper her voice. "Where is he?"

The girl gaped back at Carter through tears streaming down her cheeks.

Helpless.

Hurt.

Badly hurt.

Rozzetti slipped into the room to the right of Carter and lifted his sidearm toward the ceiling. A kitchen knife was lying near the mattress, used to cut away the girl's clothing or force her compliance. He reached for the tape on Ajei's mouth but she turned her head to one side.

A sound of glass breaking came from the workshop proper. Carter slipped to the adjoining door and tested the latch. It gave but something was wedged against the door and she couldn't force it open with her shoulder. "He's out a window. Stay with her," she snapped to Rozzetti and sprang back through the kitchen to the rear door.

He was in the alley trying to hold up his pants as he lurched away from the troopers at the front of the workshop who were out of sight and unaware of what was happening.

"FBI!" Carter called. "Stop or I'll fire!" But immediately she holstered her sidearm, leapt from the stairs, ricocheted off the van and took off after him.

She tackled him as he'd made it onto the roadway. He rolled over and covered his face with his hands, rough prison tats on his fingers and arms. "Please," he cried. "Don't hurt me! Please!"

Carter rose and stood over him. "Is that what the girl said, Preston?" she demanded. "'Please don't hurt me.'" She took deep breaths to calm herself. It wasn't working. "Is it?"

"Please!" he whimpered. "Please!"

She kicked him in the face, knocking his head back violently. She thought she felt his nose break and saw his lip split and blood spray over his face and on to the asphalt. He let out a deep, wrenching groan. Footsteps were coming down the alley and she heard Rozzetti order the troopers to hold back, call an ambulance and stay with the girl. Carter was focused on Preston.

"Please!" he spluttered, coughing blood and spittle.

"Was that a turn-on for you?" she yelled at him. "Her pleading with you not to hurt her?" She kicked him a second time, even harder. "Get you hard, did it? You sick fuck!" And again she kicked, and again, working the ribcage until Rozzetti stepped in between them.

"Easy Carter," Rozzetti said. "Let it go. We've got him." He crouched down, examined Preston, winced at the sight of the man's injured face and scanned the surrounds. Carter stepped away, brushed the dirt from her clothes and unclipped her handcuffs. "Wait a minute," Rozzetti said holding up a hand. He scurried back across the road to the junkyard, checked to see if anyone was watching, and, on his second attempt, managed to scale the gate. A few moments later he clambered back, clasping a length of pipe in his kerchief. He took Preston's right hand and wrapped it around one end of the pipe, then dropped it on the ground beside the man. "He came at you with the pipe and you had to disarm him," Rozzetti said not bothering to look at Carter. Then he walked back toward the workshop without waiting for a reply.

• • •

"Thank you for coming in, Agent Carter. Would you like a coffee, a cool drink, water?"

They were in the FBI's Flagstaff agency building and more precisely the office of Resident Agent in Charge Michael Slaton. Slaton was the closest thing in this part of Arizona to Carter's boss and was asking the question. It was two days after she'd arrested Leroy Preston.

"No thanks," she replied and noticed him look expectantly at her. "Sir," she added.

She sat down across from his desk, legs crossed, arms folded tight across her chest. "Preston's lawyer has filed a complaint alleging excessive force on your part, occasioning his client severe physical and mental trauma," Slaton read from the contents of a red folder on his desk. He waited, awkward, gaze fixed on the file in front of him.

"He was raping the girl!" she said regretting the anger in her voice. "He took off down the alley," she continued in a more moderate tone. "When I caught up with him he took a swing at me. I did what I had to do. It's all in my report."

"Ah yes. Your report," said Slaton. He looked up. "And Rozzetti's report backs up yours. Of course."

Carter didn't reply, just jiggled her leg. The Resident Agent pushed his chair back, rose from his desk and walked across to the window which overlooked the building's car park. He stood silent for a moment, wiping his brow with a tissue from his pocket.

"Preston was left with a broken nose, fractured eye socket, several fewer teeth, and two fractured ribs," Slaton said. He paused. "This isn't the first time, is it Carter?"

She sat up in her chair. "First time for what? What are you implying...sir?"

This time Slaton didn't answer. He threw the tissue into a waste basket and leaned on the windowsill staring into the car park, agitated by something that had caught his eye.

"What are those damned kids doing in the visitor's car space?" He reached back over his desk and pressed the button on the intercom. "Margaret. Margaret! There are kids on skateboards clowning around in the visitor's car park. Get security and clear them off right away, will you? It's not a good look."

He released the button. "Damned kids," he said and slumped back into his chair. He closed the red folder and slid another, yellow this time, in front of him. Then he tried a smile which on him always resembled an affliction.

"How would you like a change of scenery?" he said leaning back casually in his chair. "Sort of, you know, a working holiday."

"I don't understand...sir," Carter said.

"Sara. May I call you Sara?" Slaton asked and continued without an answer. "We've had a request, Sara, to send, that is, to lend an officer to an INTERPOL operation in er—" he sat up straight, opened the yellow folder, then closed it and lent back— "in Dili, Timor-Leste. Well, that's what they call it there. Everybody else knows it as East Timor. Means the same thing but one's the Portuguese name and one's the English." He stopped. "Where was I? Oh yes. Three months max. There's a lot of stuff going on there that would interest you. Drug trafficking, people smuggling, and even a child abduction case I understand. Same as you've been doing here, Sara. You'd be perfect. Why—"

"I'm not sure I even know where East Timor is," Carter protested.

"Well, it's, um—" Slaton opened the folder and shuffled through several sheets of paper. He held one up to her on which there was a small map she couldn't clearly see. "Between Indonesia and Australia. You know. Southeast Asia." He put the map back in the folder and stared at it rather than meet Carter's glare. "Nice. An island—well, half an island anyway. Eastern half. Hence the name. Western half is part of Indonesia."

"Is this some kind of joke?" she asked.

"Not at all," Slaton replied looking slightly affronted. "Why would you think that?"

"First I get called in here to answer questions about Preston's arrest. Now you seem to be making me a job offer. Or is it some kind of order because if it's an offer the answer's 'No thanks' and if it's an order you're forgetting I'm assigned by the Phoenix office to investigate the rest of these reservation abductions—"

This time Slaton interrupted, his smile gone, his finger tapping the folder in front of him. "This request has come to headquarters from the State Department. They've received a bunch of them. Sending a dozen agents all over the place. Seems we need to pick up the slack on our international policing commitments—"

"Why us? Why here?" Carter demanded to know.

"Maybe they view us as the top cops for hopeless causes," Slaton said showing his irritation. "I gather East Timor is a lot like our reservations. You know, incurably backward. Or maybe because they see us as surplus to operations in the Southwest. How should I know? But what I do know is we must prove our worth." He tapped his finger harder into the folder. "These days every field agency needs to prove its worth."

He sat back, composed himself. "I can't send Whitman because he's an idiot. Only reason he's here is his uncle's a judge or something. Camacho is about to have a baby, as you know. Rainey and Tanner are needed to testify in that Apache murder trial next month and in the meantime they can take over from you on reservation abductions. And Rozzetti, well, you know my thoughts about Rozzetti. Besides, he's put in a lot of years and his wife's not well. Bad heart or liver or gallbladder—some damn thing. But I can't expect him to head off on some damn fool—" He stopped, embarrassed by the faux pas. "He's earned consideration," he said.

"Haven't I earned consideration as well?" Carter interrupted. "You know how hard I've been working—"

"Of course I know you work hard," he cut in and lent forward. "That's why you are perfect for this assignment," he continued less abruptly, "and that's also why I'm suggesting this…this break. And it'd be easier for you than any of the others." Slaton waved his hand vaguely at the window. "You're young, single, you're not hooked up with anyone—" He paused, gave her a quizzical look and added, "Are you?"

"That's none of your damn business," Carter said raising her voice. Slaton raised both hands in mock surrender on the point. "Anyway, how do we 'prove our worth' by sending a field agent overseas from an office as small as this already?" she asked.

"Well, with Camacho on maternity leave and you gone they'd have to give us a replacement. At least one. Regulations. When an office gets a replacement, it slips off the radar for potential closures."

Slaton closed the folder.

"None of that—" she began.

"Besides," Slaton said talking over her. "This will look good on your résumé, Sara." Carter caught the sneer but before she could react he was on his feet and back to the window. "It's all in that yellow folder. Air tickets, itinerary—everything you need. Take it. Pressure's coming down from head office on field agencies to stop dragging their feet so you leave day after tomorrow. That'll make us look good, responsive, efficient. Briefing at the local embassy on arrival. Usual stuff. Check with Margaret if you have questions. She's fully briefed on the arrangements."

Slaton had his back to Carter now indicating the conversation was over as far as he was concerned. He was staring down into the car park again. "Why haven't those damned kids—?" He turned and reached for the intercom but Carter rose and put her hand over the button.

"And if I refuse?" she demanded.

Slaton looked up at her, his teeth gritting. "Then, Agent Carter, I'll have to launch a thorough investigation into the Preston arrest, inform Phoenix I need to suspend work on those reservation abductions you seem to have made a personal crusade, and assign you to a desk counting paperclips until I'm convinced you can be trusted to operate outside of this building without becoming your own judge, jury and executioner!"

• • •

"Sounds like typical bullshit to me," said Rozzetti, trying to catch the barman's eye. "But three months on a tropical island? Why complain?"

The barman looked over and Rozzetti indicated two more drinks. They were side by side on stools in a small bar in downtown Flagstaff. Carter glanced at her partner for the first time since she'd sat down. "Why complain?" Carter repeated. "Preston abducted and raped that girl, Frank. She was twelve years old, for Chrissake. Twelve. The fucker had priors. His lawyers'll claim a psycho condition, deprived childhood, parental fucking abuse or some other crap and he'll be out doing it again in no time. That's why I'm complaining."

Rozzetti finished his first beer as the other two arrived. "Well I thought you were going to draw your sidearm and shoot the bastard," he said, chuckling to himself.

Carter gave him a cold stare. "Don't worry, I was tempted."

He shot her a sideways glance then stared into his drink. "Look Carter. We've been partners since you came to Flagstaff. And for most of that time you've been like a bomb about to explode. Three months away might do you good. Chill out. Relax a little, you know?"

"I don't want to relax, Frank," she said clenching the glass in front of her with both hands.

He looked at her, took a sip of beer and wiped his mouth. "I know you don't," he said. "And that's the problem. How many years has it been now? Bec's gone, Carter. You're never going to find her now. You have to let go of the past."

Carter sat motionless, staring at the brightly coloured bottles lining the wall behind the bar but only seeing the dark images inside her head.

• • •

It was six hours from Flagstaff to Los Angeles via Phoenix, twenty hours from Los Angeles to Singapore via Tokyo-Narita. Then it was a stopover at an airport hotel in Singapore during which she slept fitfully for a few hours, showered and boarded a plane for another four hours over the Equator, over the Java Sea, over the Flores Sea and on to Dili, the capital of the country called Timor-Leste but known as East Timor––no time to catch her breath, no time to relax or take in any sights. But that's how she'd wanted it. She figured the sooner she arrived, the sooner she could leave. As the plane made its approach to the airstrip Carter peered down apathetically on a city that stretched out along a coastline between the gun-barrel grey of the sea and the fading form of a high ridgeline. In between there didn't appear to be a building more than four or five storeys in height, the streets were dark, and there were few vehicles on the roads.

The plane taxied to a stop outside what passed for a terminal at the end of a poorly-lit palm-lined walkway. Along with the eight other passengers on the flight, Carter exited the plane. The tarmac was still quite warm underfoot. She paid for her visa at a tiny booth before dealing with the immigration and customs controls located in the main building. It was hot inside and the air was sticky with humidity. The air-conditioner apparently had stopped working. She'd only brought one suitcase which had been quickly unloaded and a shoulder bag. Just about anything else she needed she was assured she could get in Dili--except cash. Twelve years after East Timor became independent in 2002, there was only a handful of ATMs in Dili and occasionally they either didn't work or ran out of money. Large withdrawals from banks were uncommon. She was carrying two thousand American dollars—the Timorese having adopted American currency as their own, although retaining Portuguese centavos for coinage. The two thousand was to get her by until the embassy could get more to her.

Outside the terminal a small huddle of taxi drivers in shorts and flip-flops touted for her business but she walked toward a neatly- dressed Timorese man carrying a printed sign that read 'Sara Carter'.

"Welcome to Timor-Leste, Agent Carter," the man said. He took her suitcase and gestured toward a waiting embassy vehicle. "I hope your flight was a pleasant one," he added with a smile when they were seated.

"It was long and I'm tired. But thank you. How long until we get to the hotel?" Carter asked.

"Ten minutes," the man replied. "It's not far and there is not much traffic now."

Nor was there much to see on the way. The night was closing in, most of the streets were deserted. There were few signs of life aside from stray dogs and men squatting in shadowy groups smoking cigarettes. Flagstaff was not much bigger than Dili, maybe even smaller, but it was close enough to Phoenix and even Las Vegas not to matter. Dili was a long way from anywhere. And

Flagstaff was fully connected to the twenty-first century with ATMs, serviceable air conditioning, and street lighting. How had Slaton described East Timor? 'Incurably backward'—that was it. For once it appeared he might have been right.

Chapter 2

Investigator Vincintino Cordero of the Timorese national police was driving north toward the road that wrapped itself like a belt around the shoreline of Dili. Ahead, he could see the faint outline of Atauro Island, 15 miles out in the wide expanse of sea Timorese called *Tasi Feto,* or female sea to distinguish its calm waters from their opposite—Timor's southern, more turbulent, *Tasi Mane* or male sea. As he passed the elegant white *Palacio do Governo* which housed the offices of the Prime Minister, he gave a sarcastic salute to the current leadership, then turned left, rounded the harbour lighthouse and genuinely blessed himself, as he always did, as he drove by the statue of a dying Sebastião Gomes. He was now heading along the *Avenida de Portugal.* On his right the sea sparkled silver in the early spring morning light under a cloudless blue sky. On his left, new buildings— embassies, hotels, banks, government offices—were spaced here and there between the burnt-out structures from more violent times that no-one had the time or money to replace. One city: two very different eras.

Further along the *Avenida* vacant lots appeared where water buffalo grazed lazily in sunlight filtered through the bright purple and red flowers of bougainvillea vines that lent Dili its distinctive tropical appearance. Coils of sweet-smelling smoke rose from rubbish smouldering under giant fig trees. The road crossed wide stormwater canals that drained into the sea but were also used by crocodiles to venture up the concrete troughs in search of chickens, stray dogs, or food scraps washed down from restaurants in the centre of the city.

Cordero was in no hurry. He rarely was. Since his return to Timor-Leste almost ten years earlier he had settled back well into life in his native land, earning respect in his job and his community. He was genuinely liked as well and largely did as he pleased. At forty years of age he had the lean build of a middleweight and the agility of a man ten years younger. He could boast a full head of black hair and a caramel complexion undamaged by sun or sea. He also retained a youthful energy and an enthusiasm for life that belied his age. He was happily unattached, not tied down to anyone or anything. Except this country. Maybe because he'd been robbed of a childhood here and needed to fill that gap; maybe because his country of birth had set him apart in exile and accordingly had become inseparable from his sense of self.

He weaved slowly through the traffic and settled behind a dump truck with half a dozen bare-chested workers standing in its tray. Each had a T-shirt tied as a kerchief around his neck and their bodies were covered in cement dust from whatever job they'd just left. He waved to them and a couple at least returned the gesture. He was humming a reggae tune until his thoughts were disturbed as he neared his destination, the boutique Hotel Playa. Up ahead was a traffic jam and, in the middle of the *Avenida*, people crowding around what appeared to be a body on the road.

Cordero pulled off to the side and parked his car gingerly on the splintered cement of the sidewalk. He exited and closed the door without locking it, tucked his sunglasses into the neck of his shirt and walked toward the commotion, along a line of banked up motorcycles, trucks, microlets, and dilapidated yellow taxicabs. Roosters were crowing in the yards of the few houses that bordered this stretch of the *Avenida*. Enough of a breeze came off the water to disperse diesel and gasoline fumes and convey a faint odour of salt and decay. Cordero glanced across to where several people were sitting on the seawall selling fish in the rising heat. Some of it would have been caught this morning from the outrigger canoes now beached on the dark sand. The rest would have been bought frozen from the supermarket, thawed overnight and then strung out in the hope that the unwary might pay more than it cost.

"*Polisia. Sees ba sorin,*" he said calmly in Tetun and pushed his way into the middle of the crowd. He didn't bother to show his badge even though he was dressed casually in only a white shirt and casual blue trousers and neither carried any insignia. "Police. Move aside," he repeated and edged away two on-lookers bent over the accident victim. He quickly took note of a yellow motorcycle on its side, its front fender buckled, the front wheel bent out of shape, and a skinny rider lying on his side below him. A few feet away a dark blue Hummer had backed onto the roadway and stopped, its near rear side scarred with flecks of paint from its encounter with the bike. The driver was behind the wheel, talking on his cell phone and ignoring the scene outside. The Hummer's engine was running.

Cordero squatted beside the bike rider. "Are you injured?" he asked, and the rider, though dazed, shook his head. He was a young man, a boy really. His helmet was lightly scratched from where it had hit the ground. He was dressed in worn jeans, cheap, scuffed shoes, and a red T-shirt with 'HairSpray' printed across the front. The T-shirt was ripped, maybe from the fall, maybe from overuse. "What's your name?" Cordero asked.

"Ximenes Florencio," the boy said, speaking through his helmet.

"Okay Ximenes, you can call me Tino. I'm a policeman and I am here to help you. What day is it?" Cordero asked.

"Tuesday," the boy said, lifting off his helmet. "Don't you know?"

"Yes, I know," said Cordero. "I just want to make sure you know. How many fingers am I holding up?"

"Four," said the boy, doubtful about that question as well.

"Good. Can you stand?"

"Yes, give me a moment," said the boy.

"Is this your bike, Ximenes?" asked Cordero rising and again the boy nodded. Cordero looked at the two dozen or more people who had gathered around the bike and its rider. They were the assorted passers-by of any street in Dili at this time of day: office workers, university students, labourers, mothers with babies, and children on their way to school but finding a road accident far more interesting than anything their teachers were likely to tell them. "What happened?" Cordero asked and immediately regretted that he had.

"This crazy guy—" began another young bike rider, unable to contain his anger.

"The motorcycle was moving—" interjected an older taxi driver who'd left his vehicle for a closer look.

"I heard the bang when this big thing—" yelled a woman balancing on tiptoes to be heard across the heads of the others.

"One at a time," Cordero said and held up a hand to stop to the confusing rush of accounts. He looked around quickly, noticed a middle-aged woman standing quietly alongside the bike rider. She was neatly dressed and carrying a canvass bag filled with fresh vegetables purchased from a nearby market. "*Mana*," he said using the informal Timorese form of address meaning 'sister'. "What did you see?"

"The bike was coming this way. Not fast," she said in a clear, dispassionate tone. "I was walking along here from the store down the end of the block." She pointed at the driver of the Hummer. "That man was parked with the front of his vehicle facing the wall of this hotel away from the road. He reversed out onto the road without looking and the bike hit his car. There was no time for the boy to stop. It wasn't his fault." She gestured with her chin. "I think that driver is a foreigner because he hasn't come out of the car to help the boy and he hasn't said anything to anyone. He's just been talking on his cell."

The boy was now standing, holding his helmet in one hand and brushing down his T-shirt and jeans with the other. "Move your arms and legs," Cordero said to the boy who stopped brushing his clothes and did as he was told. "Any pain?"

"No," the boy replied.

"Where were you going, *maun*?" Cordero asked, referring to him as 'brother'. "To work?"

"No. I am a student. I am studying mechanics at the Dili Institute of Technology," the boy answered. "I was on my way to class. I only work nights."

"Well, you're not going to make it to your class on this bike today," said Cordero considering the three miles the boy would have to travel to the institute. "Go over there under the hotel awning for a moment and finish brushing your clothes down. Is there a friend you can call to come and get you and the bike?"

The boy nodded, took a cell from the pocket of his jeans and started to punch in a number. Cordero approached the Hummer. The onlookers shuffled in a small tight pack behind him to the driver's door, anticipating the encounter between a Timorese policeman and a foreigner. A few of the younger school children squeezed forward through the legs of the adults and began to giggle with excitement. Cordero knocked on the window, which was closed, took his badge out of his back pocket and held it against the glass. The driver, tanned, faintly manicured and wearing expensive sunglasses, wound the window down without looking at him. The smell of after-shave wafted out.

"I am Investigator Vincintino Cordero of the Timor-Leste police. Do you speak Tetun?" Cordero asked in that language but the driver said nothing and merely shook his shoulders.

"Do you speak English?" Cordero asked.

"*Oui*," the driver grunted, staring straight ahead.

"Then turn off your motor and show me your licence, please," said Cordero.

The driver rummaged through an expensive-looking leather valise which lay on the passenger's seat and handed the licence to Cordero without making eye contact. Cordero studied the licence then read aloud: "Jacques Albert Touton." The driver nodded, not looking at Cordero. "Originally from Marseilles," Cordero observed. "Do you live now in Timor-Leste, sir, or are you here on business or on holiday perhaps?"

"Holiday. I scuba dive," the Frenchman said.

"I asked you to turn off your motor," Cordero reminded him. The Frenchman huffed before complying.

"Is this your Hummer?" Cordero asked, and stepped back as if to admire the vehicle.

"Of course it's mine," the Frenchman replied. "Rented."

Cordero returned to the driver's window. "I'm told by these witnesses that you reversed onto the roadway without looking. And then your vehicle hit the bike. Do you deny this or are you prepared to accept responsibility?"

The Frenchman appeared to swear in his native tongue, grumbled and answered. "Yes, I seem to have caused the accident. I am responsible. What happens now?" he asked, checked an elaborate diving watch on his wrist and then turned his eyes toward Cordero. His sunglasses caught the sun and reflected the glare back at the police investigator. "I came here to dive not to waste time. I'm in a hurry."

"Would you mind taking off your sunglasses? I prefer to look a man in the eyes when I am talking to him," Cordero said.

The man held Cordero's stare before complying and folding his glasses into his top pocket.

"Happy now?" he said.

"Well," Cordero began, ignoring the taunt and scratching his chin for effect. "We all make mistakes. If you are prepared to recompense the boy you hit, I think we can work something out. That will save me having to write you a traffic violation and save you all the hassles that would entail." He paused for a moment and looked over at the motorcycle rider. "The boy does not appear to be badly injured but his bike is damaged—at the very least the front fender needs fixing, the wheel is bent out of shape, and the bike cannot be ridden. I would guess it would cost maybe two hundred dollars to fix the damage. He will miss his class today, and his work tonight, and he'll have to arrange to be taken home along with his bike. I expect he is likely to find he has bruising and other aches and pains tomorrow which he is not aware of today. Plus his clothes will need replacing. Nothing another one hundred dollars won't fix." Cordero paused, put on a serious face and looked back at the Frenchman. "Three hundred dollars all up. I'm guessing that would be less than the excess on your insurance. Are you willing to pay that? And if you are, do you have the cash on you now?"

The Frenchman had been tapping his fingers impatiently on the steering wheel but he stopped, swore under his breath, nodded his agreement and rummaged through his valise for the money. "I must go now, the boat I am to take will be leaving soon," the Frenchman insisted, counting out the notes and handing them to Cordero.

"One moment," said Cordero holding his hand up against the money. "The law, you know, works at its own pace. I'll have to see if the boy agrees to this arrangement."

With that Cordero left the Frenchman red-faced with anger at the delay and clutching his wad of cash while the crowd of people looked on enjoying his discomfort. He walked over to the boy who was now examining the bike which a couple of onlookers had wheeled over to him. "If you are willing to let the foreigner off without a complaint, he will pay you three hundred dollars for the damage," Cordero told him.

"Three hundred dollars!" the boy cried in disbelief. "Are you kidding?"

"Quiet. Keep it down," urged Cordero. "Yes, three hundred cash in the hand. Where do you work at nights?"

"The Yellow Lotus restaurant in Lecidere. I'm a kitchen hand. Washing, cleaning, you know, that sort of thing," the boy explained.

"Aren't you meant to study at night?" Cordero asked.

"I have big tuition fees to pay, *maun*. And lots of textbooks to buy," the boy protested. "My family does not have a lot of money." An excited look came over his face, he leaned in and lowered his voice. "Is he really going to pay me three hundred dollars? That's fine by me."

Cordero thought for a moment. "Yes. A little more perhaps." He turned and walked back to the Hummer and its driver. "The boy says three hundred and fifty and you have a deal," he said. The Frenchman looked annoyed. "It's less than your excess I think," Cordero repeated. The Frenchman gave him a cold stare. "If that is not satisfactory to you then I will get his statement, write you a ticket and—"

"Okay. Okay," said the Frenchman.

"I will take down your details and take some photos of the bike and the scratches on your vehicle. I will also take down the details of witnesses who saw the accident. But I won't file a report if you pay the boy now and nothing else comes of this incident. Do you understand?" asked Cordero.

"Yes, alright, get on with it," the Frenchman said making a show of looking at his watch again. Then he retrieved the additional fifty dollars from his valise and shoved the notes through the window to Cordero.

Cordero was in no hurry to write down the man's name and address. After he had, he pretended to take several photos on his cell and to get the details of the woman who had told him what had happened. When he had finished thanking her for her help—which is all he actually did—he handed the three hundred and fifty dollars to the boy who gave him a broad, excited grin. Only then did Cordero wave the Frenchman on.

As he pulled away from the hotel, the Frenchman noticed the boy he'd hit waving the money above his head and those around him mocking the foreigner in his big, expensive car.

The traffic along *Avenida de Portugal* was soon flowing smoothly once more. Trucks rumbled by east and west, microlets festooned with gaudy images of young Asian girls rattled passed, motorcycles jostled for position, and taxis without fares blasted loud music from open windows ventilating their hot interiors. The hum, clank and rasp of the traffic drowned out the gentle rush of the sea. The smell of diesel and gasoline filled the air once more.

Cordero walked back to his car, the reggae tune in his head again. What he had told no-one at the accident scene was that after his years of policing in Timor-Leste he still didn't know how to write a traffic ticket properly, what he did know about motorcycle repairers in Dili made him confident that Ximenes Florencio would get his bike fixed for less than fifty dollars, and that he had always thought that foreigners who could afford to rent luxury vehicles to go scuba diving could also afford to help a struggling Timorese student with the cost of bike repairs, a new pair of jeans and a year's tuition at the Dili Institute of Technology.

Chapter 3

The thought of Ajei Billy's violent rape in the workshop in Flagstaff continued to torment Carter in her sleep. For different reasons the way she'd been bundled off on an INTERPOL mission to Timor-Leste also troubled her. As a result, after another restless night, she found herself on Tuesday morning not only tired and resentful but also very grumpy while she waited to meet her Timorese contact at the Hotel Playa in Dili.

She was finishing her morning coffee when the policeman Cordero came up the stairs. The only other patrons in the lounge now were an elderly Australian couple absorbed in a map of Timor-Leste spread out between them on a table and a stern-looking European who had earlier looked up from his laptop as Carter arrived for breakfast, offered a cursory good morning, and then returned to his graphs of rainfall, crop yields and other things indecipherable to the FBI agent.

At the top of the stairs Cordero greeted the boy who worked as a waiter with a handshake and a friendly slap on the shoulder. The two talked in a language Carter didn't understand for a moment and broke into laughter. Then Carter noticed the boy point in her direction, heard Cordero mention the word 'espresso', and waited with an expression of feigned indifference while he ambled towards her. "Agent Carter, I presume," he said and held out his hand. "I am Vincintino Cordero of the Timorese police. Welcome to Timor-Leste and good morning—or *bondia* as we say."

"You're late," replied Carter raising her gaze from the papers that had replaced her toast and bowl of cereal, yoghurt and fruit on the table in front of her.

Cordero, looking mildly embarrassed, took back the unaccepted hand. "Yes. I apologise. There was an accident—"

"I saw that from the balcony," said Carter cutting him off. "Or rather I saw you sorting it out. The Frenchman driving that Hummer is staying here. He was very rude to the boy over there this morning, complaining in French that his toast was cold as if the boy should understand. Then he swore at him and virtually threw the toast back at the boy. Trying to humiliate him."

"He did seem arrogant," Cordero agreed. "Not to mention bad-tempered. But I gave him a short lesson in humility."

"I gathered that. But that's not what I am talking about," said Carter. "You were meant to come to the embassy briefing yesterday. I was told I would meet my Timorese police liaison there."

"Well, I'm more your collaborator than a liaison person," he said by way of gentle correction. She held his gaze. "But, yes, again I apologise. My sister is not very well and yesterday she asked if I could take her son to school and mind her younger one until the neighbour came back home. By then it was too late to make the briefing," Cordero explained. "Her husband is deceased you see," he added hoping that fact would add weight to his excuse.

The boy brought Cordero's espresso and the policeman thanked him. "May I sit?" he asked, gesturing at the table.

"Of course," Carter replied. "Cordero was it?"

"Yes. Vincintino Cordero. But you can call me Tino. Most people do," Cordero said as he sat and took a sip of his coffee. "How was the briefing? And your trip to Timor-Leste?" he asked, registering as he did that this American woman was around 30 years of age and much more attractive than he'd expected.

"I arrived Sunday night and went straight to bed," Carter began. "It was a long trip from Arizona. But mosquitoes kept me awake most of the night. And those roosters start very early." Cordero smiled. Carter didn't. "At the briefing I didn't learn much about what it is I am supposed to do here. The embassy was more excited that Washington seemed to be taking an interest in the posting by sending an FBI agent out. The local press was there, of course, and there were a lot of photos taken with the Ambassador, that kind of thing." She paused for a moment and flicked the pile of papers in front of her. "I've been reading these background papers they gave me but they are very general and not very helpful." She moved the pile of papers aside. "No-one from INTERPOL turned up either," she added—and which he took to be another complaint.

"May I take sugar?" Cordero asked and waited for Carter to gesture her permission. "The INTERPOL office here is very small and understaffed," he said as he spooned sugar into his coffee and stirred it. "I imagine that's why they requested your secondment and maybe why no one was available to turn up at the embassy. But we have a meeting with the director in fifteen minutes and we should both learn much more about this case they have in mind for us then. I know it's to do with missing babies and has quite a few people on edge. But I know nothing of the details either."

Carter considered the expression 'have in mind for *us*' but couldn't decide what she thought about that.

"Fifteen minutes—should we leave now?" she asked.

"There's no rush," he answered.

"You speak good English," she said.

"You as well—for an American," he responded and gave her a cheeky grin hoping to break the ice between them. "I spent twenty years in Australia," he explained. "First at school in Darwin, then at university in Melbourne. I came back here a few years after independence in 2002."

He took another sip of his coffee, found the sugar had sweetened it to his liking, leaned back in his chair and started to relax. "And you?"

Carter shrugged her shoulders. "Born in Sedalia, Missouri. Know it?" she asked but Cordero couldn't decide whether it was a serious question. "Small town. Few people have ever heard of the place. Joined the police force there. Made detective. Went to the FBI training academy in Washington. Then posted to Flagstaff, Arizona. Another small town but better known. Been there about a year."

And that was as much as she'll tell me, he was thinking, *which is a pity because there's something very appealing about her beneath the scowl on her face.* "What do you think of Timor-Leste?" he asked to make conversation.

"I've been here less than 48 hours," she said, "and spent most of that time trying to sleep."

"Sorry," he said. "Bad habit I picked up in Australia." He waited a moment. "You know, when American celebrities arrive in Australia they are usually asked what they think of the place the moment they step off the plane. They have a strange need for constant reassurance down there."

She looked at him without comment.

"Australians," he said. "Funny lot. They drink a lot of beer but at least they generally don't carry guns."

"Do you?" she asked. "Carry a gun, I mean."

"No," he said. "I'm an investigator. I investigate. Others do the rest." They were silent for a moment and then he gestured with his coffee cup. "You must find the sea out there a pleasant change from the scenery you're used to. In Arizona, I mean. Dry, desert country."

Out from the shore a lone fisherman was casting his net from a canoe on water that was a blue lacquer in the sunlight. Beyond him and further out a small cargo ship lay motionless.

"It has its good points," she replied without looking over the water. "And bad," she added as though she might actually be weighing up Cordero. She hesitated a moment. "I took a walk along the beach yesterday after the briefing," she said raising a hand in the direction from which Cordero had driven. "A Timorese man followed me and slapped me on the ass," she added. The abruptness of her language caused Cordero to gag on his coffee.

"Unfortunately, that can happen," he said wiping his lips. "Rare, but it can happen to foreign women. Especially young, and may I say attractive, foreign women walking on their own. I blame the influx of Westerners after independence. They were quite a novelty. Their looks, their clothes. In many ways they remain a novelty. Then of course there is the influence of Western movies and music videos. Oh my God. But I apologise on behalf of my country. Were you injured? Distressed?"

Carter ran her fingers through thick brown hair that hung loose across her shoulders and let the 'attractive' remark pass. She'd learnt that descriptions like that revealed more about male appetites than female appearances. "I kicked him in the groin," she said. "Hard. And left him there to lick his wounds—if you'll pardon the association."

She looked at him with a poker face but Cordero fought to hold back a chuckle. "Usually Timorese will come to the aid of any foreigner—"

"Two Timorese women did come to my assistance. Not that I needed any. One berated the man and the other hit him on the head with her shopping bag," said Carter, raising an eyebrow. "Repeatedly, I might add."

"Timorese women can be very...forthright," Cordero remarked. "Especially since independence. Perhaps that is why I am a single man," he added and laughed.

The two sat in silence for a moment, Cordero finishing his coffee, Carter watching him but slightly less guardedly now. The jousting between them appeared to have ended, or at least been put on hold. "Shall we go then?" he asked. "If you like I will wait while you put those briefing papers in your room and get ready."

"It's okay," replied Carter. "I have a briefcase here and I am eager to get the details of this assignment." While Cordero paid for his coffee she collected her things in the case, stood and turned toward the sea. It was quite a pleasant view, she conceded to herself. When she turned there were skittish sparrows on her table pecking at what remained of her breakfast. She'd always admired how daring sparrows were for their size and felt a slight sense of relief that they could be found in this country as well.

They went downstairs. As they made the sidewalk the Hummer pulled up with a jolt that raised the dust in front of them. The driver got out, slammed the door and stormed straight up to Cordero his face aflame with fury, fists clenched at his sides.

"*J'ai raté ma plongée à cause de toi, connard*," he shouted.

Cordero wiped a droplet of the man's saliva from his face and smiled. He had no idea what the man was yelling at him. Carter stood to Cordero's left side, saying nothing.

The man unclenched his fist and pushed a finger into Cordero's chest. Cordero ignored it and kept his hands in his trouser pockets. The man pushed his finger in harder.

"*J'espère que cela vous rend heureux, vous et votre petite pute,*" he spat.

"Would you mind talking to me in English?" Cordero said, unruffled by the man's threatening tone and behaviour. "I don't understand what you are saying."

"*Connard!*" the man repeated and then sniffed in Carter's direction. "*Pute,*" he said.

Cordero turned away from the man which only made him angrier, as if his yelling and finger-pointing had had no effect. Carter saw the punch coming.

The Frenchman's right elbow flexed and his shoulder dropped slightly as he swiveled to strike. But before his fist could come up she whacked the narrow side of her briefcase between his legs and he doubled up in pain. She dropped the case, grabbed his right wrist and bent it forward. She shifted left, twisted the Frenchman's arm behind his back, and slammed him onto the bonnet of the Hummer. He screamed in agony as she kept pressure on the wrist and said calmly into his ear: "*Restez immobile ou je vais vous casser le poignet.*"

The man dare not move. Carter looked at Cordero. "He was going to punch you, for fuck's sake. Why did you take your eyes off him?"

"I wanted to see how you handled it," he said, unable to come up quickly with a better excuse. "What did he say—and what did you say to him?"

"He said you made him miss his dive. I told him to stop struggling or I'd break his wrist," she answered. "What do you want to do with him?"

"Let him go. I don't think he'll bother anyone else today," answered Cordero.

Carter released the Frenchman and he skulked off into the hotel swearing under his breath. Without further comment she picked up her briefcase. Cordero went to open the car's passenger door for her but she took hold of the handle ahead of him, opened the door, sat, placed her briefcase on the floor and clicked her seat belt into its lock. Cordero walked around the front of the car and sat behind the wheel. He didn't bother with the seatbelt. He switched on the car's ignition, reversed carefully onto the *Avenida*, quickly did a U-turn and drove back the way he had come.

"Thanks," he said.

"I didn't do it for you," she replied, staring straight ahead. "He called me a whore."

He coughed a little awkwardly. "When did you learn French?" he asked to change the subject.

"My stepmother was French," she replied. "Wanted at least one person she could talk to in her native tongue. Couldn't force my father to learn but she could force me." Then she gave him a stern look. "You never take your eyes off them. Didn't they teach you that?" He said nothing. She held the stare. "He called you a cunt by the way," she added to drive home the indignity he had suffered.

The fish mongers had left the sea wall and had been replaced by mangy dogs scrounging for whatever scraps they could find. The day was growing hotter, the tide was heading out, and the storm water canals were spewing rubbish onto the beach. They drove in silence for several minutes, Cordero had settled and was in no hurry to get to wherever they were heading.

"Where's our meeting?" Carter asked.

"At the headquarters of the Scientific Police for Criminal Investigations in Caicoli," he answered. "That's the unit I work for and it's also the building where the INTERPOL people are located. I guess that's why I was assigned to you. Also, I speak English, as you've gathered. Caicoli is only about five or ten minutes from here, depending on the traffic."

There was silence until they approached the statue of Sebastião Gomes. It comprised two figures: one on the ground wounded and dying, the other kneeling, holding the head of his companion and looking up appealing for help. The statue was larger than life, heavy, and immovable as though its point should never be forgotten. Cordero blessed himself as they passed the statue, more discretely this time but with enough of a gesture for Carter to notice.

"That statue," she said after they had passed it. "I was approaching it yesterday when the ass slapping incident occurred. After that I headed back to the hotel. I never did learn what the statue represents."

It was a question statement. Cordero straightened his position behind the wheel before he answered. "The figure lying on his back is Sebastião Gomes," he began. "He was a young teenager protesting Indonesia's occupation of Timor-Leste when Indonesian soldiers took him from the church we just passed on the other side of the road and shot him there in the street." He gestured back toward the statue. "Indonesia invaded in 1975—"

"I gathered that from the briefing papers," she interrupted him.

He glanced across at her, pondering her impatience. "Okay, the shooting of Gomes is what the statue represents. Gomes' funeral at the same church a few days later was attended by thousands of Timorese. After the Mass they all walked behind the coffin to the Santa Cruz cemetery two miles from here where the Indonesians had positioned several army trucks."

He paused a moment, then blew out his breath.

"When the people were inside the cemetery, the flaps on the trucks were rolled up and machine guns opened fire and mowed down the mourners. Then Indonesian soldiers walked through the cemetery shooting anyone they could find including the wounded. Women, children, old people. It didn't matter to them. All up, nearly three hundred were killed." He ran a hand through his hair. "My older brother, Trinidade, was one of them. He'd stayed after I'd left for Australia because he was determined to be a priest here and had been accepted into the seminary."

"I'm sorry to hear that," she said.

"That was 1991," he went on. "The massacre made it hard for the international community to continue to ignore what was happening here. You know, the repression, forced relocations, the use of food supplies as a weapon. Thousands died. Tens of thousands, in fact. But it was another eight long years before Indonesia agreed to the referendum that finally gave us our independence."

Carter made no comment and Cordero fell silent. A few moments later he made a right turn off the *Avenida de Portugal* and into the graceful tree-lined *Avenida Mertires de Patria*. He inched the car through heavy traffic that was merging slowly at an intersection. A hundred yards on from the intersection he turned into a side street.

"We're here," he said and drove into a parking space in front of a nondescript office block flying a large Timorese flag. They left the car, entered the building and Carter followed him down a corridor lined with photographs of dour men in uniform. At the end of the corridor two offices had 'INTERPOL' stamped on their doors. Cordero knocked on the door of the first office and opened it without being invited to enter.

Chapter 4

"*Bondia,* Tino," said a sturdy middle-aged woman in a blue INTERPOL uniform rising from her chair. "Or is it *botarde*? I can never work out when you Timorese decide morning has passed and the afternoon has arrived."

"*Bondia,*" Cordero said emphasising the '*dia*', which signalled 'morning'. "May I present Danique Jacobsen," he said inclining his head toward Carter, "director of INTERPOL operations in Timor-Leste but really the advanced guard of the Dutch attempt to colonise the eastern half of our island having already colonised the west and found it not to their liking." He stood aside. "And this is FBI Agent Sara Carter."

Jacobsen ignored the jibe. It was clear that she and Cordero knew each other well enough to be practiced at this game. "Agent Carter," Jacobsen said approaching her. "Welcome. We have been expecting you. Sorry I couldn't make it to your embassy yesterday. We had an unexpected issue to deal with and I couldn't get away." The INTERPOL director offered no details. "Please sit," she said.

Jacobsen indicated pink plastic chairs set along the wall of the room. Carter noticed that Jacobsen's own chair was wooden and padded. Her desk was also made of wood, big, heavy and piled high with files surrounding her computer terminal. Through an open door Carter could see a smaller, metal desk in another room where a young black woman dressed in a similar blue INTERPOL uniform sat on a plastic chair making unpractised taps on a keyboard. Carter thought of her Resident Agent in Charge back in Flagstaff, his expensive desk and fancy office chair, the TV monitor he'd had attached to the wall, the bar fridge in the corner. *Managers are everywhere alike*, she was thinking, *with their pathetic distinctions of rank.*

A few flies circled a light bulb hanging from the ceiling and an air-conditioner above the back door wheezed in its struggle to keep the room cool. Maps adorned the walls of the office— maps of Dili, of Timor-Leste, of Indonesia, of Southeast Asia— and between the maps were bookshelves packed with files and directories of a drab, official-looking kind. On the young black officer's desk Carter noticed a small ornamental cat, its paw rising and falling continuously. It was the only personal touch in either room.

"About the embassy briefing," Carter said. "It was a public relations event. Don't worry about it."

"Good," Jacobsen replied. "I know you've only just arrived and haven't had time to settle in. But this case we'd like you to help us with has just taken on a degree of urgency. And as you'll be working closely with Tino here, there'll be no need for orientations or inductions. Nor will you need a uniform—even if we had one to spare which we don't. This is a small office with an even smaller budget," Jacobsen said stating what seemed fairly obvious. "Drug trafficking is our main focus. We'll have you sign a few forms— mainly for insurance purposes—hand you some manuals which you don't really need to read but which we are obliged to give you, and issue you with an INTERPOL identity card which you may find that you require although I doubt that you will." She looked at Cordero. "After that it is my hope that you and Tino can go straight to Suai and begin your investigations."

"Today?" Cordero asked, surprised. "Surely you can't mean—"

"Yes," said Jacobsen, cutting off his protest.

"But my sister—" he began.

"Today," Jacobsen interrupted. "You have been assigned to this office Tino with orders to take instructions from INTERPOL. That means me, not that boss up the corridor you ignore. And as I said, this case now involves an urgent matter." Cordero looked morose. "I have arranged an SUV you can take," Jacobsen added.

"Clapped-out UN surplus, I suppose," Cordero complained.

"A year old, I believe," said Jacobsen who then turned from him and back to Carter. "But let me fill you both in from the beginning."

Carter lent back in her chair, found the plastic too soft to support her, leaned forward, as Cordero was doing. Only the African seemed able to accommodate herself with poise on these chairs as though she came from a country which knew no other type. Jacobsen had moved to the large map of Timor-Leste near her desk and was indicating an area to the south of the island.

"This is Suai, in the district of Cova Lima which borders Indonesian West Timor. There have been twelve children—babies actually—that we know of who have gone missing in this area in the past several months. Eleven have not been seen since. One turned up recently in Florida. Dead. A girl less than a year old. Her body was found in a dumpster. Police tracked down a couple who were paid to re-house the girl but they detoured to wager the money in a casino, left the baby in the car during the heat of the day, and the poor thing died of heat exhaustion. Autopsy revealed she'd come from this part of the world. Apart from everything else bacterial infections led to that conclusion, I believe." She turned to Carter. "You'd be familiar with the term re-house?"

"Absolutely," answered Carter. "It means an unwanted child is being passed around, perhaps sold, because whoever is supposedly responsible no longer wants it."

"Correct," confirmed Jacobsen. "Many children who are taken like this for one reason or another disappoint the people who pay for them and since there are no authentic records of any kind they're simply disposed of."

"What do you mean 'taken like this'?" Cordero asked.

Jacobsen turned to face him. "Stolen, Tino. In this case for adoption. The female of the couple who dumped the girl worked for a wealthy American businessman. His wife had lost a baby, couldn't have another, and nearly drove him crazy mourning the loss of her child. The man's business involved him making regular trips to Indonesia. On one of them he was drinking with Indonesian associates and complaining about his wife. One of the

Indonesians took him aside and said he could put him in touch with someone who would arrange a child of an age and sex of his choosing, with forged documents attesting to its adoption, and all within a matter of a few weeks. For a price, of course."

"Offered by? And how?" Carter asked.

"Those are questions we have no answers to," said Jacobsen. "The businessman has lawyered up. Isn't talking. All we know comes from the couple who were supposed to get rid of the baby. And that's not much. But it tells us that the man to whom this particular girl was initially delivered had connections in Indonesia, and Indonesia borders Timor-Leste, and the whole thing was done quickly and professionally from abduction to discovery inside the US. That leads us to believe there is some kind of established network dealing in illegal adoptions."

Jacobsen looked at the map. "You may know that Indonesia has not signed the Hague Convention on inter-country adoption and consequently US authorities have not checked, approved or registered any adoption agencies there—the usual source of any child being adopted into the US. That makes it easier to forge paperwork. The international nature of the abduction brought INTERPOL into the equation but the US angle had us ask Washington for additional support. You have worked in the area of child abductions Agent Carter and that's exactly the kind of expertise we need."

Carter shifted in her seat. "The FBI believes several hundred children are stolen in the US each year," she recounted. "Several hundred stolen by strangers, as distinct from a parent or relative, that is. But it is a rough estimate only. Children don't always turn up in figures for child stealing because if they're abused they can be categorised under child assaults instead. Some are simply not reported if they're taken from traumatised or addictive home environments."

"As I said," Jacobsen began, staring at her map, "your experience in this area is the primary reason you are here. Our suspicion is that a person or persons is responsible for stealing all those babies down there near Suai and has started doing it again."

Carter was silent for a moment. Then she asked, "Have you found any pattern in the abductions?"

"We're short on resources in this office," Jacobsen answered her with a hint of disappointment in her voice. "And short on officers. And as I said our priority at the moment is drug trafficking or rather preventing East Timor becoming a transit point for drugs. We simply haven't had time to look for a pattern in these abductions," she turned to face Carter. "Which is not to say there isn't a pattern. Perhaps you can uncover it for us."

"Any leads, any suspects?" Carter asked.

Jacobsen shook her head. "Nothing," she said.

She sat back heavily in her wooden chair and glanced at Cordero. "I have rung Modesto. He's expecting you this evening. He will give you what help he can."

"Superintendent Basilio Modesto of the Cova Lima police district," Cordero explained leaning toward Carter. "We call him 'Buzzi'. He hates the name, which is more reason to use it."

"You mentioned an urgent matter," Carter prompted.

"We hadn't had reports of new abductions for six weeks," said Jacobsen. "Until three days ago, that is. A six-month-old baby girl appears to have been taken from the *suku*—that is Tetun for 'village'—of Fatuloro on Saturday. You may know it Tino. She is the daughter of the *xefe*." Jacobsen looked knowingly at Cordero.

"The village chief," Cordero explained for Carter's benefit.

"Modesto immediately increased police patrols along the border," Jacobsen continued, "and it's possible the abductor or abductors don't want to risk smuggling the baby out of the country until police lose interest and the patrols die down. If that's the case, it's possible the girl could be hidden somewhere in the area." She let that thought sink in. "Or they might decide the whole gambit is too risky now and—"

"Dump the girl or kill her," Carter said finishing the statement for her.

"Exactly," said Jacobsen. "Hence the urgency," she added looking directly at Cordero. "I can't give you more details. Modesto will have them, if there are any." Jacobsen paused in case

Carter had any further questions. She didn't. "Any assistance you can give us Agent Carter will be most welcome," Jacobsen added. "Your experience in these kinds of cases will be invaluable." She stood. "As you know INTERPOL has no actual enforcement powers in Timor-Leste. That's why you'll be partnered with Tino." Jacobsen adjusted her tone back to informal. "I'm sorry your welcome has had to be rushed, Agent Carter," she said. "Perhaps when you return from Suai in a few days we could have dinner and a few drinks. The food in Timor is generally excellent and a few cold beers are a welcome relief from the heat. Now, Officer Furaha Oodanta will take you to sign those papers and get you your identity card."

The young black officer rose at the mention of her name and entered the room. Her lips moved slightly in what might have been a smile for Carter's benefit but her expression quickly went blank. It was clear that she understood the modest limits of her role. Carter rose now too, shook the director's hand and began to follow Officer Oodanta to the door.

"I just have a few operational matters to go over with Investigator Cordero," Jacobsen said as the two were leaving. "Good day Agent Carter and again, I'm sorry our first meeting could not have been warmer and more welcoming."

Officer Oodanta ushered Carter out and closed the door behind her. Jacobsen came around from her chair, threw a leg over her desk and stared gravely at Cordero. "There's another matter, Tino, and it comes straight from the Prime Minister." Jacobsen paused for effect. "It's getting dangerous where you're going," she said. "There are fears among the villagers north of Suai that demons are active."

"Demons? What have they to do with stolen babies—and the PM?" Cordero asked.

"A rumour has taken hold down there that demons, ogres, devils—call them what you will—are engaged in construction sacrifices," she explained.

"You mean killing babies to bury under buildings to appease land spirits?" Cordero questioned.

"And ensure things don't collapse," Jacobsen said. "Exactly. Centuries ago this was folklore throughout Asia and Europe. Timor's just been slow to catch on. And here demons are regarded as the culprits."

"My father used to say the Indonesians spread the idea that their death squads were demons with supernatural powers that made them impossible to defend against. I knew the fear persisted in a handful of remote villages but what's this to do with me?" he asked.

"While you were on that junket in Portugal learning to be an investigator, the police conducted a major operation along the south-west border ostensibly to root out demons," Jacobsen replied.

"Yeah I heard. It was a fuckup. The government was accused of using the operation to intimidate its opponents. And instead of putting an end to panic about demons the operation only increased the concerns as word went around."

Jacobsen nodded her agreement. "The PM doesn't want a re-run of that. On the other hand he's worried that demon panics could turn violent toward foreigners—since they're the ones the villagers hold responsible for the actual constructions. At the very least, talk of human sacrifices or vigilante responses could raise local opposition to the developments down there and hostility toward foreign investors and technicians." Jacobsen stood and looked down at Cordero. "And any violence toward foreigners, any hint of widespread unrest—"

"Could sink the government's plans for the area and its chances of re-election, right?"

"Right." Jacobsen took a deep breath. "Could also sink plans to transform Timor from its reliance on foreign aid to pay for just about everything—including your salary, Tino—to a self-reliant economy. Now you know why the PM is anxious, especially with a *xefe's* daughter taken and the added trouble that could cause."

"You haven't explained what this has to do with me?"

"When the PM learned that you would be assigned to work with the American on the abductions he specifically requested, well insisted actually, that you keep the lid on things down there. I'm just the messenger."

"'Keep the lid on'?"

"Recovering the *xefe's* baby and finding whoever is responsible for these abductions will go a long way to calming the villagers. For starters, work with the American to solve this thing quickly. But keep her focused on babies rather than chasing demons or getting caught up with vigilantes. They're two different problems and she's not here to fuel the second."

"How could she do that?" Cordero asked. "She's a stranger here."

"Precisely. If she gets herself tangled up in folklore she doesn't understand she may make matters worse. She's an outsider, the kind of outsider most villagers would regard with suspicion—white, female, assertive." Jacobsen leaned toward Cordero. "She could get herself killed, Tino!" She stood upright. "But even if she is only distracted by the demon issue, it will pop up in her reports back to the US Embassy that locals are opposed to the government's plans down there. Opposed enough, in fact, that they're actively trying to stop the developments. Or she may tell reporters much the same thing and either way cause alarm among foreign investors."

"Aren't you exaggerating?" Cordero said more as a statement than a question.

"We've had reports of suspected demons being beaten in several villages. And the beatings are increasing in number and severity. There was even a suspected execution of a subsistence farmer near Beko recently."

"I haven't seen anything about that," Cordero said.

"It's under wraps for now. Tight wraps, I might add," Jacobsen said. "The fear is that news of the beatings could lead to payback attacks by relatives of the victims who've moved to the city for work. Before long a lot of people could be killed. The whole thing could spiral out of control. If a panic spreads to Suai itself, foreigners could be targeted. Or simply scared off. Either way work on the projects then grinds to a halt. All I'm saying is the American's here to solve the mystery of why babies are being stolen, not to involve herself in anything to do with policy issues or local unrest."

"And are you also warning me to keep an eye out for demons?" he asked.

"I'm telling you that when people are scared, things can get out of hand. Fast."

Cordero made to rise and leave. "Is that all?"

"No. The PM also wants you to help Modesto deal with the problem."

"Buzzi? Me? Why? I have no jurisdiction over Buzzi."

"No, but you know him well enough that he may listen to you. I'm also told Buzzi gets the jitters and over-reacts when things get difficult. We don't need anyone losing their heads down there. You're a senior police investigator. Offer advice. That's all. But make sure he takes it." She glanced at the ceiling. "INTERPOL steers clear of politics, Tino, and I do as well."

"Politics?" he queried.

"INTERPOL is politically neutral. But we've been able to work well with this government and we've achieved a lot. The opposition parties may not be as cooperative," Jacobsen said.

"You don't want to be seen rescuing the government's development plans? Is that why there's no INTERPOL uniform for the American even though I know you have a cupboard full of them?" Cordero asked. "And an INTERPOL identity card? Why not a big, bright, hard-to-miss badge like the one usually attached to your belt?"

"The PM wants to keep a low profile," Jacobsen said ignoring his questions. "That's why he's keen for INTERPOL to take the lead role in this investigation rather than the Timorese police. But I'm keen on as little visibility as possible." She lent in toward him. "If things go bad, we could all end up wearing the blame. We need some kind of insurance against a screw-up. The American is our insurance policy." Jacobsen lowered her voice. "If things go wrong a lot of Timorese in Dili at least will be prepared to direct their anger at Americans rather than their own government. The Americans *did* give the Indonesians a green light to invade in 1975, remember."

Cordero looked down at his shoes and started tapping them on the floor. "Let me get this right. Plan A is to keep the FBI agent in the dark about the real problem down there but use whatever experience she has to solve the crime," he said. He glanced up at Jacobsen. "And Plan B is to hang her out to dry if things go wrong." He blew out a faint whistle. "That's a little under-handed, even for you."

"Don't get all ethical on me, Tino," Jacobsen said. "It complicates things too much. Give the American all the information she needs and all the assistance you can to play her part. Keep her out of danger for God's sake. But yes, keep her in the dark about what you call 'the real problem' as much as you can." Jacobsen walked back behind her desk and sat. "And we don't *want* to hang her out to dry, Tino. Do your part properly and she won't need to be."

Chapter 5

"You'll find policing in Timor interesting," Cordero said as he drove them away from Carter's hotel. "For many years the criminal code was written in Portuguese. Not many officers could speak or read Portuguese. That meant a lot of them had no idea what the laws were they were supposed to be policing." He suppressed a laugh. "A lot of it was ad hoc. You might be arrested for something in one village, say beating your wife, that was perfectly okay in another down the road. That's Timor-Leste for you."

"Portugal colonised the place for what, five hundred years?" said Carter. "I gather the impact was fairly marginal."

Cordero had driven her back to her hotel to pack enough for four or five days away from Dili. He then headed back to the small house he rented on the western side of town, threw clothes into a bag, several maps, a toothbrush, cell phone charger, and a flat screen television unopened in its cardboard box. He drove back to the INTERPOL office to exchange vehicles. The SUV had been fuelled but he stopped on the way back to Carter's hotel for pastries and bottled water as there would be no time now for lunch. It was already past midday and the distance by road from Dili to Suai, though only a little over 100 miles, could take just under four hours on Timor's poorly-maintained roads if he took the most direct route inland. But Cordero preferred the faster coast road to Batugade which would allow him to drop off the television to his cousin in Balibo. Moises had been pestering him about the TV for weeks. From Moises' place, he would drive to Maliana, across the mountainous spine of the island to Bobonaro, then down to the coast and Suai. If he had to go to Suai, he figured he might as well

43

make use of the drive for his own purposes even if it added to the travel time. With the stop to stretch their legs in Balibo he figured it would take about six hours if they were lucky.

"Well you see the Portuguese never bothered much with educating the locals, except for a privileged few Timorese they thought might be useful to help administer the colony. Many of those people were able to flee when Indonesia invaded. Most went to Portuguese-speaking countries like Mozambique."

They passed Cordero's neighbourhood, over the wide expanse of the Comoro River, through the crumbling round-about leading to the airport and on to the outlying settlements around the city. Big, bright posters advertised American brands and Chinese electronics from the many shop fronts lining the road. From side lanes and alleyways children emerged in neat school uniforms singing and laughing. Several walked in groups of three or four, others congregated in small packs at points on the main road to catch microlets home. School was out for the day and for many people the heat of the afternoon meant that work was over until sunset as well.

"During the Indonesian occupation," Cordero continued, "Tetun became popular with the Timorese who couldn't leave because it was a language the invaders didn't understand. But when the exiles returned after independence, they brought Portuguese back with them. Of course, they took many positions of power in the country. They insisted on pushing Portuguese to emphasise their own importance and because it pleased Portugal, which provides a backdoor for Timorese to get work in Europe and send back remittances. Together with Tetun, Portuguese remains a national language but the insistence on using it in virtually every official capacity has had to be moderated."

Carter wasn't in the mood for too much lecturing of this kind. She changed the subject. "Jacobsen seems competent enough," she said.

"Oh yes, she is that. Too Dutch for me. You know, all business," he said and glanced over at Carter briefly. "But I'm working on that. She knows her stuff. Her term was extended last year with support from our government. She's been here close on three years. I don't think she's in a rush to go back to a country that's built below sea level," he said and laughed freely this time. "Not in an era of global warming."

"How effective is INTERPOL here?" she asked.

"It's been here quite a while and its record is good. Small operation, small achievements but it's earned a lot of respect."

"And the police unit you work for?"

"Only just established. When I applied to join I was sent for training in Portugal along with a few others. We're professional investigators and we take the role seriously. You won't find too many countries of Timor-Leste's size or stage of development with an interest in a sophisticated unit of our kind."

Carter wondered just how sophisticated Cordero's unit could be but she didn't pursue it. "What's this place like we're heading to?" she asked.

"Suai? If you read a travel brochure it'd emphasise unspoilt beaches, sunshine, coral reefs, and crocodiles. About ten thousand people live there and maybe as many crocodiles." He glanced at her and smiled. "Just joking—but there are a lot. On the other hand the government looks on Suai as a gateway to an economically viable future. There's a great deal of construction work going on there because off shore are large oil and gas deposits that are ripe for processing in this country rather than just selling-off the raw product to outside interests. But most people are quite traditional and in the villages where these babies have been taken they largely live off the land still."

"Jacobsen said the Indonesian border was close by. How close?"

"To Suai? About twenty kilometres—around twelve miles."

They had drawn behind a construction truck lumbering up a slight incline. About two dozen people were in back, men standing on the rear bumper and holding on to the tail gate while women sat inside the tray itself. There were too many bends in the road here and too many vehicles coming from the other direction to risk over-taking and, short of options, they slowed to a crawl.

The price they paid was to endure black smoke belching from the truck as the driver changed down in gears to make the rise.

"Any thoughts about what's going on down there?" Carter asked rolling up her window. "With these babies I mean?"

Cordero pushed back against the steering wheel, stretching his back. "It could be as simple as couples off-loading one too many kids," he said.

"That's your *first* assumption?" Carter was surprised by the suggestion.

"Definitely," he said. "When Timor-Leste became independent it was the poorest country in the world. Even now it ranks down the bottom of the list. And where we're going is among the poorest of the poor. Oh there's money for development projects and well-paid work for labourers. But the area Jacobsen indicated won't benefit much from any of that for years. Instead it's an area of subsistence farming—like I said, you live off what you can grow in your garden plot and supplement by foraging in the forest. Maybe you make a few centavos each week in the market as well. In communities like these, people marry young, thirteen, fourteen years of age often."

"Is that legal?" Carter asked as Cordero closed his window and the interior of the vehicle began quickly to get hot and sticky.

"Well it happens regardless. The Church doesn't condone it, I mean bless it with a formal marriage, but it turns a blind eye. Nothing else it can do. Nothing the government can do either. And people have a lot of children. That was customary when times were much harder than they are now but now there's the added influence of the same Church—you know, no contraception. A woman can have ten, twelve kids by the time she's thirty and have many productive years left."

"How much say do the girls have in in all of this? You know, marrying that young? Becoming a full-time baby production line?" Carter asked, looking with more interest now at the women in the back of the truck up ahead.

"Not much," answered Cordero. He glanced across at her. "Boys don't have much say in it either. It's the traditional way, the custom, what's expected."

"You seemed to imply that the Church has a degree of influence though," Carter said. "If you could call its influence modern."

"A degree, yes. It came with the Portuguese," he explained, "and has been here a long time. But the Indonesians are the real reason it took off. They made everyone sign up to a monotheistic religion and the only practical options were Islam or Catholicism. As a consequence most Timorese are Catholic. That's the main difference between Timorese in the east and those across the border in the west. One is Catholic, the other Muslim. But scratch the surface and most are actually animist, especially in the rural districts. What that means is that on this side of the border the Church's ban on contraceptives actually reinforces age-old practices. Ironic, huh?"

Carter nodded as she thought about what he was saying. He waved a hand at the people in the truck up ahead. "Well, by the time you have your thirteenth, fourteenth kid, it's getting hard to feed them all. The last few are even more malnourished than the others with all sorts of developmental and health problems. The parents might give one or two away or sell them if they can. In their minds, they're doing the kids a favour." He glanced over at Carter who sat there expressionless. "Lots of kids are raised in orphanages in Timor not because they don't have parents but because the parents don't have the means to raise them."

"Hard luck for the kids," she said.

"Except that it's a kinship society," he responded. "Everybody is connected in some way to just about everybody else. The Western idea of the nuclear family is very…well very foreign here. It's not as though a kid in an orphanage has been wrenched away from his or her only point of connection. Even the idea of individual rights is quite novel—a product of the new Timorese state not the old Timorese culture."

She wiped sweat from her face and the back of her neck. "I see that kind of thing in the Native American communities I work in back home. Although I guess they've had a lot longer to get used to the 'white man's ways', as they say."

"Well we could end up in villages that have yet to see a white man—much less white woman for that matter."

"Even these days?" she asked.

"Even these days."

"The Indonesians made no difference? The briefing papers said—"

Cordero waved a hand about. "They built roads and bridges. Even tried to develop commercial farming in the coastal areas at least. But they did it for their own sakes, not for the sake of Timorese. We were little more than an inconvenience to be pushed aside. And their scorched earth policy when they left really showed that."

"I read that around seventy percent of the country's infrastructure was destroyed by pro-Indonesian militias in 1999," Carter said.

"Yeah but figues never really tell the story. Try to imagine them in terms of houses, schools, churches, bridges, livestock... pretty much everything that could be destroyed was destroyed. Timorese had to start again from scratch."

"Okay. What's your second assumption?" she asked to move the conversation along. "About the stolen babies, I mean."

"It could be a gang from West Timor. A lot of Timorese who supported incorporation into Indonesia went over there when the country voted for freedom. Thousands of them. They remain there to this day. And they don't have any love for their fellow countrymen—well actually they don't see us as their fellow countrymen at all. They regard themselves as Indonesians." He blew out a deep breath. "And they don't have many sources of income over there. They're basically permanent refugees. Like Palestinians." He inclined his head out the driver's window to check for on-coming traffic.

"Or it could be a Timorese gang that know where to get the kids they want and one or more Indonesians who have the connections to take it from there. Young people who find life growing food for a living too dreary drift into population centres and from there into criminal gangs. It happens in America too they tell me," he added with just a hint of sarcasm. "Smuggling is a regular thing down around Suai because of the nearby border and the rough terrain that makes it almost impossible to police. If it's that scenario, identifying the Timorese involved won't be easy. Could be anyone. Of course targeting babies that the parents want to keep suggests a callousness unusual for Timorese."

"Unusual? I understand children were regularly victims of violence in the lead up to the vote on independence," Carter countered.

"True. But that was in a different context. It was just possible for those opposed to independence to believe they were serving a cause rather than participating in a crime. As I said, many of them believed Timor's future was best served as part of Indonesia. Plus—and this is a big plus—the Indonesian army supplied drugs to a lot of the people they employed to terrorise the population. That's why many of their attacks were incredibly brutal."

Cordero saw his chance and overtook the truck on a straight stretch of road with no other vehicles or motorcycles in sight. Several people waved to them from the back of the truck as they passed. A swam of motorcycle riders who had been caught behind the truck as well had the same idea and quickly accelerated around the truck and off ahead of Carter and Cordero. Both rolled their windows back down immediately and were thankful for the rush of fresh cool air.

"And if Buzzi has stepped up patrols along the border," Cordero added, "the smugglers will lie low. That will make things doubly difficult."

"Difficult for that latest girl who's been abducted, certainly," Carter said to herself as much as to him.

"Uh-huh," Cordero agreed. They drove on in silence for a while. "If it is an illegal adoption thing, what I can't figure," said Cordero, "is the attraction of Timorese children. I mean would a rich, white American family really want such an obviously untypical son or daughter?"

"You'd be surprised," said Carter. "You have couples that are just desperate for a child, any child. And legal adoptions can take years. Others think non-Caucasian kids are trendy or will give them an edge over their peers. Kind of, 'Look at us, we're different, we're cool, we're into saving the world one kid at a time'. Makes me want to puke. I was mainly working on reservation abductions in Arizona before I came here. Navajo, Hopi and Apache kids have become as valuable—that is to say fashionable—with some people as rare artworks. Remember those FBI figures I quoted to Jacobsen on kids in the States stolen by strangers? Indian child theft is a sizable sub-category."

"This case interests you then?" Cordero asked.

"All cases interest me," she replied.

"Equally?"

"No. Not quite," she said and cut the discussion short by leaning over to the back seat. "I noticed you bought pastries when I first sat down."

"Yes," said Cordero. "You like Tahini? There's an Indian baker near where I live. I think he left India because he isn't a very good baker but he does do a nice Boyoz—you know, a Turkish scone full of tahini. The guy had a Turkish grandmother, you see. Get them out, open them up."

She did just that and they ate the pastries while they drove on. After her second—which she had to admit was surprisingly light and flavoursome—Carter brushed the crumbs from her slacks and said: "Did it ever occur to you that I don't speak Tetun or Portuguese and may not be any use to you at all?"

Cordero laughed. "You needn't worry about that. I told you Tetun is a national language but not everyone in Timor speaks it or at least speaks it well. Even fewer speak Portuguese even after twelve years of independence." He pointed a finger up ahead. "The town we're coming into is Liquica. A lot of people around here, particularly the older ones, speak Tocodede. But not me. As we head down to Suai we'll go through areas where people speak Bunak, Kemak, Habun and Mambai. East Timor is a small country. About the land area of Hawaii but fewer people. Just over a million. Nonetheless it's a patchwork of languages and cultures. The rugged terrain has seen to that. Seventeen languages to be precise plus over sixty dialects a lot of which are incomprehensible to each other. You'll be fine. I'll interpret for you where I can." He chuckled to himself. "Where I can't, we're both in the same boat."

If Cordero saw the humor in the situation, Carter didn't. Her involvement in this investigation seemed to her absurd. After all, what could she possibly bring to it that the locals couldn't? She folded her arms tightly across her chest. Three long months, she lamented, on an assignment in a foreign country she had little knowledge of and even less interest in and where she had no enforcement powers at all.

She fell silent. As they entered the outskirts of Liquica a hand-written sign on a corner wall read 'Redus velosidade'— 'Slow down'. Next to it was also scrawled: 'Ka ita bele oho ema ruma'— 'Or else you could kill somebody'. Cordero translated the mix of Portuguese and Tetun for Carter's benefit. "Everything out of the ordinary has to be explained to rural Timorese," he said, "and especially the old ones. The older ones can't read. The younger ones can and they tell their parents what they've learnt. Everything is new—motor vehicles, radios, cell phones, electricity—and has dropped into their world almost overnight. Western people have gone through stages in which information was shared through reading and writing, then through listening to the radio, then through television and finally computers and cell phones. Here people have jumped all those stages and gone straight to the cell phone. That can really mess with your mind."

Carter made no comment. They drove through the half-dozen streets that comprised the centre of the town without stopping and soon rejoined the coast road. As they did Carter surveyed the beachfront to their right where clumps of children in raggedy shorts and T-shirts ran along the sand either chasing a deflated soccer ball or hitting empty plastic bottles with a stick. On their left were neatly-fenced yards around small vegetable gardens, spaced out in a way that meant most houses—which were becoming little more than huts—were no closer than twenty yards from each other. Clothes were hung here and there on bushes to dry. Outside one house Carter noticed a small girl, bare-foot, climbing a tall coconut palm tree and cutting fonds with a heavy machete while below an even younger girl was stacking them as they fell. Outside another house a man sat on a wooden chair while a boy cut his hair with a knife. The scenes reminded Carter of some of the more depressed Native American settlements she had visited where time had come to a stop and progress was a hollow term.

She awoke two hours later, the violent swaying of the vehicle having disturbed her. She had fallen asleep and left Cordero to drive without company. "Where are we?" she asked yawning, blinking and pressing against the passenger's door to stabilize herself.

"We're heading up the hills into Balibo. Can't help the windy road, I'm afraid. Over on the right is Indonesia. The border runs just down there. Did your background papers tell you that this is where the Indonesians began their invasion in 1975?" he asked, not really expecting an answer. Carter said nothing. "My cousin Moises lives with his wife and four children in Balibo. I must call in and give him that television in back."

"I had been wondering about that," she said.

"He asked me to buy it for him in Dili weeks ago. He not only has electricity now but a satellite dish as well. From slash-and-burn farming to satellite dishes in barely twenty years. Who could have imagined! Like I said, jumping all the stages in between can really play with your mind."

Cordero eased the SUV off the main road and onto a gravel excuse for another on the outskirts of the small town. "It's just down here," he said. "This'll only take a minute."

In a yard shaded by banana trees, their big leaves flapping in the breeze, stood a neat, whitewashed cement block house with three young children playing in the dirt out front. When Cordero pulled up, turned off the ignition, and stepped out of the vehicle the children looked up and cried "*Tiu!*" or "uncle" in Tetun with excitement. They ran to him and he lifted each in turn high above his head.

"*Botarde, botarde,*" Cordero said smiling broadly. "*Ita nia apaa iha nebee ka?*"

"*Lae!*" the children sang in unison. Their father was not there at the house.

"*Amaa?*" asked Cordero.

"*Sin!*" sung in unison. Their mother was home and just then she appeared from the house carrying a baby in her arms. "*Mana* Cipriana," Cordero said greeting her with a kiss. By now Carter was also out of the vehicle and drawing the attention of the children away from Cordero. He introduced her to Cipriana, a woman of about the same age as Carter but weather-beaten, barefoot and dressed in an old pale green nylon dress.

"*Ita nia namorada husi Australia ka?*" Cipriana asked grinning.

"She wants to know if you're my girlfriend from Australia," Cordero said laughing. Carter was taken aback by the question.

"*Lae, lae. Nia husi Amerikanu. Polisia hanesan ha'u,*" he looked back at Carter. "Relax. I told her no, you are an American and a police officer like me."

Cipriana suggested coffee but Cordero knew they had hours yet of driving and declined the offer. He carried the television into the house while Carter was listening to the children explain something to her that she had no way of understanding. She smiled and tried to look in turn curious, surprised and happy—taking her cue from their expressions. Then, almost as soon as they had arrived, they were off with a handful of bananas Cipriana had found for them to eat on the way. "She assures me Moises will be able to connect it," Cordero said shaking his head. "But I'll believe that when I see it."

They drove through the hilly country beyond Balibo, Cordero tapping the vehicle's horn as they approached each bend to alert any chickens, pigs or feral children straying onto the road ahead. Carter's father would often tap his car horn to neighbours driving past on the back roads in Missouri but to acknowledge people rather than warn them away.

Eventually they came to a wide green valley and drove down through the outskirts of Maliana where rice fields and vegetable gardens were interspersed with run-down houses and ponies standing motionless in vacant lots. In the centre of town the streets seemed largely deserted as though the people here had no time for loitering like many seemed to do in Dili.

Cordero stopped at a gas station and eventually a female attendant ambled out, pocketing her cell phone in her jeans.

After the customary 'Hello' and 'How are you?' she topped up the vehicle's fuel tank with diesel. Cordero paid her and thanked her too profusely Carter thought and then he climbed back behind the wheel and they started up a snaking mountain road toward Bobonaro. The sky was pale blue but clouds banking on the western horizon had turned a light shade of pink on their fringe. They reminded Carter of the sky around Flagstaff. She wondered how the little girl who Preston had violated was faring. She wondered if Rainey and Tanner really had been assigned to pick up the investigation into other reservation abductions. On a lighter note, she wondered whether Sanchez had given birth and whether it was a girl or a boy. Then she stopped daydreaming. It had only been a few days—although it felt to her like more—and they probably hadn't yet realised that she'd even gone.

The cleared fields of the valley soon gave way to a forest of eucalypt, mahogany and teak as they ascended into the foothills on the south side of Maliana. Carter noticed the further they climbed the more they seemed to travel back in time. Cars became fewer, structures less frequent and cruder in their construction. Higher up and trees overhung the road as though the forest was trying to reclaim it.

They twisted and turned through tortuous bends and progress was slow as they made their way through a pass at more than two thousand feet above sea level. Soon she saw smoke rising from the embers of open cooking fires in the centre of clustered huts. Unfenced gardens of what Cordero said were sweet potato and cassava were dotted here and there through the trees and in what looked like newly slashed plots men and women finished the day's tilling by hand. Often the side of the road was marked by what Cordero pointed out were borders of coffee plants. "Timorese coffee is ranked in the top one percent in the world for quality," he boasted. "It's the volcanic soil, the hybrid variety of arabica and robusta beans and the organic nature of the farming. A lot different to the kind of country you're used to, I bet," Cordero said.

Carter didn't answer immediately. "I've gotten used to dry country," she said. "But I could take some of this greenery every now and then to break the monotony of dust storms."

They passed more children playing on the road, two men carrying a wild boar they had killed, trussed up by its legs to a pole, and a man standing by the side of the road talking to another who had a dead snake draped around his neck. At the village of Bobonaro—less a district centre than a collection of huts and ramshackle buildings—they had to slow to a crawl for a group of elderly women monopolising the centre of the road as they lumbered in single-file. The women wore blankets wrapped around their bodies and covering their faces. Baskets of vegetables were balanced on their heads. The one in front carried a staff; the one at the rear led a goat by a frayed rope. As they made their way around the vehicle, Carter noticed the women's faces looked like tanned leather and their teeth and gums were red from chewing what she guessed was betel nut. The tableau was like a scene she recalled from an illustrated Bible she'd been given as a child where a group of Galileans watched Jesus heal a leper they'd all shunned as unclean.

It was getting darker. Cordero said he would call Superintendent Basilio Modesto and suggest they meet first thing in the morning. They were only twenty miles from Suai but road conditions on the other side of the range after recent heavy rain could make it a drive of almost another hour. Cordero pulled the SUV over to the side and stopped. "We should have coverage here," he explained and took out his cell. Carter stepped out of the SUV to stretch her legs while he punched in numbers and she strolled along the road a little. Up ahead she saw an old woman in a grubby shawl splashing water on her face from a pipe coming out of the side of the embankment. A man equally old in shorts but shirtless walked up to the woman, machete in hand and dogs straggling around his feet. He waited, she joined him, no words were spoken and the two of them trudged doggedly on.

By now heavy clouds had blanketed the sky and it started to rain, at first only a few drops here and there, then a sudden deluge that stopped almost as soon as it had started as though it had been a mistake. Carter ran back to the vehicle and settled herself inside. The man and woman didn't seek shelter or break their stride but pressed on as though getting drenched was too regular an event to worry about. The scent of wet, black, fecund earth had wafted into the SUV with Carter and she contrasted it to the arid smell of dry rock and sand more familiar to her back home. "Buzzi says he'll meet us for a meal tonight," said Cordero interrupting her thoughts. "He's anxious we get started on the case. He's also arranged accommodation for us in Suai." He cast an eye over her damp clothes. "Buckle up. If we hurry we should have time to clean up and get you into something dry before dinner."

Chapter 6

Superintendent Basilio Modesto—Buzzi—proved to be a short, rotund man of about fifty years of age. He had big round eyes like a cow's beneath a greying head of frizzy hair and above a long day's stubble on his chin. He also had an overbite which tended to draw attention to his teeth when he spoke. He wore the uniform of the Timor-Leste National Police complete with the insignia of his rank and what appeared to be a medal for distinguished service that seemed meant to elevate his status even more.

"I am sorry, Agent Carter," he said by way of introduction, rising from his chair to greet her. "I speak a little bit English only."

He also apologised for the Indonesian restaurant where they were meeting and for the guest house in which he had booked them two rooms. Neither was up to American standards, he confessed. "All hotels full up," he explained. "Too many engineers, surveyors, tradesmen, all from China. Even here," he said and gestured around the restaurant, where the overflow crowd from the Chinese eatery down the road had ended up.

"It's fine, really," Carter reassured him. "Why don't you order for me, I can't read the menu in Tetun anyway."

Buzzi nodded and called over a wizened old woman who was sitting impassively on a stool by a door that led into the kitchen area. Without looking at the handwritten menu which hung on the wall, he listed off a number of things and the woman shuffled away expressionless. Then Buzzi sat in silence, scratching the blue plastic covering that passed for a cloth on their table while Cordero and Carter hungrily eyed the food being eaten at the tables around them.

Soon the woman returned with three welcome cans of cold beer which she placed in the centre of the table. Cordero took one and finished half of it in a series of uninterrupted gulps while the woman was wiping down their table. "Twenty years in Australia," he said by way of explanation to Carter. She took her beer and sipped it more sedately. Buzzi left his can sitting untouched on the table and began scratching the plastic covering again when the woman had left.

They sat in an uncomfortable silence for several minutes. Then fish dishes of two kinds arrived together with a plate of fried chicken, beef in a pleasantly pungent gravy, and a large serving of boiled potatoes, fried tofu, bean sprouts and yellow noodles with a peanut sauce which Cordero said was *gado-gado*—a typical Indonesian salad. Another simpler tomato salad and a pot of boiled rice completed Buzzi's order. While Carter and Cordero were salivating over the aromas, the woman fetched plates, knives and forks and placed a small jar of crushed chili on the table.

Buzzi stopped scratching the plastic and gestured to Carter to eat. He then spoke rapidly and non-stop to Cordero who translated for Carter's benefit between attempts to satisfy his own hunger and further quench his thirst.

"The budget hasn't been passed," Buzzi began. "How am I supposed to pay my officers? Do they understand these things in Dili, Tino? Do they? I haven't had money for new equipment since June last year. And you've seen what the price of diesel is now. Imagine what that is doing to the little spare cash we have."

Carter was trying to follow the translation but Buzzi was competing with her appetite for attention.

"And these young officers they're sending me. They think they know everything because they finished middle school. The men just want to stare at their cell phones all day and the girls just want to paint their fingernails!"

An electric fan in the corner was meant to cool the dining area but it was only spreading the warm moist air around and all the patrons were sweating. A bright green gecko ran up the wall next to where the old serving woman was sitting but she ignored it. A table of Chinese men who had finished their meal lit cigarettes and were soon creating a haze of pungent smoke that was blown across the room by the fan as they joked and laughed in their high-pitched staccato tongue.

The one consolation was that the food was fresh and full of flavour.

Buzzi had stopped complaining and now focused on the child abductions. "Come over tomorrow, both of you, first thing in the morning. Read the reports. They are very basic—the work of those new young officers mostly—but they will have names, villages and dates for each of the babies that've been taken."

He said that police inquiries had been made in the stores in and around Suai and there had been no suspicious purchases of things needed to care for a baby at the time that any of them had been taken. Then again, he added, things like baby formula could be bought in most of the small village kiosks and often even in roadside stalls which were usually unattended and relied on an honor system of payment.

"I ordered more patrols along the border. You know, where forest tracks cross over. And I asked my counterpart over there to do the same," Buzzi said referring to the Indonesian police. "I'm getting no reports of anything suspicious but that country is full of forests, ravines, rivers. You could drive a herd of buffalos across and not be seen."

"What about the coast?" asked Cordero.

"Same thing," Buzzi replied. "I've increased port inspections here in Suai but I don't have the resources to patrol the coastline. Small boats could pull in anywhere and be gone before anyone knows about it."

Buzzi could see that Carter was becoming more choosey about what she ate as her hunger abated. "Have you had enough to eat, *mana*? Is the food okay?" he asked.

She shook her hand to indicate she'd had enough but he was already talking to Cordero again. "I worry about that little girl taken last Saturday," Buzzi was saying. "There's no telling what those bastards might do to her now. After you read the reports tomorrow you should go talk to the mother. Maybe we can find the girl before she is harmed."

Buzzi apologised for not having more he could tell them and said he would help in any way he could. He had chosen a young female police officer to work with them. She spoke English and knew a couple of the local dialects in the areas where the babies had been taken.

"Estefana dos Carvalho," he said. "A good girl. She doesn't paint her nails. She will be waiting for you at the office tomorrow morning." Out of deference to Carter he added his hope that Officer dos Carvalho could help her bring all her skills and experience to the investigation.

When Carter and Cordero had put down their forks Buzzi ate what was left of the food on the table. He attacked it ravenously and had consumed what was left in a matter of minutes. He drained his beer, sat back, took a toothpick from his pocket and casually cleaned his teeth. He asked Cordero if he or the FBI agent had any questions.

Cordero conveyed the invitation to Carter who said she'd rather wait until she had a chance to look over the reports.

"Will you excuse me while I go to the bathroom?" she said and looked toward the back of the restaurant.

"*Mana, sintina nebee?*" Cordero asked the old woman who was now cleaning the table next to them. The woman pointed to the kitchen and went about her work. Carter took the cue, stood and made her way gingerly through the door. "Tell me about the village beatings," Cordero said to Buzzi when she had gone. "I don't want the American to hear this."

"The attacks are getting worse, Tino," said Buzzi.

"Why's that?"

"Damn traditionals," grunted Buzzi in between picking his teeth. "Probably think the earth is flat. Can you believe this crap? It's all to do with these babies going missing. They're on edge."

The old woman came to clear their table. Buzzi ordered three more cans of beer.

"They don't understand this in Dili," Buzzi continued when the woman had gone. "They never do because they never go up into the mountains and talk to these people where they live. Dili thinks this is just a fucking policing issue. It's not a policing issue. Have you ever tried to tell a traditional that what he's believed for generations, what his people have believed for centuries, is nonsense? You and I are modern men, Tino. These people live in the Dark Ages. Most of them can't read or write and haven't traveled more than twenty miles from the village they were born in." He slammed a finger into the table. "And that was to talk to someone even more ignorant than they are!"

"Can't you at least find who's doing the beating? Arrest them?" asked Cordero.

"I'd have to arrest whole villages. They're all happy it's done. The demon's been dealt with. No more babies go missing. They all believe it, Tino!"

"How widespread has this idea become?"

"If it wasn't all over those mountains last week, it will be by now," insisted Buzzi.

"Have you been up there?"

The old woman returned with the beer and they waited for her to leave.

"Me? What for?" Buzzi answered. "No-one is going to take any notice of me."

"You have to reassure them, Buzzi. You're the police commander. You have to let them know that there's a major investigation into the abductions and that this demon talk is nonsense. It may not simply be a policing problem as you say but the police have a role to play. Because they're scared, Buzzi," whispered Cordero leaning in. "That's what this is about and that's why you have to go up there."

"If you know so much, why don't you go and talk to them?" Buzzi shot back.

"Because they don't know me," Cordero said. "And besides, I didn't bring a uniform with the braid and fancy medals on it." Cordero sat back in his chair. "Show the badge, Buzzi. Only you can do that out here. Let them know the police are working—and watching. Don't leave it to a young, inexperienced officer up there who probably shares their superstition."

Just then Carter came back from the bathroom. Buzzi gestured to the new cans of beer he'd ordered but she declined. She was very tired now despite, or perhaps because of, the nap she had taken on the drive from Dili, and the effects of the first beer hadn't helped. She made a polite show of yawning. Buzzi rested his toothpick on the table and lent in. He whispered to them in Tetun. Carter gathered what concentration she could and lent over the table as well.

"We must put an end to these abductions," Cordero translated in a matching whisper. "He says if foreigners like these Chinese here think we can't protect our own children we'll invite another invasion before too long."

Chapter 7

Carter had enjoyed a deep, uninterrupted sleep—her first in nearly a week. She'd allowed herself to forget about people and events in Arizona, been unaware of any mosquitoes in her room through the night and heard no early-morning roosters crowing in this part of Suai. She rose from the bed, went to the window and inhaled the cool sea air. She remained apprehensive about the investigation and what, if anything, she could bring to it but for the first time in days she felt refreshed at least.

Where they were staying was called 'Suai Guest House'—a functional name and nothing more, much like the establishment itself. It had twelve rooms, all but one of which were now occupied, and four bathrooms that had to be shared. The furniture was spartan, paint was peeling off the interior walls and several of the floorboards needed replacing but it was clean and close to the centre of town and what restaurants and shops Suai had to offer.

The owner of the establishment was a Syrian named Akif Nareem. He had lived in Timor for ten, maybe twelve, years—it was unclear. Many things in Timor were unclear and stories and their details often changed depending on who was doing the telling and who the listening. Nareem was close to sixty years old, tall and lean but with an ashen look about him. This morning he was smoking a cigarette, as he did first thing most days, and looked like he was wearing the singlet and shorts he had woken up in. He spoke Arabic, Tetun, Bahasa Indonesian, and rudimentary English and was speaking to Cordero in the last of these languages in order to practice it. The two were standing on the front verandah when Carter came from her room and they were looking into the street where skinny stray cats were lazing in the sunlight.

"The boat from Kupang didn't come again this week," Nareem was saying. He took another drag on his cigarette and then flicked the butt at one of the cats. "Perhaps I will have new linen next month."

Carter was wearing the slacks she had worn the day before but had replaced the blouse with a simple white T-shirt. It was tight against her body. Nareem examined her with a baleful look. *The T-shirt will cling to her with sweat in the heat before midday,* he was thinking, *and it would be nice to be close by when it did.*

"*Bondia mana,*" said Cordero. He too was dressed less formally in jeans and a simple blue shirt which hung out at his waist. "Meet our host, Mister Nareem."

Carter nodded and pressed passed the two men straight to the vehicle. Nareem's gaze followed her and Cordero had to jog a little to catch up. "Did you sleep well?" he asked across the roof of the SUV but she only made a sound that could have been 'uh-huh' or 'humph', he couldn't tell.

"A slight diversion," he said letting it go and unlocking the doors. "I received a call this morning to drop by the hospital on our way to Buzzi's office. It's where they do autopsies. They heard I was in town and want to show me something. As a member of the scientific investigative unit I couldn't say no." He settled into the SUV after her and drove off without waiting for her reply. "It shouldn't take more than ten minutes," he added.

They drove several blocks through the centre of Saui. In parts it resembled a town that had been hit by a small hurricane or a minor tsunami. Carter's attention was drawn to gutted buildings, piles of rubbish rotting outside shuttered stores, broken sidewalks, and cracked roads sprouting weeds.

But then they turned a corner and passed newly-tiled shop fronts and the impressive new Ave Maria church, built on the site of an older church where more than two hundred people had been massacred by a pro-Indonesian militia at the time of the referendum on independence in 1999. As in Dili, hopes for the future were intermixed with wounds from the past.

Cordero drove on, dodging trucks that were picking up bunches of men on street corners, eager to work as labourers on the projects—the airport being built to the north of town, the port to the south, a petro-chemical plant to the east which was meant to process the oil and gas that would one day be piped in from the rich field beneath *Tasi Mane*. Carter noticed neatly dressed women on scooters or in twos and threes on motorcycles ride pass on their way to offices on the outskirts of the town where the mountain of paperwork detailing the developments would be produced, filed and forgotten. Children were walking off to school in clean white shirts or blouses and neat blue pants or skirts. Many walked hand in hand, singing and laughing as they went. She noticed a man ride down a side street on a pushbike, apparently unconcerned that his front tire was flat and rubber was tearing against the rim of the wheel.

It was early but the sun was now high enough above the horizon to make its progress felt. "Did you sleep well?" Cordero tried again. Carter nodded.

"I did too," he said. "But I need coffee."

"Top one percent in the world for quality, right?" she said. "You read my mind."

They picked up strong, freshly roasted Timorese coffee from a corner store that had already been open for hours and they drank it as he drove. At the hospital he parked their vehicle and led the way around the side of the main building to the mortuary. They walked into an office with a hand-written sign on the door that read: '*Ezaminador mediku*'—'Medical Examiner'. Cordero knocked but as was his habit entered without invitation.

"*Bondia, maun*," Cordero said opening the door but the office was empty and there was no reply. "*Maun!*" he called more loudly.

An inside door off the office swung open and a stream of cool air escaped carrying a faint chemical odour. The sound of classical music drifted out as well. A man in his late sixties appeared in the doorway. He wore a blood-stained butcher's apron with a tattered yellow T-shirt beneath it. The man had a shock of grey hair, bushy eyebrows, rimless glasses and wore big red rubber gloves.

"Tino," he beamed. "How nice of you to come." He admired Carter. "And you've brought a very pretty lady with you I see."

"May I introduce Doctor Howard Brooks," Cordero said to Carter as the man lowered the volume of the music on an old cassette player. "Doctor Brooks is our chief pathologist and medical examiner. He comes all the way from England via Portugal, Brazil and several marriages. Doctor Brooks, Agent Sara Carter, FBI, seconded to INTERPOL."

"A pleasure to meet you my dear," Brooks gushed. "Welcome to my humble place of work. I don't do great things here, you must understand. I simply do what I can."

"Don't let appearances deceive you," Cordero said to Brooks as much as Carter. "He may look like a butcher and if he operated on you, he'd leave you convinced that he was. But the police on the south coast would be lost without him."

"The last medical apron I had was chewed up by a dog," Brooks explained. "Right here in the hospital would you believe? Boundaries are very fluid in Timor, my dear. But you are too kind, Tino. I trust your family is well and you are not yet missing the bright lights of Dili. If you are staying in town for any length of time you should both pop around to my even more humble abode for a drink one night. But at the minute we are not here to exchange pleasantries. What I have will interest you, I think, Tino. Follow me." He turned to go but then stopped and spun back on his heel. "Are you squeamish, my dear?" he asked Carter with a ghoulish smile on his face.

"Not in the least," she replied.

"Good, then please, come this way."

They entered a large, cold windowless room with a worn poster of muscles in the body and another of the human skeleton along one wall. Both charts were in English. Nothing adorned the other walls but a dust-free mark on one indicated where a crucifix had once hung.

A man's body was laid out uncovered on a metal table in the centre of the room. He appeared to be forty or fifty years of age but the damage to his face made it hard to tell with any accuracy.

The damage to his body, in fact, made it hard to tell much at all, such was the trauma it had suffered. He had a stocky build, mostly muscle, little fat. The skin was greenish in parts where sulphurous gases had corrupted the red blood cells in the body and grey or black in others where the process was more advanced. Dark hair was matted to the skull but there was little body hair. The right arm was missing and there were deep gashes along the torso and remaining limbs. The body's modest height and weight and the lean build suggested he could have been Timorese or Indonesian but it was hard to tell. There seemed to be markings on his left arm and on his upper legs but the cuts and abrasions to his body made it impossible to be sure whether they were tattoos or old injuries. On the floor beneath the man's feet were two metal trays brimming with a discoloured liquid. Around the table the chemical smell was intense.

"This gentleman came in last night," Brooks began. "One of your fellow police officers, Tino, found him on a beach late yesterday down by a western branch of Rio Tafera. Says he was in the process of being eaten by a crocodile, which is not hard to believe from the look of him. A very big crocodile I might add. The thing appears to have torn off the chap's right arm as you can see. May even have swallowed it because it hasn't been found. Your man—that is, your police officer—shot at the croc several times with his service pistol," Brooks said raising an eyebrow as he glanced at Cordero. "Said he hit the thing in the stomach and the neck. The croc beat a hasty retreat back into the water."

Brooks was enjoying telling the tale. It was the most interesting examination he'd been asked to do in months. "The officer, wisely, didn't follow it," he continued. "Instead, he collected what he could of our friend here and brought him in. Dragged me away from a little party I was having with my old friends Gin and Tonic. I assembled the remains as best I could and gave it a quick clean up. That's why I rang you. This morning I'm getting ready to examine it properly."

"Do you know who he is?" Cordero asked, inspecting the body closely.

"Not in the least."

"Where are his clothes, shoes?"

"What's left of them I've put over there on that bench behind you," Brooks said indicating a jumble of black pants, dark shirt and dirty boots collected together in a heap. "No ID, nothing in the pockets, nothing distinctive that might indicate who he is."

"How long dead?" asked Cordero, standing back and addressing Brooks directly now.

"When he came in, I'd say twelve, fifteen hours."

"You think the man was walking along the beach and was attacked by the crocodile?" Cordero asked. "Why should that be of interest to me?"

"More likely he was murdered elsewhere and then his body was dumped on the beach," Brooks said moving to the far side of the body. "The crocodile is not our culprit. Not for the killing, at any rate. If you discount the damage done to the torso and look carefully at the centre of the chest here," Brooks pointed to the spot with one red-gloved finger, "you'll notice a cavity." He then reached over to a bench along the wall on which were laid out several surgical instruments and aluminium basins. From one of the basins he picked up a four-inch iron nail the head of which had been fashioned into a barb and held it out to Cordero across the dead man's body. "I took this out of him this morning. This is what killed him, shot straight into the heart. The crocodile was only cleaning up the carrion."

"A *rama ambon*," said Cordero taking the nail in his kerchief. He turned it in his fingers examining it and handed it to Carter. "A nail fashioned into an arrow, usually shot from a home-made cross bow. Common weapon here in Timor or at least it was before firearms became more readily available."

"A *traditional* weapon," added Brooks with emphasis. "Or weapon of choice for a gang."

"What makes you think he was killed elsewhere and dumped on the beach?" asked Carter, who was examining the nail.

"The police officer said there were drag marks along the sand," Brooks answered. "The killer may have been trying to dispose of the body via the crocodile, who knows?"

"Who is the officer who found the body?" Cordero asked.

"Jose dos Santos," Brooks answered.

"I don't know him. You say he shot twice at the crocodile?"

"Several times. Hit it twice. He's new here. From Ainaro. A Pentecostal."

Cordero moved around the body, peering down closely at it while nodding. "Ordinarily a Timorese would never harm a crocodile, what we call *lafaek*," he explained to Carter. "We believe *lafaek* to be our ancestor. Many call crocodiles 'Avoo' meaning grandfather." His tone now lacked the usual levity she had come to associate with him. "Our creation story has it that a boy once saved a crocodile from dying and, by way of thanks, the crocodile transformed itself into our island."

He stood up from the body. "The point being that someone who converts to Pentecostalism probably underwent a degree of cultural re-programming. Customary beliefs would no longer be seen for what they are, namely myths, but instead be viewed as abominations before God. As a result, unlike most Timorese, he would have had no hesitation in firing at the crocodile."

"Moreover, my dear," Brooks added, "the locals believe that anyone who is harmed by a crocodile probably deserved it. Crocodiles have ways of identifying bad people not normally available to the police, you see. And then they eat them."

"But that isn't much help in working out who this man is, or rather was," said Cordero, pushing both hands deep into his trouser pockets.

"Prints, dental records," suggested Carter.

Brooks explained that the one remaining hand was too badly mauled to retrieve fingerprints even if there were records against which they could be checked—which in Timor there weren't. As for dentals records, he said the only dentists in Timor came with the United Nations forces around the time of independence and left with them a decade later. They had treated very few Timorese.

"You can see why I called you in, Tino," Brooks said. "This is a perfect case for a member of the scientific investigation unit or whatever fancy name you give yourselves."

Cordero was slowly examining the man's clothing. "Why boots," he wondered aloud, "and not sandals? Could he have been a construction worker? But even many of them wear sandals."

Carter waited, growing impatient. "Cordero," she said eventually but he ignored her. "Cordero!"

"Hmm. What is it?"

"We're here to find a missing baby, remember?" Carter said. "And we don't have much time."

"What? Yes." Cordero straightened. "Ordinarily this would interest me Brooks but Agent Carter and I are here to look into the theft of babies in the mountains around Suai. A more urgent priority I'm afraid. One of them may still be here, alive and needing to be found. And we're late for a meeting at Buzzi's office. I'll see what he wants to do about our friend here and I'll have a chat with this dos Santos. Oh, and I'd like you to keep me posted if there are any further developments." Cordero took another look at the dead man's clothes. "You are right, it *does* interest me," he said.

• • •

"So the Suai travel brochure wouldn't have been entirely wrong," Carter said as they climbed back into the SUV.

"Wrong?"

"In mentioning crocodiles—remember?"

"Oh yeah," he said. "You're right. Well I did say there were quite a few crocodiles around here."

When they reached police station on the other side of Suai, Buzzi had not yet arrived. A female officer was sitting quietly in the reception area and she rose and straightened her skirt over her knees as Cordero and Carter walked down the corridor toward Buzzi's office.

"*Bondia, maun,*" she said to Cordero following behind them. "*Bondia, mana,*" to Carter. They both stopped, conscious of her for the first time. The officer looked at Cordero and said: "I am Officer Estefana dos Carvalho. I have been told to work with you while you are in Suai."

She was an attractive girl, perhaps no more than twenty-one or twenty-two years of age. She had a slight build, unblemished light brown skin, long dark hair tied in a tight bun and the faintest hint of lipstick around a set of near perfect teeth when she smiled. She was dressed in a neatly-pressed police uniform and was obviously nervous. As they turned she had dropped her notebook, then her pen, and was now having trouble juggling the two with the police cap she was also carrying under her arm. Carter wondered how much experience in policing this young woman had had.

"*Bondia, mana*," said Cordero and introduced himself to her. "This is FBI Agent Carter, from America. She doesn't speak Tetun."

"I understand," Officer Estefana dos Carvalho said switching now to English. "I will only speak English to you, *mana*. I mean Agent Carter."

"Thank you," said Carter. "That's fine. You speak good English?"

"Oh yes, *mana*. I was taught by Filipina nuns. All through school." She took her gaze to the floor. "And my mother says I watch too many American movies."

"And you know the area north of here, I'm told," said Cordero to refocus her attention.

"Yes, *maun*," she said, looking up. "I spent a little time posted to one of the villages there."

"Do you know much about the babies who were taken?" he asked.

But before Estefana could answer Buzzi strode through the front door of the police building with a troubled look on his face. Cordero suggested that Estefana go over the reports of baby thefts with Carter while he spoke to the superintendent and the two women disappeared into a small room Estefana indicated at the back of the building.

"You heard about the shooting on the beach, I understand," Buzzi said when he and Cordero had entered the superintendent's office. "More trouble I have to deal with."

"Yes, I saw Brooks. Looks like a crossbow," Cordero replied.

"Not that," Buzzi corrected him. "I'm talking about that fool dos Santos shooting at the crocodile. A couple of fishermen saw it. Spread the word around fast. Exaggerated things, of course. I've just come from a meeting with locals down by Tafera. They're pissed off. Blaming the police—me, the whole damn office here."

"I was afraid this sort of thing might happen," said Cordero, "although I didn't think it would be this quick."

"I just hope it doesn't get up into the hills and mix with that other idiocy," Buzzi said and threw his hands up in the air. "But who am I kidding. Word spreads like a bad smell around this place. And if that crocodile dies and washes up, God knows what sort of backlash we're in for." Buzzi sat down heavily in his chair. "For the moment we can pretend that the police officer just shot *at* the damn thing but didn't hit it." Buzzi nodded for Cordero to sit as well. He took a packet of cigarettes from the top drawer of his desk, flipped them open, sniffed the contents, tossed the packet back in the drawer. He reached into his pocket and withdrew a toothpick, then realised he already had one in his mouth and put the new one back.

"Where's dos Santos now?" Cordero asked.

"Home. I gave orders he was not to show his face around town today."

"I was hoping to talk to him," Cordero said.

"Why? He can't tell you anything you don't already know if you've talked to Brooks. Besides, I don't want to involve the fool any more than he is already."

"Well, to be fair Buzzi, he probably thought he was saving a man's life," Cordero protested.

"Saving a life my ass," Buzzi said waving the suggestion away. "He's an idiot. Some sort of Bible nut. Why can't he just be a Catholic and ignore the Bible like the rest of us?"

"What do you want done about the victim?" Cordero asked.

"Oh leave it," said Buzzi, calming himself. "We'll circulate his photo, keep an eye out for a missing person's report. Sooner or later we'll find out who he is. Or maybe we won't. If that's the case, who cares? Don't waste your time on it. Probably a dispute over a woman or a gambling debt that got out of hand. A one-off." He began fidgeting with the papers on his desk. "Where's the American?"

"With that young police officer, dos Carvalho, now. They're going through reports on the stolen kids."

"Good. Stick with that. Officer dos Carvalho is a good girl. Not too bright but eager to please. You have her as long as you need her."

Buzzi stood, laid his toothpick on the desk and adjusted his belt. "We must find that baby girl and fast," he said. "It's been almost a week since she was taken and her father will be stirring up trouble. That'll ignite all that unrest up in the mountains. As I told you last night I've had no reports of people crossing the border where they shouldn't be crossing it. That means there's a good chance the girl is alive. But almost a week, Tino," he repeated. "A lot can happen to a baby in that time. We must solve this and soon. I don't want Dili on my back. Get me a result, Tino!"

Chapter 8

Officer Estefana dos Carvalho had gathered the reports on the stolen babies into a thin pile and put them in a green manila folder. She had placed the folder on the table in the middle of the room together with a map of the Suai district, a pad, two pens, and two glasses for water in case they were needed. Two plastic chairs sat side-by-side against the table. As in the INTERPOL office in Dili, these chairs were made of poor quality plastic. A plant of some kind in a pot lay wilting from lack of water in one corner of the room. A cabinet, largely empty, and a stand-up fan that had not been turned on were the only other objects in sight. Officer Estefana stood by one of the chairs, waiting for Carter to sit before she did.

"As my colleague said I can't speak or read Tetun," Carter pointed out.

"That's alright, *mana*," Estefana said, a smile lighting up her eyes. "I'm here to help."

"If I speak too fast for you or you don't understand what I say, just tell me. Okay?" Carter said.

"*Bele*," said Estefana which from her expression Carter took to mean 'okay'. Then Carter sat and Estefana did the same, pulling her skirt down over her knees again.

"Let's start with the earliest report and then work through to the latest," Carter suggested. "See what things we can find are common across the reports." She pointed to the map on the table. "And as we work through them, perhaps you could mark each with a number on this map—'1' for the first report, '2' for the second, etcetera—and show me where they are."

"*Bele*. Oops. I must stop saying that. I mean okay," Estefana said and rifled through the folder for the first reported abduction. She took out one page, only half of which had any text on it. "Valeria Rate Falur," she read concentrating carefully on each name. "Six months old. From the *suku* of Lailua." She studied the map in front of them a moment and pointed. "Here."

Carter lent across and looked at the map. The village was on a small stream, isolated, close to the Indonesian border and surrounded by heavy forest. The forest held her gaze for a moment. "This area," she said to Estefana, indicating the forest, "who lives there?"

Estefana inspected the area where Carter was pointing. "I don't think anyone lives in there, *mana*. I think it is *lulik*. That means sacred, taboo. No-one can go there without the permission of the village headman."

"Why is it taboo?" Carter asked.

"Spirits of the ancestors live there, *mana*," Estefana answered.

"Would everyone be likely to observe the taboo on going there?" asked Carter.

"Everyone *should* obey it, *mana*," Estefana replied, her brow creasing. "But there are always people who don't do what is right."

"Tell me about it," agreed Carter. "When was the child taken?"

Estefana checked. "January 14."

It was now September 18. Carter checked back on the calendar on her cell phone. January 14 had been a Tuesday. "How was she taken?" Estefana looked puzzled by the question. "Okay. Where was she taken from?" Carter asked.

Estefana looked at the report. "Her home. Her mother had gone out to buy something."

"What did she buy?" asked Carter.

Estefana checked the report. "It doesn't say."

"What time of day did she go out?" asked Carter.

Estefana looked, frowned. "It doesn't say."

"Does the mother shop every Tuesday?" Carter asked.

Estefana checked the file. "It doesn't say, *mana*."

"Was anyone unfamiliar seen in the village at the time? Or any vehicles not usually there?"

"It doesn't say, *mana*."

"Did anyone hear the baby cry?"

Estefana just raised her shoulders to indicate that there was no comment on that in the report. She looked embarrassed.

"Was the family interviewed by a male or a female police officer?"

"Male," Estefana said, checking the name on the report and relieved that she could answer that question at least. *That figures*, Carter was thinking.

"Was a search of the village and surrounding areas undertaken?"

Estefana looked at the report. "Yes the police conducted a search with the help of a few villagers."

"When?" asked Carter.

"When, *mana*?"

"Yes. How soon after the report came in that the baby was missing?"

Estefana checked. "The next day." *Far too late*, thought Carter. She could remember cases back home where a child had been taken across a state border, raped, killed and the body dumped within hours of being abducted.

"Is that all there is on that file?"

"Yes, *mana*."

"Okay. Mark that location on the map and let's look at the next one," Carter told her.

Her name was Merdiana Esperanca. She was five months old and taken from the village of Belematai. Again, small, isolated, surrounded by forest and close to the border. As with the previous baby, Merdiana had also been taken from her house while her mother was out—tending the garden plot nearby. That was January 28. Another Tuesday. There were no details of regular routines, strangers in the village, or unfamiliar vehicles. The distance between the garden plot and the house was not indicated. A search was conducted, but again it was done the day after Merdiana had been taken.

"Did any of the neighbours report anything unusual?" Carter asked.

"No *mana*, not from what is in the report," answered Estefana. "Did the same police officer make this report?" asked Carter. Estafana checked. "No. It was a different officer."

"Was the officer—"

"Male," Estafana jumped in. "I think I was the only female police officer in the area at this time and then not all the time." *Learns fast*, Carter told herself.

"Okay. Mark it on the map," she said. "Next."

Third case: A boy. Manuel Fonsela. Eight months old and from the *suku* of Camoreno. Similar location. But went missing from his home on a Monday—not a Tuesday—in early February while his mother was dropping food to a sick relative. Another belated search. No further details. Nothing about neighbours.

And on it went. Miranda Tilman, seven months. Joao Guterres, eleven months. Luana Ruiz, eleven months…until they came to the ninth child taken. The babies had been abducted across several different days of the week—no pattern there—but all while the parents were briefly absent from the house. No-one reported seeing or hearing anything unusual.

"Julieta da Silva," read Estefana and her tone expressed excitement. "I did this report, *mana*. She comes from the *suku* of Lotarai. It is a very poor village, much poorer than the others. There are less than fifteen buffalos," she said as though that would explain how poor it was. "I checked. It too is near the border. Here," she said and pointed on the map. "There is *lulik* forest nearby and although there is a church the people are very traditional. Julieta was six months old at the time. She was taken from under a tree by the side of the road near her house. Her brother Julio, who is nine years old, was meant to be caring for her while their mother went to check on one of the buffalos. That's why I asked how many were in the village. I thought it might be useful to know. There may have been a, what is the word, ransom? Or maybe taking the baby had something to do with a ritual. Buffalos are often used in rituals, *mana*. But I couldn't find any connection like that."

Estefana wasn't reading the file because she had memorized the details of her report. "Julio said he saw a friend and ran off to play. He was not gone long, maybe twenty minutes. When he came back, he couldn't find Julieta. He said he saw nothing and was crying when I talked to him because his mother had slapped him in her anger when she found the baby gone. I was nearby the village that day. That's why I took the report. I organised a search immediately and was able to confirm that the baby had gone missing. But we found no traces."

Maybe not, Carter thought, *but at least you went straight into action and at least you thought to get some details unlike the male officers in the other eight cases.* She was beginning to warm to Estefana. She reminded Carter of herself as a rookie—keen, attentive to detail, respectful, and probably ignored by her male colleagues for all those reasons. Maybe in time she'd learn that being nice didn't get you far in a male environment.

"Did you interview the neighbours?" Carter asked.

"Yes, *mana*. But no-one saw or heard anything that was helpful. Instead, they just asked me questions. They wanted to know what I knew."

"When you say this was a very poor village, are there other villages in this area that are wealthier or at least more developed in terms of, say, cell phone access, a police presence, that kind of thing?" Carter asked.

"Not many, but yes," said Estefana. "This is a large area and it is difficult to access all of these villages. Government services are concentrated in one or two, like Matalawa." Estefana pointed to it on the map. "And that means people have access to things there that they don't have in villages like Lotarai."

"Things like what?" asked Carter.

"Better cell phone reception, better roads, better schools and shops with more goods in them."

"Are there reports of babies being stolen from those places?"

"No, *mana*."

They looked through more reports of abductions from other villages and marked the locations on the map. Finally they examined the latest case, Elisanda Soares, taken from the village of Fatuloro the previous Saturday—September 13. Her mother was at Mass with six of her children at the time. Her father had not gone to Mass because he was supposed to be minding the boy of theirs who was sick. But he was the village chief and was called to a brief meeting with a few villagers down the road over a matter they had been complaining about for several days beforehand. When he returned Elisanda had gone. The boy who had been in the house was asleep. He'd seen and heard nothing. A search of the village was conducted. Nothing was found.

Carter sat back as far as her plastic chair would allow but it began to buckle. She stood and paced the room, thinking.

Estefana collected the reports back into the manila folder and placed them on the side of the table with a heavy weight on top. Then she secured the top ends of the map with the two drinking glasses and the bottom ends with two more glasses she took from the cabinet against the wall. The air-conditioner was not working and it was hot in the room now. Estafana turned on the fan that she had brought in to compensate. Then she sat, corrected her dress, and waited with her hands in her lap.

"Good work, Estefana," said Carter. "I mean with the reports, especially the one you did. Now, let's consider what we have." She came back to the table and lent over the map. "Apart from the ages of the children, which are more or less similar, the only things that seem common are that all the babies are taken quickly, from small, isolated and relatively poor villages near the Indonesian border, and their homes are near forests that are largely uninhabited and unused. That suggests the person or persons taking the babies know what they are looking for, know the area well, and want to get the babies quickly out of sight and across the border."

"Whoever takes the babies could just act quickly, when the chance arises," offered Estefana.

"True. An opportunity has to present itself," agreed Carter. "But the fact that the babies are taken quickly and without any crying that would attract attention suggests prior knowledge and maybe a degree of familiarity with the baby."

Estefana took a while to digest that but then nodded at the point. "It also suggests that they may be targeting villages with only basic infrastructure and government services in order to get away before a proper search can be conducted," Carter concluded. She looked down at Estefana. "And that doesn't help us very much, does it?" Carter said and started tapping her fingers on the table.

Estefana appeared ready to apologise for that conclusion when Cordero walked into the room. Carter went to the fan and pinched the T-shirt from her chest to cool down in the breeze. Outside the glare from the sun off the sea was blinding and the palm fonds hung motionless in the heavy air. Carter flapped the T-shirt in and out as best she could in a vain attempt to dry the sweat. She was wishing she hadn't worn a low-cut bra which was now clearly visible through the damp cotton fabric.

"Does it get this hot in Arizona?" Cordero asked.

"Hotter, actually," she replied, "but never this humid."

"Anything?" he asked to change the subject, aware of her embarrassment.

"Not much. I think police investigating and reporting procedures could be more methodical in this part of the world," she said.

Cordero ignored the comment. Carter went through the little that the reports contained and showed him the location of the villages where babies had been taken on the map.

"If babies are being stolen for illegal adoptions—which, from what we know, seems likely—then it's possible they're chosen—males, females, ages—to match some sort of request or order, if you like," said Carter. "That would give us a motive for each particular baby. What we don't have is any idea about the means or sense of opportunity."

She thought for a moment. "How many people would live in these villages, Estefana? A rough guess."

Estefana screwed her face up considering the question. She looked at the map. "In the smaller villages, maybe two hundred, counting children," she said. "In the larger ones, up to five hundred people perhaps."

"And what is strange is why no-one seems to have seen, heard, or noticed anything," Carter said. "I've worked cases in communities of that size back home and everyone knows everyone else's business. One person hangs their washing on a line; before long it's common knowledge that so-and-so is wearing new blue pyjamas or has just bought a new red dress. Then the speculation starts that there's a new girlfriend or boyfriend on the scene. Nothing much else to do, you see, but watch your neighbours and exchange gossip. But if we believe these reports—" and she slapped her hands forlornly against her thighs.

"Well everyone in these villages is working," Cordero pointed out. "As I've said before these are subsistence farmers. Nearly all of them up there. You eat what you grow and that doesn't leave much time for snooping or for gossip." He frowned. "Or maybe they just weren't questioned properly."

"Quite likely," Carter said. "In most cases at least," she added for Estefana's benefit. "Either way, I'd like to visit these places myself. You know, talk to the parents of the babies, talk to the neighbours. Thoroughly," she emphasised. "And get the lie of the land."

"Of course," agreed Cordero who had thrown one leg over the table and was leaning in, looking at the map. "Starting in Fatuloro," he said pointing to it, "in case there is a chance we can find the little girl taken on the weekend. Then we'll work back through the cases from there."

He waved his hand in a circle across the map where Estefana had marked the case numbers. "We could leave now and base ourselves in Fatuloro. The nuns there have a small guest house next to the church. I could ring ahead. You two might have to share a room," he said. "If that's not a problem."

"That'd be fine," Carter said on behalf of both of them. "Let's throw a few things in a bag and go without wasting time. That okay with you Estefana?"

Estefana looked excited. "I always keep a bag packed here in my locker," she said and rose from her chair. "It is for when I am called out on duty at short notice." Then she excused herself to text her mother that she would not be home for dinner.

Chapter 9

After they had packed for the trip north from the coast, Cordero fuelled the SUV and put additional diesel into two jerry cans he carried in the back just in case it should be needed. Carter and Estefana bought fried chicken and rice in polystyrene containers for the three of them to eat on the way. The sealed road out of Suai quickly became a gravel one, then a very rough dirt one, then a carriageway hard to distinguish from the many wash-aways, rockslides, and deep potholes that scarred the way. Nonetheless, by the standards of travel in rural Timore-Leste, they made reasonable progress. They climbed quickly into hilly country, motorcycles better able to negotiate the terrain overtaking them along the way. Microlets jammed tight with passengers and large hessian bags of who-knew-what piled high on their roofs were a lesser challenge and they passed them in turn along with trucks lurching up the road heavily laden with agricultural gear and concrete pipes or crowded with people in back clutching chickens, goats, and assorted produce.

"What do you think of Suai?" Cordero asked to make conversation. She glowered at him. "Sorry," he said. "I'm doing it again."

They drove on a little more in silence.

"How long have you been a police officer?" he asked Estefana, expecting a more enthusiastic response.

"Almost two years, *maun*. If you count the training," she replied.

"And do you like police work?" he asked.

"Oh yes, *maun*. I like to think I am doing something to help my country. I like that very much."

"I like that too," Cordero said. "But I also like beer, boxing, music, and comfortable shoes. What do you like?" he asked Carter, trying to encourage her to join in.

"I like to put bad guys away," she said and looked out the side window. Then she reminded herself it wasn't their fault she'd been uprooted and sent to East Timor. "And spicy food when I can get it and the Blues," she offered.

"Blues, *mana*?" asked Estefana.

"Blues?" echoed Cordero.

"It's a style of music, Estefana." She turned to Cordero. "Or didn't you know that?" she asked with a slight grin.

"Yes I know what the Blues are but you don't seem like a Blues type to me," he said.

"And what is a Blues type?" she asked.

"You know…a bit negative, self-absorbed—" He could see where this might lead and stopped.

"We may not get spicy food in the villages, *mana*," Estefana said coming to his rescue.

"Anything will do," said Carter staring out her window.

They stopped briefly to stretch their legs at what appeared to be a lookout.

As they got closer it proved to be a small grotto overlooking the river which ran about sixty yards below them. Fresh flowers had been placed in a plastic container by a statuette of the Virgin Mary, her hands joined in prayer and her blue robe fading in the harsh tropical sun. What looked like prayer cards of various vintages, together with offerings of one kind or another, had been placed at the base of the statuette. A wooden railing bordered the grotto where the land dropped off abruptly and the three of them drifted over to take in the view.

"Look, there!" said Estefana pointing toward the river. On the far bank a large crocodile lay stretched out in the sun. The bank itself was cleared of heavy trees and brush for about a hundred yards along its length and not a third of that distance from where the crocodile lay were three young children playing at the water's edge. A man stood among the children but with his back to the crocodile and his gaze fixed on an eagle soaring off into the distance.

"They come up the rivers, quite a long way inland," said Cordero of the crocodile, showing no concern for the kids.

"But those kids!" cried Carter. "That thing could pounce on them in seconds."

"Crocodiles only attack bad people, *mana*," Estefana said as though it was common knowledge.

"I've heard," Carter said. "But really?"

"And science tells us they calculate the risk," added Cordero. "That croc's about five feet long at best. The man's taller. While he's with the kids the crocodile won't risk taking on any of them. The man's too big." Cordero turned to go. "Or maybe he's just eaten his quota of bad people for the day," he added and strolled back to the vehicle.

• • •

A few miles further along on a deserted stretch of road they passed a battered red utility that had pulled over to the side, its bonnet raised. Cordero slowed as they passed, checking his rear vision mirror.

"It's an old guy," he said. "Probably knows little about engines and how they work. Let's stop and see if we can help." He reversed, stopped on the verge in front of the utility and they all piled out. "*Botarde tiu*," Cordero said, paying the older man due respect by calling him 'uncle'.

"*Botarde maun*," the man replied. He had a white moustache and eyes showing signs of advanced glaucoma. He was wearing shorts, an old soiled, sleeveless shirt and sandals. Resting on their haunches beside the utility were two elderly women, their heads covered in shawls. They gazed at Cordero but said nothing.

"What's the problem?" Cordero asked.

"The engine keeps cutting out," the man said pointing under the bonnet.

"Let me see." Cordero sat in behind the wheel of the vehicle and started the engine. No problem with the starter motor. He checked the fuel gauge to eliminate the possibility of an empty tank as well. But after a few seconds the engine stalled and died. He stepped out to check under the bonnet.

Carter and Estefana had walked to the edge of the road near where the women squatted. They exchanged cursory greetings. Leathery faces and red gums, Carter noticed. "Start it up," Cordero instructed and the old man wriggled himself in behind the wheel and did as he was told. Cordero worked the accelerator cable—no problem there. He poked around a little more, collecting oil and dirt all over his hands.

"Do you have any pliers, a wrench, tools of any kind?" he yelled. The old man scurried around to the tray of the utility, rummaged through bags and assorted boxes and produced pliers, a screwdriver, and a hammer. The engine died a second time. Cordero rose and selected what he needed then bent down to work under the bonnet. "Try it now," he said a few minutes later, "and keep your foot on the accelerator."

The old man did as he was told. This time the engine did not cut out. "Don't take your foot off the accelerator," Cordero told him, slamming the bonnet and returning the tools to the tray of the utility. "I've disconnected the wire that controls your idling. If you keep a bit of pressure on the accelerator you'll make it to the next village. Don't reverse or it'll cut out again. A mechanic will have to take a better look at it but this will get you home."

Cordero was wiping oil and grease off his hands with his kerchief. The old man was smiling and bowing his thanks through the driver's window. He shouted through the passenger's window to one of the women who rose, went to the back of the utility and came back with a grubby sack. She handed the sack to Carter, also bowed her head in gratitude, and then slid into the front seat along with the other woman.

The old man drove off, the engine revving, and Carter and Estefana looked at the sack. It was heavy and inside, at the bottom, was what looked like a large, dark clump of vegetative matter. "I think it is an edible bulb," Estefana said. "I've seen them in the markets. I have never tried one but they say they are very good to eat when cooked."

"Perhaps the nuns will know how to cook it," suggested Cordero.

They put the sack on the floor in the back of their vehicle and headed off, thinking no more about it. Five minutes later Estefana started to scratch her legs. Then Carter did as well. Then Estefana was scratching her stomach and arms. "Ants!" she yelled from the back seat. "They're coming out of the sack!"

Cordero stopped the car. They scurried out onto the road. He placed the sack on the ground outside the vehicle and opened it. The driving motion had disturbed the ants which had made a nest inside the bulb. Carter and Estefana were brushing themselves down frantically and stomping to kill ants that had gotten into their boots. They looked to be dancing a wild jig on the side of the road. Cordero laughed. "Well that's one piece of Timorese hospitality we might leave behind," he said. Estefana then broke into a giggle. And Carter, for the first time since she had arrived in East Timor, couldn't help but do the same. The sack, the bulb, the ants stayed where Cordero had put them on the side of the road when they left.

• • •

Fatuloro was a little over fifty-five miles from Suai by road and they made the journey in just under two hours, arriving around 4 pm. The village was positioned around a ridge that dropped off sharply into a wooded ravine to the north. Isolated huts of wooden slabs beneath thatched roofs were scattered on both sides of the ridge. Just below the ridge line on a flat area of ground was the main collection of several dozen cement block buildings with rusting iron roofs. They were arranged along two poorly kept streets that ran from a fork in the main road into the village at a crumbling monument erected to mark a local feat accomplished long ago.

On one of the streets were two stores. From the tables and chairs that could be seen through the doorway and the smoke curling upwards from a chimney out back, the first appeared to be an eatery. The other clearly sold groceries, cigarettes, clothes, and assorted bric-a-brac. Next door were a string of drab structures that served as government depots and offices. At one time these had been painted a light blue to just below the windowsills and then yellow, green or red beyond there to distinguish one from another but the weather had taken its toll and the paint had faded and peeled. One of the buildings, from a sign above the door, was evidently the police station but it was closed when they passed.

The second street contained houses across from a field on which about twenty children were playing soccer. Saplings set in the ground loosely at either end served as goalposts. The children yelped and bawled unconcerned about their bare feet on the rocky ground. Stray dogs, chickens, and small pigs were roaming about rummaging for food scraps through the rubbish that had piled on the side of the field. On a slight rise overlooking the centre of town but along its own dirt track was a church made of white-washed brick with a red tin roof and simple bell tower. To the right of the church within a fence surrounding its grounds were a large house and a smaller one also of brick and tin. A sign on the gate read 'Capela de Santo Eulogio'—the 'Chapel of Saint Eulogio'. Cordero drove up the track and through the open gate, passed a grotto framed by yellow and red flowering vines and on toward the larger of the two houses where he stopped the vehicle and cut its engine.

"We're here," he said and rubbed his eyes from the strain of driving. "At last."

Carter was the first out of the SUV to work her legs after sitting for so long. Estefana remained seated for a moment checking her cell reception. Cordero stepped out, stretched, walked to the door of the house, and knocked. After a few moments an elderly nun in a white habit and blue veil opened the door, steadying herself on a walking cane. She was Filipina and spoke English. Cordero knew this as he had met her on a previous visit to Fatuloro several months earlier.

"*Botarde, madre*," Cordero greeted her. "*Diak ka lae?* I am Vincintino Cordero. We met once. I rang you earlier today."

"*Botarde senyor*," the nun replied in barely a whisper before glancing at Cordero's companions. "*Diak, obrigada*," she added with more volume in her voice.

"Allow me to introduce my fellow police officers," continued Cordero in English, "*Mana* Carter and *Mana* Estefana. *Mana* Carter is from America. She doesn't speak Tetun. This," he said motioning to the nun, "is Sister Theresa."

"Good afternoon," said Sister Theresa in halting English. "We are happy to have you staying with us here." She looked back to Cordero. "May I ask what brings you to Fatuloro, *senyor*? You didn't explain when you called this morning and I am curious—one of the many vices of an old nun, I'm afraid."

"We are investigating the abduction of children in this area," explained Cordero. "Here in Fatuloro last Saturday and in other villages nearby in recent months. I'm sure you know about that. We should only trouble you for two, at most three, nights."

"You are no trouble, *senyor*, no trouble at all," insisted the nun. "But oh, those abductions. Yes, we do know about them. How could we not? Terrible. Simply terrible. Who would do such a thing to innocent children, to little babies?" she said then crossed herself and kissed the crucifix that hung from her belt. "Father Timoteo is saying a special Mass this Sunday for Elisanda Soares that God may intervene and return her to her parents. My sisters and I have been saying a rosary every day to the Holy Mother of God that all the children will be found, unharmed, and given back to their mothers." She paused. "Do the police have any more information about the whereabouts of Elisanda, *senyor*?"

"I'm afraid not, *madre*," Cordero said. "That's why we've come."

"And God bless you and help you in your efforts too," the old nun said.

"We can pay you in advance—" Cordero began to say reaching into his pocket.

The old nun held up a hand. "There is no rush, *senyor*," she said. "It's only money." She turned. "Come, I will show you to your rooms. You must be tired and here I am prattling on. Is that the right word in English—'prattle'? I don't use English much any more up here." The nun did not wait to be reassured and led them along a path by the side of the house. "Here, next to what we like to call the office you will have your meals," she said pointing with her cane. "But first, I'm sure you will want to freshen up after a long drive from Suai."

They had each grabbed their bags from the vehicle and followed behind Sister Theresa as she hobbled along. She showed them two small guest rooms at the end of the house. Each room was lit by a naked bulb and contained two single beds and assorted bits of furniture, here a night-stand, there a lowboy, two unmatching chairs. Both rooms contained a window, neither of which was screened, and one of which was slightly cracked. Mosquito nets were draped alongside each bed. The rooms smelled of dust and stale air as though they had not been opened in quite a while. "The two women will sleep here," Sister Theresa instructed, "and you, *senyor*, in the next room. Along there," she said pointing with her cane to the end of the building, "is a wash-room. There are clean towels on each bed. Dinner will be in one hour. We have early devotions tonight."

Carter and Estafana chose their respective beds and unpacked clean clothes. It was decided that Carter would use the wash-room first. It consisted of a squat toilet and a bucket behind a poorly-fitted wooden screen and a slightly sturdier door that opened on a cubicle where a tap fed a large concrete basin full of water. In this cubicle were also a ladle and another drain. It was what passed for a shower. Carter undressed, completed a body wash, and then cleaned her T-shirt and underwear. She dressed in a clean blouse and modest skirt, left the wash-room and hung her washed garments on a line that ran from the end of the building to a pole nearby.

Estafana appeared from their room to take her turn in the washroom and noticed what Carter was doing. "*Mana*," she said blushing. "Perhaps you'd like to hang your washing in our room. I can make a line for us both." Then she glanced across toward the smaller of the two houses beyond the pole and back to the flimsy black bra and panties on the line. "The priest lives there," she whispered.

"Oh, of course," Carter agreed. "But you have your wash. I can rig up a line inside."

While the two of them waited for Cordero to take his turn in the washroom, they strolled over to the chapel, which was open. As they entered Estefana dipped her hand in a font beside the door, blessed herself with the holy water it contained and knelt at a pew in silent prayer. Carter followed her in, hesitated at the water font, quickly dipped a finger in and blessed herself. She stood at the back of the chapel and looked around. It was the same as any other church she had visited except for the quaint addition of a dozen swifts that flew in and out from open windows high up along the walls and a banner of black, red and yellow—the colours of the Timorese flag—that had been strung around the lectern.

Estefana completed her prayer, crossed herself, rose and rejoined Carter. "Are you Catholic, *mana*?" she asked after a moment.

"Well, not really," said Carter. "I was raised Catholic but—"

"But you do believe in God?"

"Well—" Carter began but paused. Maybe she did and maybe she didn't. She wasn't sure. But Estefana certainly did and Carter respected that. "I—" but she was cut off."

"We call him *Maromak, mana*," Estefana explained. "When I was young, at school, the nuns told us that *Maromak* came to our ancestors through rocks and the trees but now he comes to us more clearly through the Church. Through Jesus and his Blessed Mother. But many people speak to him out there," she said pointing through the door, "and they continue the old rituals to keep him and the spirits of our ancestors—how would you say—on side."

"You mean supportive?" asked Carter.

"Yes, *mana*. That's the word. Supportive in order for crops to grow as they should. For babies to be born without their mothers dying and for those babies to live to become children and then adults. For protection from floods and landslides and snakes. All of those things."

Carter nodded but didn't comment. She turned toward the door and the two women walked out of the chapel to find Cordero. He was waiting for them outside his room. "Let's eat," he suggested, and they went to the room where the nun had told them their dinner would be served.

It consisted of rice and beans, fried eggs, and boiled green vegetables that Cordero said were pumpkin leaves cooked with lemon. The meal was simple but tasty and filling, especially for Cordero and Carter who had effectively skipped breakfast and lunch—again. A young Timorese nun served them. She came in and out of the room without saying a word or looking directly at any of them, setting down bowls of food and collecting the plates.

When dinner was over and they were preparing to leave the table, Carter asked Estefana to inquire about her name. "*Madre* Valeria," the nun answered in a barely audible voice looking up directly at the visitors for the first time.

Carter smiled. "Would you thank *Madre* Valeria for dinner, please Estefana? And tell her it was excellent."

"*Obrigada, madre*," Estefana obliged. "*Hahan furak*." The praise made no impression on the nun who gathered the used cutlery and left the room without saying another word.

"Right," declared Cordero. "It will be light enough for another hour at least. I suggest we talk to the parents of Elisanda Soares this evening. They can't live far from here and they are both likely to be at home now."

"Good plan," said Carter.

"I'll ask Sister Theresa where the family lives," said Cordero, "and grab a torch in case we need it on our way back. Hopefully we can leave the SUV here."

A few minutes later the three of them regrouped outside the house. "It's not far," Cordero reported. "We can walk after all."

As they headed out of the churchyard gate a boy, not more than eight or nine years old, ran past them rolling a hubcap down the road with a stick. He was bare footed, in baggy shorts and shirtless with a runny nose. "Hullo mister," he said to Carter as he passed. "Where you from?"

"America," Carter called out after him.

"Oh, very good mister," the boy yelled back and then ran on chasing his hubcap. Carter wondered if he knew what she had said or was just repeating lines of English he'd learned by rote in school.

The three of them walked on. Along the way to the Soares' house, Cordero dropped back from Carter and spoke to Estefana in Tetun. *Odd*, Carter was thinking, *because on the way to Fatuloro and since their arrival the two of them had spoken only in English for my benefit.* Cordero appeared to be giving Estefana instructions about one thing or another and Estefana appeared to be arguing with him until a stern rebuke caused her to fall silent. Then Cordero quickened his steps to catch up with Carter. Estefana held back with a slightly troubled look on her face.

Chapter 10

Napoleao Soares and his wife Veronica lived in a three-room cement block house on the far side of the improvised soccer field. Napoleao had been elected village chief two years earlier for a term that would last another several years but his title earned him little other than authority in dealing with certain local matters and the respect that flowed from that. His house at one time had been painted yellow from the foundations to the bottom of the two windows that fronted it and white above that to a red corrugated iron roof. But like the buildings in the centre of town, time and wear and the lack of maintenance had seen the paint wither, many of the cement blocks crack, and the roof rust badly. The three rooms of the house accommodated the family of two adults and eight children—now minus the baby Elisanda. A make-shift kitchen was attached to the back wall and a privy had been built twenty yards from the back of the house in the yard.

Napoleao was sitting on the steps of the small porch out back, shirtless, smoking a hand-rolled cigarette when Cordero, Carter and Estefana arrived. He appeared to be in his thirties, all muscle and sinew, an old scar that looked like a stab wound prominent on his chest. "*Bonoite, senyor,*" Cordero began with the deference due a village chief and before introducing himself and his two companions.

"*Noite,*" Napoleao grunted and he took another drag on his cigarette.

"We were sorry to hear about your baby daughter being taken," said Cordero. "We are police investigators and we're here to try to get her back." Napoleao looked past them out into the yard and showed little interest in what Cordero was saying. "Can we ask you and your wife a few questions?" Cordero put to him.

"What for, *maun*?" Napoleao asked. "We've spoken to the police. It did no good. I don't have my baby back. This is something you people have no power over."

"Well answering our questions may do no good but it can't do any harm," replied Cordero. "And we have come a long way to talk to you," he added in the hope the man would feel obliged for their journey. "Each one of us," he added.

The man took one last drag on his cigarette and threw the butt into the yard. "Veronica," he called. "Come out here and talk to these people about Elisanda." Then he looked up at Cordero. "You can ask me questions here," he said. "Those two," gesturing toward Carter and Estefana, "can go with the woman, over there under that tree."

Cordero agreed and explained the arrangement to Carter. She protested that it would be better if all three of them talked to each parent together in turn but Cordero said the husband would insist on the split and he wasn't a man to be challenged. At that moment, the woman appeared in the open doorway of the house. She was not old but she was hollow-cheeked, her eyes were bloodshot from lack of sleep, her hair hung untidily below her shoulders and she was kneading the hem of her heavily mended skirt like a child. Behind her three small faces were peering at the strangers while from further inside the house came the sound of other children thrashing about at play.

Carter greeted the woman with a friendly nod of her head. "I am Officer dos Carvalho of the Timor-Leste National Police," said Estefana. "This is my colleague *Mana* Carter. She is a policewoman from America. That is our senior officer Vincintino Cordero." She waited for the introductions to register with the woman. "We are sorry to hear that your baby was taken." The woman seemed to be straining to hold back tears. "Could we ask you a few questions, perhaps over there, under the tree? I will have to translate for my colleague," she said indicating Carter, "as she does not speak Tetun."

The woman wiped her eyes quickly with the back of her hand, reassured her children she would not be gone long and started off across the yard ahead of Estefana and Carter. She stopped under the tree looking as though she had forgotten why she was there. Carter arranged three plastic chairs that lay in the grass and dirt so that they were facing each other. She wanted to see the woman's reactions to questions, watch her expressions as she told her story, gain what insights she could from closely observing someone whose language she did not understand. She was practiced at this; it was something she often had to do among many older Native Americans back home.

"Could you ask her to tell us what she did last Saturday?" Carter said to Estefana. "Starting with why she went to Mass on Saturday rather than Sunday."

The woman hesitated. "My name is Veronica," she began. "Saturday was the feast day of Saint Eulogio. Our church is named in his honour." Carter remembered the sign on the gate leading into the church grounds where they were staying. "That's why I went to Mass. I went on Sunday as well."

"Okay," said Carter after Estefana had translated. "Now ask her to tell us what she did that morning. And when you translate make sure you mention all the details of what she says however small and try to summarise any emotions she expresses."

Veronica had woken at dawn, checked on the boy who was sick, prepared coffee for her husband and a small serving of rice porridge for the children, and fed Elisanda. Then she gathered eggs from the chickens while the children ate, filled the water troughs for the animals around the yard, and come back to sweep the house and porch.

"Like every other morning," she said.

The woman's hands were playing with the hem of her skirt again as she recalled the day. She dressed the children for Mass in clean clothes, washed their faces and combed their hair. Then she dressed herself, checked on the sick boy and gave her husband instructions on what to do if the baby started crying or the boy woke feeling ill. She looked up from her hands.

"Then I kissed Elisanda on her head and walked to the church." Her face contorted. "That was the last time I saw her."

Estefana touched her gently on the knee. "It's alright, *mana*. Take your time," she said.

"When I returned," the woman began and sniffled, "my husband had been called to a meeting down the road, not far."

She pointed vaguely through the trees. "My son who was sick was asleep. Elisanda was gone." She looked directly at Estefana then, a mixture of sadness and guilt in her eyes.

"I searched the house, the yard and sent for my husband to come. He didn't know where Elisanda was. We both searched the house and the yard a second time and my husband went to each of the neighbours in case one of them had come and taken the baby. A short time later we went to the police station but it was closed."

The older, more senior, police officer was sick at home in bed, she said, and the young officer had fallen off his motorcycle and broken his leg. He wasn't in the police office either but also resting at home. Napoleao went to his house and demanded he come back with him but the officer complained his leg was aching. Finally her husband managed to persuade him to come. By this time it was two hours after the baby went missing. The officer spoke to Veronica and, with Napoleao's help, organised a search of the village by several men and women. Then he went back to the police station saying he had to write a report.

"But I think he just went back home and we haven't seen him since," Veronica added.

She looked at Estefana, then at Carter, and wiped back tears. The three sat in silence for a moment while she collected herself and, at Carter's suggestion, Estefana asked Veronica to describe her baby.

"Oh she is beautiful," she began, sniffling. "She has big eyes and a head of thick black hair even though she is only six months old. Her fingers are small and delicate. Everyone says how pretty she is. All the time." She wiped her eyes and stared at nothing in particular.

Carter asked Estefana which one of them had been using the present tense—her in the translation or Veronica in what she had said. The Tetun language didn't use tense, Estefana explained, but the context of what Veronica was saying indicated she was talking in the present. *Good*, thought Carter, *she hasn't given up hope of the little girl's return.*

"Ask her for a photograph of Elisanda," Carter said.

"We don't have money for such things," the woman replied when Estefana put the request to her. "We are poor," she added looking faintly embarrassed.

"Ask her if it was unusual for Veronica's husband to leave Elisanda and his sick son as he did that day and walk off," Carter said.

"No," the woman said appearing slightly riled by the question. "He is chief of this village and is often called out to settle disputes."

"Had he been gone long?" Carter asked. The answer was no.

"Ask her about her relations with her husband," Carter said.

The question led to a long exchange between Estefana and Veronica. As delicately as Estefana could broach the subject, the woman seemed angered by the implication that the relationship with her husband had anything to do with the baby's disappearance. Eventually Estefana summed up the response as best she could by reassuring Carter that husband and wife were living happily together and that Veronica had never entertained any suspicions that her husband might have harmed Elisanda.

"I don't blame him for anything," the woman had told Estefana. "He is very proud of the baby and loves all our children."

No one had been asking about the baby or any of Veronica's other children who ranged in age from three years to twelve. And none of the older boys' friends could have come to the house because Veronica had seen them all in the church that morning. "The feast of a saint is a big occasion for all of us," she added as though Estefana at least should know this.

"Had her husband locked the house when he stepped out to go to his meeting?" Carter asked.

"The house has no lock," the woman said but nothing had been taken.

"Had anyone unfamiliar been speaking to her recently?" Carter asked.

"No, no one," annoyance showing in Veronica's voice again.

"Did she or her husband have any enemies in the village, or nearby?"

Veronica hesitated for a moment then appeared angry. "Of course not," she said. "Why do you think my husband was elected village chief? He is liked by everyone. He doesn't drink palm wine or gamble with the other men. We don't borrow money. We are simple farmers."

"Had any of the neighbours heard the baby crying while Veronica was at Mass?"

"Babies always cry because they are always hungry in this village," the woman said, this time looking at Carter as though the answer was obvious and it was a stupid question to ask. "If Elisanda was crying, no one would have taken any notice."

"I think she is becoming impatient with our questions," Estefana said to Carter.

"Just a few more," Carter replied. "Ask if she, her husband, their children or any the neighbours noticed anyone or anything unfamiliar near the house, in the village, driving through Fatuloro that morning?"

"No," the woman said as she shifted restlessly in her chair and looked over at her husband who was talking to Cordero.

"Just one more question," Carter said. "Ask what she thinks happened to her daughter."

Veronica sat motionless, staring at Carter for a moment. Then tears welled in her eyes again and her voice became a rasp. "They say a demon took her to Suai," she said looking at Estefana and there was fear in her eyes and desperation in her voice. "Help me find her before the demon cuts off her head and buries it!"

Estefana's voice was flat when she translated. "A bad person took my baby," she told Carter the woman had said. "Please help get her back."

• • •

Napoleao pulled a small pouch filled with loose tobacco from his trouser pocket, extracted the amount he needed plus a small piece of paper, and rolled another cigarette between his fingers. He licked the paper to seal it, brushed flies away from his face, picked up an orange plastic lighter from the porch and lit the cigarette. He took a deep drag, held it in his lungs, then blew smoke out of the side of his mouth. He didn't bother to look directly at Cordero but gazed passed him into the yard.

"I told everything I know to that police officer," he said. "When the fool finally came."

Cordero squatted on the ground next to the porch steps. "I know. I don't want to ask about that. The American woman over there has investigated a lot of cases of children who've been taken from their homes. That's why she's here with me. If there are any more important details she will find them."

Just then one of the man's older sons came out of the house and plonked down next to his father on the steps. The father ruffled his hair playfully, told him to go back inside and take care of his brothers and sisters. The strangers would be gone soon.

The boy stood up and ran back inside. "Then what do you want to ask?" Napoleao said.

"I want to ask you what you think really happened to Elisanda," Cordero said.

The man took another deep drag of his cigarette and let the smoke drift from his nostrils but said nothing.

"This will not go into any police report," Cordero assured him. "What you tell me will stay with me."

"Why should I believe that?" Napoleao asked.

"Because you are the village chief and I respect that. And because your baby girl has been stolen and I may be the only person able to get her back."

The man wrestled with that thought for a moment as he took another drag on his cigarette then threw what was left of the butt away and wiped his mouth. He looked up at the fading light in the sky, the first stars appearing, and then at Cordero without showing any emotion.

"Around here people are talking, getting angry," he said. "Children have been taken from that village down by the river, Bunik, and from Beko and Lotarai. Their parents can't find them, the police can't find them." He turned away again from Cordero. "They disappear into the air without a trace."

"And what are people saying about that?" Cordero asked.

"What do you think they're saying?" the man replied.

"You tell me," said Cordero.

The man sniffed, looked away again, then glanced back. "Down around Suai there is a lot of building going on," he said. "Many foreigners are there with trucks and machines that disturb the land and cut down trees. Trucks come in every day. They say big roads are being built, a place where giant airplanes can come and go, another where big ships can unload. Across the River Tafera they are building a giant bridge. I've seen it with my own eyes. It's as big as this village. But the last bridge there was washed away. After a storm, you know?"

"All of that is true but what has it to do with your daughter and the others?"

"How do you make sure a bridge of that size stays up? What will stop the big new roads from washing away when the rains come or stop the place for the ships from being blown away in the storms?" He looked squarely at Cordero. "Nothing has stopped these things happening before when the spirits are disturbed."

The two men fell silent for a long time. Cordero waited. Napoleao took the pouch of tobacco from his pants pocket again.

"But children aren't being taken in Suai," he snapped. "They're being taken from up here. Because we are poor. We don't matter."

Cordero waited for the man to calm down. "What are you telling me?" he prompted him.

"I'm only telling you what they are saying around here," Napoleao said and rubbed the tobacco with more force into his palm. "That's all."

"Who are they who are saying these things?" Cordero asked.

"Everybody," said Napoleao.

"Do you know about demon activity around this area?" Cordero asked. The man's face hardened. "And the men who take action against the demons?" Cordero added.

The man looked off again to where the women were sitting, brushed the tobacco from his palm onto the ground and then stood to re-enter his house. "You'd better go before it is dark," he warned. "Ghosts walk this village at night."

Chapter 11

"Nothing," Cordero complained after they had returned to the guest house and were sitting in the room shared by Carter and Estefana. Cordero had brought a chair from his own room as well as a bottle of gin and one of tonic from their vehicle, and he had poured a drink for himself and Carter. Estefana had declined the offer and was sipping water from a glass. "Napoleao seems to genuinely grieve for his daughter, I think, and he's certainly angry but he told me nothing useful. What did you learn from the wife?"

"About the same," said Carter downing a large measure of her drink with her first quaff. "She doesn't suspect her husband or any of the neighbours. Says they have no enemies or debts. No-one was asking about the baby in the days before she was snatched." She finished her glass. "She says nothing else was taken from the house, which is curious."

"In what way?" asked Cordero, swatting a mosquito on his arm.

"Because it suggests the abduction was either a spur of the moment thing—which seems unlikely given the number of earlier cases—or that whoever did it had everything they needed to take care of a baby for the next few days. Change of diapers and clothes, feeding bottles, blankets, that sort of thing."

"All of this of course assumes that Veronica and Napoleao are telling us the truth," Cordero said.

"Yes and we might've arrived at a better sense of that had we all had a chance to talk to both of them," Carter replied.

"But let's assume they are," said Cordero ignoring the complaint. "Whoever did it certainly picked a good time with most of the villagers at church."

"Most but not all," Carter added. "And not the father. Maybe his meeting was known about in advance. What do you think Estefana?" Carter asked, bringing the young policewoman into the conversation.

Estefana thought for a moment, a serious look coming over her face. "You would think that someone would have seen something," she offered. "If not a person going into the house then one leaving the area with a baby. It's like a picture where something's happened but nothing changes."

Cordero considered that. "I suppose whatever people saw might not have seemed unusual," he said. "You know, what sticks in people's minds is what stands out from routine, from everything they're used to which has become familiar."

"That's true," agreed Carter, motioning Cordero for another gin. "And with lots of kids around here whoever took Elisanda might have been counting on nobody thinking twice about someone walking off with a baby."

Cordero had stood and was refilling his and Carter's glasses.

"Perhaps I will have a little to try," said Estefana. "If *maun* allows."

"Of course," said Cordero and he prepared a third glass. Just as he sat down again the light in the room went out and they were plunged into darkness.

"A power failure," Cordero said looking up toward the light bulb. "It happens all the time, even in Dili."

They sat in the gloom for several minutes quietly sipping their drinks until a faint knock could be heard on the door even though they had kept it open for decorum's sake. It was the same young nun who had served them dinner and she was carrying a kerosene lamp, her face almost angelic in its glow.

Estefana looked at Carter and said, "Come in, *madre*". The nun entered the room. She placed the lamp on the night-stand without saying a word. The lamp lit up the underwear drying on a line strung along the wall from the window to the door and Carter registered the embarrassment on the nun's face. They thanked her and she quickly slipped out of the room.

"Early tomorrow I think we should have a talk with the police officer," said Cordero. He yawned, picked up what was left of the gin and headed for the door. "It's been a long day," he said. "Good night."

The two women prepared for bed. Carter unfolded the mosquito netting then unself-consciously stripped down to her panties. She slid on a faded black FBI Academy T-shirt from which the sleeves had been cut off. Estefana turned her back to Carter as she stepped out of her uniform and into an oversized pair of pale blue pyjamas. Then she folded her uniform neatly onto a chair. Carter's bed creaked as she lay down and then each time she tossed to find a comfortable position. Estefana blew out the lamp and settled down beneath her mosquito netting making hardly a sound.

"*Mana*," she said after a few moments.

"Yes Estafana," Carter replied.

"What is America like?"

"Well," said Carter, thinking she'd never been asked that question before. "It's big. Much bigger than here. And what it's like depends on which part of it you live in."

"What's it like where you live, *mana*?" Estefana asked.

"I live in a place called Arizona. Now. But I was brought up in Missouri. That's east of there. Arizona is in the southwest of America. It is mostly desert country, hot and dry."

"Do you live in a city or in a rural area, *mana*?"

"A city. It's called Flagstaff, like the pole you run a flag up. But I work a lot in the surrounding area. Near Flagstaff is a place where Native Americans, you know, Indians, live on reservations. They're called Navajo, Hopi and Apache. I have mainly been working cases there for the past year. Most recently stolen children cases like here."

"I have seen Apache Indians," Estefana said, sitting up excited. "In a movie I saw once at a friend's house. The soldiers, what you call the cavary, were fighting them. The Apaches were shooting lots of arrows. They seem very angry and aggressive."

"*Cavalry*. We call those soldiers 'cavalry'," said Carter. "Indians are only aggressive in movies. I find them very peaceful people. Most of them anyway."

"Have you ever been to New York?" Estefana asked, lying back down again.

"Only once," said Carter. "When I was at the FBI Academy. They sent us up for a three-day conference."

"What was it like?"

Carter considered that. "Boring. So boring I can't remember much of what it was about," she said smiling to herself. "Like most conferences, I guess."

"No. I meant what was New York like, *mana*," Estefana said.

"Oh. Well, it was all work. The conference, I mean. No time to sight-see. We only went out of the hotel one night for dinner. All I remember are the lights, noise and people crowding the streets. Where I come from in Missouri we only had one streetlight and most of the time it wasn't working. People didn't go out much at night. The Native American communities are a bit the same."

"I would be scared I think to go to a big city like New York," Estefana said. "Too many people. And too many cars. And tall buildings way up into the sky. And I can only imagine the noise! I have only been to Dili twice and I think there are too many cars there and too much noise. But not tall buildings. Not like New York."

Estefana was quiet for a moment. "I read that Americans only have small families. Maybe only two or three children," she said. "How many brothers and sisters do you have, *mana*?"

Carter took a second to answer. "None," she said.

"My family is big. I have four sisters and three brothers. Five live with my mother and me. We have fun. And then there are all the friends who come to visit us." She giggled softly and paused. "What are your friends' names, *mana*?"

"Friends?" Carter asked.

"Yes, *mana*. Your friends," Estefana insisted. "What are their names?"

"Well," Carter yawned, buying time. "There's ah, Sanchez. Barbara Sanchez. And then, er, let me see. Rozzetti. Yes, Frank Rozzetti."

"*Mana*," Estefana said.

"Yes."

"Do you have a husband, *mana*?"

"No," replied Carter.

"A boyfriend?"

"Not right now."

"I have a boyfriend," Estefana said, excitement in her voice. "His name is Josinto. Josinto Centavo Veddo. *Centavo* like the coin. He is the same age as me. Twenty-one years. We met in high school. He plays the guitar and works for the coffin maker in Dili now. He is studying carpentry. We plan to marry when he finishes his study. I hope to have a big family. Maybe only six children though."

"Will you stay in the police force after you marry?" asked Carter.

"I don't know," Estefana answered. "Sometimes a police officer must do things you don't want to do," she added. Carter thought she heard a dog howl in the village below the church grounds. She waited and listened but Estefana, along with the night, fell silent.

Chapter 12

Dr Brooks, Suai's medical examiner and chief pathologist, had rung early, obviously exuberant and rushing out his words.

"A handful of fishermen said they'd heard the distress call of a crocodile through the night and the thing washed up dead on the beach at dawn," he was telling Cordero. "I came in twenty minutes ago. A crowd of people have gathered outside and they don't look happy. But you should see this thing, Tino—"

"Slow down Howard," Cordero said. "I was asleep when you rang and I'm still not fully awake."

"This big, beautiful, terrifying thing. It's over sixteen feet in length, Tino! I'd say two thousand pounds in weight. It took six police officers and some hospital orderlies to manoeuvre it in. It's huge!"

"You said there were people outside. How are they taking it? What's the mood?" Cordero asked.

"Well they're not too happy, I can tell you that, dear boy," replied Brooks. "But that's Buzzi's problem. He phoned me to expect the carcass. I just called him back to say I need a police presence in case things turn ugly."

"Well that could easily happen, Howard, if there's any evidence that the crocodile was killed by that police officer."

"Oh it was, dear boy. It most certainly was. First thing I looked at." Brooks explained that the outer skin on the left side of the neck, just behind the jaw and in front of the left leg where the police officer said he had shot the creature two days earlier, appeared to be healing from a previous wound, perhaps suffered in a fight over territory with another crocodile or the result on an encounter with a shark.

The new skin was tender and had not yet dried into the hard, leathery protective coating across the rest of the body. After he had made a quick incision to provide access to the inside of the neck, Brooks had pulled the outer skin on either side of the cut apart. He saw that the jugular vein along with its carotid artery had been punctured by the police officer's bullet. The crocodile had bled to death.

Cordero blew out a deep breath. "Wow," he said.

"Wow indeed, dear boy," replied Brooks. "But Tino, what a creature!"

Cordero knew that Brooks was fascinated by anatomy. And an animal this big and this powerful was sure to excite the inner child in him. But it didn't excite Cordero anywhere near as much. He tousled his hair in an attempt to become more alert.

"Why are you telling me all this and at this time of the morning, Howard?"

"Because it's a magnificent thing, Tino! If you could see the webbed feet tucked into the side of the body, the scales along its back as armor plating, the muscles bulging from each side of its jaws that work them like a steel trap. Ancient, Tino, but a perfect killing machine and that's why it's changed so little down through the eons. And the teeth! I counted nearly eighty, many as long and thick as a man's finger."

"That's all well and good, Howard—"

"The eyes, Tino! I opened one and shone a torch into it. A yellowish-green light reflected back like a cat's eye in the darkness. For a moment I shuddered at the thought it might still be alive!"

"I've another call coming in, Howard. Enjoy your autopsy."

"Oh I will, dear boy, I will. But the real reason I called? You asked me to keep you posted on any information to do with our body on the beach."

"Yeah."

"Well inside this thing might be more of the body."

"Then call me when and if you find any."

With that Cordero ended the call. He was lying about another call coming through but no sooner had he thrown his cell onto the bed then it lit up again. He checked the caller ID. Buzzi.

"Hello Buzzi," he said. "I was just on another call with Brooks."

"The fucking thing's turned up, Tino!" Buzzi said ignoring Cordero's greeting. He sounded unnerved, frantic.

"Yes, Brooks just told me."

"Did he tell you that idiot dos Santos killed the thing! Bloody fool. He didn't have to kill it, Tino. He could have fired a warning shot. Now they'll blame the police! Me!"

"Calm down, Buzzi."

"Oh that's good advice," he mocked. "All very well for you to say 'Calm down'. You're up there in the mountains. I'm in the middle of a fiasco down here, Tino!"

There was an interruption on Buzzi's end of the call. He heard someone say "Sir!" and then Buzzi issue an order to whoever had entered his office to go to the home of Officer Jose dos Santos and tell him to leave for Fatululic immediately, report to the officer in charge of the post and stay there until further notice. Fatululic, Cordero guessed, was a safe distance from Suai. Cordero could just make out the other person ask when he should go and Buzzi bark 'Now you fool!'

"I rang one of the elders this morning, Tino," Buzzi said back into the cell. "I asked for a meeting. And do you know what he said to me? He said a meeting of elders had already been called and I was to stay away! Stay away! Do you know what that means?" Buzzi was near hysterical now. "It means they're planning something, Tino! And it won't be a party to congratulate the police on killing a fucking monster!"

"Buzzi—"

"I'm canceling all leave and ordering all officers to stand by. This is going to get bad, Tino. You hear me! Very bad. Find that kid and fast. That's the only chance we have to prevent a damn riot. And keep your eyes and ears open. If there's any sign that news of the crocodile is stirring things up in the mountains I want to know about it."

And with that Buzzi was gone.

• • •

Carter had woken to the sound of soft voices in unison—people singing, a small choir. From the haze of sleep it took her a moment to clearly recall exactly where she was and what she was doing. Then it came to her like a series of mental slides that she was in Timor-Leste, on a baby abduction case, and that the voices were nuns who ran the guest house where she was staying. She figured they were in a private prayer room at the other side of the building reciting their Divine Office. They were singing in Latin and what they sang was familiar: 'Tota puchra es O Maria/Et macula non est in te'.

The memory resurfaced. She had heard it sung with her father on the television one rainy day when she was sick and he stayed home to mind her because their mother was busy elsewhere. She couldn't have been more than five or six years old. They'd watched daytime movies—her father breaking his own rule of never watching television before dark—old black-and-white movies, snuggling up on the couch with pop-corn he'd made. A special treat, he'd said. The movie was The Bells of St Mary's and the hymn was sung by someone called Bing Crosby—she'd laughed at the name 'Bing'—dressed in the black cassock of a priest. She had always remembered the beauty of the hymn or perhaps its beauty was mixed with the happiness and security she'd felt that day with her father. And she remembered the name of the hymn, strange to a child but for that reason, on that day, also precious: 'Ora pro nobis'. 'What does it mean, dad?' she had asked him and he answered 'Pray for us' and seemed to be holding back tears.

Carter looked over at Estefana who lay asleep on her side. She stared out the cracked window until the nuns had finished their prayers and she could hear them going about their chores. She sat up, shivered slightly at the thought of a cold body wash this early in the morning, threw a towel over her shoulder and headed for the wash-room leaving Estefana to wake in her own time. Outside Carter noticed a clear blue sky. It would be another hot day. On the way to the wash-room she saw Cordero's door slightly ajar. She tapped on the door and popped her head inside the room, wrapping her towel around her waist. He was sitting on the bed staring at his cell phone.

"*Bondia, mana,*" he said and smiled. "Sleep well?"

"I was woken by the nuns singing," she replied and leaned against the doorframe, hands cushioning her rear from the hard wood. "For a moment I thought I had died and gone to heaven."

Cordero laughed. It was the first wry comment she'd uttered since they'd met.

"I don't think police officers go to heaven. There's nothing for them to do there. But in the other place—" he said and let the thought hang there.

Carter smiled at that. She nodded at his cell phone. "Everything okay?"

"Brooks called. The crocodile he showed us yesterday washed up dead this morning. He's performing an autopsy on it now." He rubbed a hand across his face. "Then Buzzi called." He looked up at her and grinned. "The crocodile turning up dead has made the natives restless and he's demanding a breakthrough in the case to calm things down."

Carter pushed herself off the doorframe. "A breakthrough would be nice," she said. "I'll be ready in ten." And with that she strode off to the wash-room.

• • •

They found officer Juno Ximenes sitting on the porch of the house in which he was staying, his injured leg raised on a wooden crate, and a coffee mug in his hand. He was young, perhaps not more than twenty-two or twenty-three, clean-shaven, and dressed neatly although not in uniform and therefore, Cordero reasoned, not intending to show up for any kind of work today.

"*Bondia, maun,*" Cordero said approaching the porch and introducing himself and his colleagues. "We are here investigating the abduction of Elisanda Soares. You are the officer who filed the report I understand."

The man looked defensive. "Yes, I am. My superior, Sergeant Olivares, is sick with malaria. Says he caught it years ago when he was posted down on the coast. It comes and goes, you know."

"What can you tell us about the abduction?" Cordero asked.

"It's in my report. Have you read it?" the young man replied.

"Yes, we have. But there are details you may have left out. Tell us again, please."

Juno shifted in his chair. He looked nervous about being confronted by three officers he didn't know and had no reason to trust. He drained his coffee and placed the mug beside his chair, calculating how best to answer. Then he began in a rush about his motorcycle accident the previous Thursday and how he had swerved to avoid a child in the middle of the road, fallen off and broken his leg.

"Parents should keep their children off the roads," he said. "There are dozens of motorcycles and trucks using them now, you know. Maybe even hundreds." He added that children should be taught these things in school as well. "My leg hurts," he said. "A lot. It was a bad break. The medical clinic only opens when the nurse comes to the village and no one has come for days. I wasn't in the office last weekend, and won't be today." He looked at them defiantly. "I don't expect to be fit for work for another week or more and then only for light duties."

They listened patiently to him sheet blame in all directions and try to raise what sympathy he could. Then Cordero asked again: "Perhaps now can you tell us what you know about the abduction of the Soares girl and what you did when her father reported her gone."

"Of course I wanted to help Napoleao and Veronica find their baby," he said sitting bolt upright. "I wanted to go to their house as soon as I could. I immediately called a friend to come for me on his motorcycle. He took me to Napoleao's house."

"And what did you find when you got there?" Cordero asked.

"Well, I got into the house as best I could." He was avoiding eye contact with Cordero now. "I looked around the premises. Then I questioned Napoleao and Veronica and gathered several neighbours to do a search. I told them to look in Napoleao's yard, his garden plots, and nearby houses and fields. Then I sent them into the village to look there. They found nothing."

Cordero ignored those parts of the account that varied from Napoeao's version which had Juno reluctant to act in the first place and lacking interest when he did. "Napoleao said that at the time his daughter was taken he had gone to a meeting and Veronica said she was at church. Do you believe them?" asked Cordero.

"Yes, of course. Although you can bet I checked," Juno insisted. "Several men confirmed that they had met Napoleao a short distance from his home. Said their meeting had lasted maybe fifteen minutes and that he brought nothing and left with nothing. As for Veronica, I asked Father Timoteo. He remembered giving her communion at the special Mass for Santo Eulogio." Juno turned his gaze to Estefana imagining a woman might understand this detail better. "Father Timoteo prides himself on noting who comes to Mass and who takes communion and who doesn't."

Estefana merely nodded and glanced back to Cordero.

"You have no idea who took the baby, how it was taken, where it went?" Cordero asked.

Juno looked surprised by the question. "None at all."

"And no theories?" Cordero asked.

Juno's defensiveness returned. He reached for his coffee mug, looked into it, shook it as though that might produce more to drink, and said "No".

"And your Sergeant? He took no interest in the theft of a baby?"

"Like I said, he's down with malaria. Says he's too sick to care about anything."

Cordero had been translating this for Carter. He looked at her now but she had no other questions and indicated as much by a shake of her head. *Uncooperative as well as inexperienced*, she was thinking to herself.

Cordero nonetheless suspected that Juno was holding back. He'd noticed an edginess in the officer's eyes.

"Why don't you two head back to the nuns' house and gather the things we'll need today?" he said to Carter and Estefana. "I just want to chat to Juno about policing resources in Fatuloro and I'll be along shortly. I'll walk back."

"Policing resources?" queried Carter.

"Yeah. Favour for Buzzi," Cordero told her and left it at that.

When they were gone, Cordero turned to Juno.

"Policing resources? There are none. Why do you want to know about that, *maun*?" the young officer asked.

"I don't," replied Cordero. "Napoleao Soares is the village chief. Why weren't you more eager to help find his daughter?"

"What do you mean, *maun*?"

"I mean exactly what I said."

Juno stalled for a moment. "Napoleao thinks he is the law around here. He's always questioning what we do. He and Sergeant Olivares have run-ins all the time," he said.

Probably because the two officers are lazy, incompetent, or both Cordero figured. "I want you to tell me what you know about demon talk," he said.

"What?"

"You heard me," Cordero said. "Between you and me, what do you know?"

Juno hesitated again. "I asked you a question," Cordero said but Juno made no reply, just wiped his hands on his pants. Cordero walked up the steps of the porch and stood directly in front of Juno.

"Well?" he said.

"You're crazy, *maun*. I know nothing."

Cordero kicked the crate out from under Juno's broken leg and the injured limb dropped and hit the porch with a thud.

"Ow, fuck *maun*!" cried Juno. "That hurt!"

"I get impatient when people don't tell me what I want to know," said Cordero leaning in. "I'll ask once again: What do you know about the demon talk in this area?"

Juno rubbed his leg, grumbled, looked directly into Cordero's eyes and saw the determination there.

"They say demons are taking those babies. They beat demons to scare them off. They killed one a few days ago out Beko way. Hung him on a cross. Like Jesus, *maun*."

Cordero could see the fear on the young officer's face. "I wouldn't go there, *maun*. They don't like strangers. And no one's going to know you're a police officer without you wearing a uniform. Even then they wouldn't care. They could cut you up with a machete real quick."

"You said 'they' say these things about demons and 'they' beat anyone suspected of being one. Who are 'they'?"

Juno hesitated again and Cordero touched his foot lightly on the officer's sore leg.

"Everybody, *maun*," Juno said and waved an arm around vaguely.

"Is Napoleao spreading that rumour?"

"Spread it? No need to spread it. Everybody in this whole region knows it."

"And what are you doing about the beatings?" Cordero asked.

Juno hesitated. "Nothing. What do you think I can do? One man can't stop the whole village."

"Well you are trained. And educated, I'm guessing. What do you think about demons stealing babies?"

Juno fell silent. "Well?" Cordero insisted and put more pressure on the officer's broken leg.

"I think it could be demons," he said. "Who else would want to steal a baby around here? People have more than they can feed now." He moved his leg away. "They can't stop having them," Juno said as though the reasoning was obvious.

Cordero considered a moment. "You won't need your motorcycle for a few days by the looks of it," he said. "Is it serviceable?"

"What? Yes, why do you ask?" Juno asked, puzzled by the request.

"Where is it?"

"It's locked inside the police office. But what's this about?"

"I will need to borrow it," replied Cordero.

"But—"

"A baby has been stolen," Cordero said. "We aim to find it. I'll need the keys to your office and to the bike and no 'buts' about it."

Juno sulked but reached into the pocket of his pants and tossed the keys to Cordero.

• • •

Back at the nuns' house Cordero announced they should split up. "You and Estefana take the SUV and head down to the villages of Metidade, Bocali, and Leho. You should be able to make Lotarai as well. I'm going to borrow the policeman's motorcycle and head to Beko, Rotia, and Uma Daiso."

Carter thought they should stay together. "Standard procedure—" she started to say but Cordero was already checking his pockets and would entertain no disagreement.

"We don't have time for standard procedures," he said. "By splitting up we'll cover the eight most recent abduction sites faster. If I get a chance, I'll go on to Camereno and Fanasi as well. I can move fast on a motorcycle. We need to cover as much ground as quickly as we can. There may be a chance to find the missing girl if we get some kind of lead." And with that he left, ignoring Carter's glare.

Estefana noticed the exasperation in Carter's face. She was quiet for a moment then asked: "You are not happy with *maun, mana*?"

"No," said Carter. "Not at all. If we all stay together one of us may hear something important that the others pass up as trivial or one of us may make a connection between what one person has told us and what another has said. That's why police work in teams, Estefana. This way we only get his version of half the information and he only gets our version of the other half."

Carter slammed various items into a bag. Her hair fell over her face and as she brushed it back she noticed Estefana's embarrassment. It wasn't Estefana's fault that Cordero had split them up and it wasn't fair to undermine her senior officer's authority in her eyes. Besides Carter had learned the hard way that textbook policing methods didn't always get you very far when working with Navajos and Apaches and the same was surely true in Timor-Leste.

"Sorry Estefana," she said. "He may be right. Time is critical and we don't have much left. You and I will do just fine. Come on let's go."

Chapter 13

Metidade was a village about six miles from Fatuloro heading north, down the ravine by way of a steep, zigzagging road that led to a river at the valley floor. Estefana drove. She'd asked the nuns for provisions in case there was no food to be bought where they were going. This early in the morning the nuns could only give them a few bananas, two cans of tuna, and a few slices of bread one of the sisters had baked the day before. But that was enough. Estefana had also managed to fill a thermos with coffee. Lunch would be less of a problem than the road.

The trip took almost forty minutes as they avoided potholes, negotiated washaway, and kept alert for fallen trees and rocks. There were few vehicles on the road though they were passed by three motorcycles signalling their intentions with a beep of their horns.

"I think *maun* Tino knew what he was doing when he took the motorcycle," Estefana said and chuckled. "Are your roads in Azona like this, *mana*?"

"*Arizona*," Carter corrected her. "'Arizona'. They're not as bad as this because we get very little rain. But they aren't good either. Sometimes you can't see ahead of you for dust. And they can be just as steep and winding at times."

They drove into a cluster of perhaps twenty traditional huts— single room structures of wooden planks and thatch. A doorway at the front seemed to provide the only entry and exit and the one or two windows a small number boasted lacked glass panes. The huts were spread out through a sprinkling of acacia trees on a flat stretch of land near the river's edge. Dogs, goats, and chickens roamed freely. Off in the distance they glimpsed garden plots along the river and up the hill on the far side more huts, their round brown shapes like giant hazelnuts among the trees. They stopped next to an old man sitting on the roadside puffing contentedly on a cigar.

"*Bondia tiu*," said Estefana. It was getting hot now and she wiped her face with a kerchief.

"*Bondia, mana*," the old man said showing nicotine-stained teeth when he smiled.

Estefana asked him where they could find the house of Ana Menezes.

"Not here," he said spreading his arms wide and laughing at his own joke. "Go to the last house down there," the man said gesturing with his cigar. "Through the clearing, just off the side of the road. Near the market. She has two pigs."

They drove slowly avoiding children playing in the dirt, past a house with one pig, another with two goats and a third with two dogs lying in the shade and several chickens scratching through the yard. Finally, they came to the market and decided the house should be near and they'd best walk or they might miss it. Estefana parked the vehicle and they both stepped out into the harsh glare of the sun.

The market was around a rickety structure built in a clearing on the near edge of the village. Crude hewn benches had been thrown together below a roof of rusting tin that sat on rough poles about eight feet off the dirt floor. The roof covered an area smaller than a tennis court.

The people earliest to arrive had claimed the bench tops and laid out their meagre wares. An old woman was selling twelve clumps of garlic, another slightly younger woman four onions and two cabbages. The older woman was chewing betel nut, the younger smoking the stub of a cigar. Both sat in silence, their faces grimy and their eyes in a permanent squint. Around the benches on the ground sat younger women with children and old men who had arrived late at the market. The men sat adjusting little piles of raw tobacco on sale in various shades of brown. The women sold small servings of peanuts in paper bags, or chilies and peppers, a handful of dirty potatoes, or mandarins. In time the women who were young now would graduate to the top bench. The old men would grow very old and simply come no more.

The stall holders, if that's what such simple traders could be called, ignored Estefana and Carter and sat impassively brushing the flies away from their produce. Only the children stared. Estefana bought mandarins from a heavily pregnant woman who kept herself wrapped in a heavy shawl despite the heat. Estefana handed over ten centavos which she rummaged from her pocket. She thanked the woman who hid the money quickly under her shawl and said nothing. Estefana then handed one of the mandarins to Carter as they continued through the market. Carter noticed that the mandarin was an unappetising pale yellow in colour but Estefana had already bitten into hers and seemed to be enjoying it. Carter followed suit, took a bite, and was surprised by the sweetness of it. She had to lick the juices off her hand.

Estefana stopped again, this time to watch a group of men gambling with a soiled pack of cards. "*Tolu!*" one demanded and the dealer laid down three cards. The other men threw old coins to the centre of the ring around which they sat, mostly one and five but even a few ten *centavo* coins. Carter watched the game for a moment but was unable to decide what it was they were playing. She looked around the market area and noticed a small corral about forty yards off where more men had gathered and were squatting on the ground. She wandered toward it without telling Estefana. The sound of cocks crowing grew louder as she approached and when she neared the railing one of the men noticed her, stood up, and spoke to the others. They all stood then, some holding roosters tight against their chests and walked quickly and silently away.

Estefana caught up with her. "They are cockfighting, *mana!*" she said. "It is only for men. They stop if a woman approaches."

As they walked back to the market, Estefana spotted a hut with two pigs tied up by the side of the front doorway. "That must be the home of Ana Menezes," she said to Carter pointing with half a mandarin and they headed toward it. Estefana finished her fruit, wiped her hands quickly on the grass and checked her uniform.

"*Bondia, mana,*" Carter heard Estefana say to the woman standing in the doorway and Carter stood patiently while her colleague went through the introductions and explanations for their visit.

Ana Menezes was a woman of about thirty. She wore a thin cotton dress and sandals and her hair was tied loosely in a bun at the back of her head. Her expression was joyless, her eyes sunken and dark. She had once been pretty but worry and wear had aged her. She'd given birth to five children, she told Estefana, aged twelve, ten, nine and eight. Bibi—the name she gave her daughter—was ten months old.

"Why the gap in age between the last one and the next oldest child?" Carter asked and Estefana put the question to Ana Menezes.

The woman looked off in the distance and replied that her husband had died of tuberculosis four years earlier. Bibi's father was a visitor to the village and he'd never come back. Estefana related this to Carter who looked puzzled. "I think perhaps she might have been violated by a man, *mana,*" Estefana explained.

"Violated? You mean raped?" asked Carter.

Estefana looked embarrassed. "Yes, *mana*. It happens sometimes when a woman has no husband."

They were sitting on a log in the shade of a flame tree now, out of the heat of the day. Estefana offered a mandarin to Ana who took it absently and played with it without peeling it. "Tell us about the day that Bibi was taken," Estefana asked at Carter's direction. "Where were you and the other children?"

Ana said it was about ten in the morning. She had gone to the river for a short time to wash clothes. Her younger children were playing in the trees behind the house; the older ones were visiting friends. The baby was asleep when she left but was gone when she returned. She searched the house and yard and then went to the neighbours. "No one had seen anything. No one knew where Bibi had gone."

"Had anyone seen a stranger in the area or a strange vehicle?" Estefana asked without prompting from Carter this time.

"No," said Ana.

The police weren't called at first because no one had a cell phone. Eventually a neighbour rode to Fatuloro to report to the police there that Bibi was missing. It was nearly six o'clock when Sergeant Olivares came. He searched several huts nearby, questioned the neighbours briefly and ordered a search along the river. But by then it was dark and they found nothing. "Is there anyone who would want to hurt you or your baby? The father perhaps?" asked Estefana.

"No. No one." The woman wiped away what could have been a tear or a bead of sweat. "As I said I have never seen Bibi's father again and he wouldn't even know he was the father."

"What do you think happened to Bibi?" Carter instructed Estefana to ask.

The woman's eyes grew large. A few of the men from the cockfight were approaching the house and the one in the lead had a severe look on his face. Ana Menezes gave Estefana back the fruit she had been offered and rose swiftly. "I know nothing of what happened to my daughter," she said loud enough for the men to hear. And then she walked back into her hut without another word.

• • •

"You don't only ask them what they saw or heard," Carter was explaining to Estefana. "You ask them how they *felt* about what they saw or heard. That way you often get more. Like 'I saw a man in black clothes'. Okay 'How did you feel when you saw him?' And they might say 'Nervous'. You ask 'Why?' And they might say 'Because the clothes were ragged and dirty and he had an angry look on his face'. Get the idea? More detail often comes through their emotional reaction to what they witnessed. Same with asking 'What do you *think* happened?' You just might get a connection between one thing and another that you hadn't thought about or an insight into the person you're asking the questions of and why they might be telling you what they're telling you. That helps you weigh up what you're being told."

Estefana nodded. She was thrilled to be getting this kind of advice. She rarely received any on the job in Suai. They had driven to Bocali which was on the other side of the ridge that had bordered Metidade and the river to the north. But the mother and father of the baby who went missing there—Dulcie Fanas Haruka—could not be found. Several people agreed the couple had left soon after Dulcie was taken. Some said they had gone to Suai, others said to Maliana. They had taken their other seven children with them and not returned.

Before they left Bocali, Carter and Estefana pulled to the side of the road, ate the bread, tuna and the bananas and finished what was left of the coffee. Carter noticed a small grave down the slope just below the road. As she finished eating she strolled over and squatted to take a closer look. A wooden cross had been dug into the ground next to the cement covering over the grave. A faded name, Jacinta Maria Branco, was hand painted on the cement. Jacinta had been eight years old when she died it also showed. Of what Jacinta had died the marker didn't say. Across the grave had run a line of red ants but they were disturbed now and running amok as though under attack from a predator. Carter was staring blankly at the grave, the red ants covering her boots, when Estefana walked up quietly. "We should go now, *mana*," she said and gently touched Carter's shoulder.

"She was eight years old," Carter said more to herself than to Estefana.

"Yes *mana*," Estefana agreed as they returned to their vehicle.

"Why do you think Ana Menezes looked worried and left all of a sudden?" Carter asked when they were back in the SUV and she had refocused on the case. Estefana looked thoughtful. Carter was treating her as a colleague not just a chauffeur and interpreter. She liked that feeling and it strengthened her desire to answer Carter's questions honestly. But she was under orders from Cordero to avoid revealing anything that might hint of demons or human sacrifices.

"I don't know, *mana*. Perhaps it was the shame of the rape. Perhaps she blames herself and thinks God is punishing her by taking the baby."

Carter nodded and looked down at the map in her lap.

"Estefana?" she said as her companion was tidying up from their lunch.

"Yes *mana*?"

"There seems to be a road from here down to where Cordero went."

"Do you mean Beko, *mana*?"

"Yes. Beko."

"There is a road, *mana*, but it is very rough. Beko is about eight miles from here but I would say almost an hour to drive," said Estefana.

"We have time to spare since Dulcie's parents aren't here. Let's go to Beko," said Carter folding the map. "I'd like to see some of the villages around there."

"But what would *maun* say, *mana*?" asked Estefana.

"Did he say not to go?" Carter replied.

"No but—"

"If they don't tell you not to do something, Estefana, you're free to do it," said Carter. "Remember that. And if you think they'll say don't do something you want to do, just don't tell them that you're going to. Okay?"

Estefana smiled. "Okay *mana*." She started the ignition and released the parking brake. "To Beko." Carter was a woman who made her own decisions and acted on them. It was something Estefana had rarely seen before.

Chapter 14

The policeman's motorcycle was a 250cc Yamaha dirt bike, strong enough to take rugged conditions and light enough to manoeuvre around rocks and potholes and edge up on the embankment when pools of mud had formed in the belly of the road. On a straight stretch the Yamaha was no competition for the larger bikes favoured by drug dealers and gun runners. But there weren't many of them and they weren't Cordero's problem anyway. As a special criminal investigator he was employed to solve more exotic crimes. That's one reason he was interested in the body that had washed up on the beach with an arrow fashioned from a nail in its chest. It was unusual, the motivation could be simple or complex, but with an unidentified body, a traditional method of killing, and what appeared to be the purposeful offering of the corpse to a crocodile, the investigation was sure to lead in interesting directions.

There were other points that intrigued him about the murdered man but none of that was on his mind now. He was enjoying the ride, enjoying the physicality of it, the breeze in his face, the trees rushing passed him and the fact that he was on his own and free to do what he liked. He had set himself the task of overtaking as many other motorcycles as he could—a silly, juvenile thing but an exciting challenge nonetheless. The contest had started on the busier road to Rotia when Cordero had realised he was being overtaken by much younger men while he was getting used to the bike. Now, familiar with the machine and heading for Beko, there were fewer motorcycles to compete with but so far he'd managed to overtake them all.

Just then he slipped trying to negotiate a pothole and had to steady himself with his left foot. A youth, who couldn't have been more than sixteen and on a blue Kawasaki dirt bike, rode around him and took off up the road in a spray of dust and pebbles. Cordero set his jaw, gripped the accelerator and revved the bike. In his mind at least the race was on.

As he drew near the Kawasaki, its rider seemed to sense the contest as well and accelerated. The shriek of their engines scattered birds pecking at the side of the road. Cordero kept pace with the younger rider, trying to gain on him where he could by cutting more sharply into the corners. On roads such as these it was a dangerous duel but Cordero was close to winning it. They overtook two slower motorcycles and narrowly avoided hitting another coming toward them. Then the two riders sped around a curve in the road, Cordero edging in front. But he glimpsed the village of Beko off on his right. He slowed and waved to his opponent. The young man replied with a toot of his horn and was gone in a cloud of dust seconds later.

Cordero turned off onto a side track and rode toward a bridge across a small stream. The bridge had originally been built of concrete but had collapsed and been replaced by durable teak logs strewn together. The bike shuddered over the logs as he rode across.

Beko was a tiny village—no more than thirty huts built from slabs of wood and thatch—clustered on a flat spur down the track from the road. Acacia trees offered a thin shading to the huts and vegetable gardens had been dug into more fertile soil below the spur. Another very rough road on the other side of the village led out of Beko and on to Bocali but Cordero had no interest in it. He slowed at the first hut he came to where a heavily pregnant woman leaned from the windowsill, expressionless. She appeared to be in no mood to greet visitors. Further on, another woman was sweeping her yard clean of debris to keep scorpions and centipedes at bay. Cordero noticed the buffalo horns tied across poles outside each hut. They were what locals called *ai-to'os* or 'farm trees' shaped like a cross but not Christian at all instead signifying strong animistic beliefs.

Off through the trees in a cleared field he noticed a single room slab and tin schoolhouse with a limp Timorese flag dangling from a pole. As he drew nearer he saw illustrated posters on the door indicating the building doubled as a medical clinic and occasional place for Catholic worship. A man who might have been a teacher or a government official was squatting on the side of the doorway smoking a cigarette. There was no-one else around. Cordero pulled the bike up in front of the doorway. He dismounted and took off his helmet. He greeted the man and asked where he might find the Guteres home.

"There are several Guteres in Beko," the man said.

"I'm looking for the home of Joao Guteres, the boy who was taken," Cordero said. "I am a police officer."

"That was many months ago," the man said. "And the boy hasn't been found."

"I know. That's why I am here."

"A bit late, aren't you?"

"Could you show me the house, please?" Cordero asked.

He had gained little from his visit to Rotia earlier that morning. Alexandrina Messakh's abduction seemed to accord with everything he knew about what had happened to Elisanda Soares and her mother and father seemed to be even more reluctant to speak about the circumstances of her disappearance. The interview had lasted less than ten minutes before the father had stood, told his wife to follow him, and walked off. Cordero had sensed that he was not welcome in Rotia and he recalled police officer Juno Ximenes's warning that he would likely find the same reception if not worse in Beko. Even so, Cordero was hoping that the abduction of Joao Guteres might reveal some useful information about what had happened. After all, Joao's was the first case of a male baby being stolen that either he or Carter would be examining.

The man pointed with his cigarette to a hut about fifty yards from them. "She goes to the grotto of the Virgin every day to pray for Joao," he said. "She wants to conduct a funeral for the boy but the priest won't say a Mass without a body."

Cordero nodded. "Is she there now? At the hut?"

"No. She'll be at the grotto. Down there, out of sight," the man said indicating a path that led off the spur to their left. "She'll be the only one wearing black. It hasn't been a year yet."

"And the father. Where would I find him?"

"That I can't say. He could be in his garden or he may have taken things to the market at Uma Daiso."

"Are you the teacher in the school here?" Cordero asked.

"You see any school children?" the man replied. "I come up from Fatuloro every other week. I work with the Ministry of Agriculture. I'm supposed to encourage the farmers to use better seed. But they are very traditional here. You can see how many people are interested in what I have to say."

"Why do you stay here, around this hut? Why don't you go to the gardens where the famers are?" Cordero asked.

"They're all on edge. Ever since the boy was taken and the dark talk began. I'm not a local and things have been known to happen in the past to strangers here especially if they wander off on their own." He tossed his cigarette away. "I'm still considered a stranger."

"What things? What do you mean by 'dark talk'?" Cordero asked.

"You mentioned school. None of the adults here have ever gone to school. None of them can read or write. They don't watch television or even listen to the radio. You see any electrical wires? Even the road doesn't come down here. When something happens out of the ordinary they go hunting ghosts or witches or devils to blame."

The man rose then and walked into the hut to shuffle papers on an old wooden desk. Cordero yelled a 'Thank you' through the doorway and headed down the path to the grotto.

Festiva Guteres was kneeling before a picture of the Virgin Mary some of the villagers had placed in a small rock shelter three hundred yards down the path out of sight of the huts. Her clothes were unkempt as if she no longer cared about her appearance and Cordero noticed that one of her slippers was held together with twine. At the side of the shelter someone had placed a buffalo's skull on a stake and there were several old, dried out maize cobs as well. A typical hedging of bets: the animist alongside the Catholic and the two combining in people's minds for extra potency.

He allowed the woman to finish her prayers before interrupting her. When she noticed him, fear showed in her eyes and she clutched her rosary beads against her breast. "*Bondia, mana,*" Cordero said. "I am a special police investigator from Dili, Vincintino Cordero, and I have come to look into the disappearance of your son. I will go if you want but I would like to ask you a few questions, if you will permit me."

She vacillated between screaming, running, and cooperating. He smiled and sat quietly at a distance from her. Finally tears streamed down her cheek. She softly moaned "Joao" and slumped in the dirt.

Festiva Guteres threw no new light on what had happened to her son. He had been taken while most of the villagers were at a hut a mile away celebrating a wedding. The wedding had been organised six months beforehand. She had stayed back with Joao because she had injured her ankle in a fall a few days earlier and while she could walk she couldn't both walk and carry him.

"My husband had gone to the celebration with our other children," she explained. "There is a very old woman in the village, *Tia* Maria. She is dying. She has no family to care for her. I go to her hut every day with rice porridge. It's not far." Each time she would be gone for no more than twenty minutes although it took thirty with her injured ankle. "I heard motorcycles and a few vehicles on the road up from the village but none came close to my hut that I noticed."

Then the woman began to cry again. "I want a funeral for my Joao. It's the only way his soul can find its rest," she said through her sobbing. "Where do I get an offering?"

"What do you mean, *mana*?" Cordero asked.

"To perform the ritual properly and to satisfy my relatives I must have a buffalo or a pig at least to kill. But we are poor, too poor for that," she wiped her eyes. "My husband has asked around for a loan but no one has offered enough. And the priest—" she began but her sobbing prevented her from finishing the statement.

Cordero waited and she had soon collected herself. "I want it done here, close to the grotto where I can come each day but the elders say no. They say Joao was taken from the village and is now buried under a bridge near Suai and the rites must be performed there if his spirit is to be laid to rest." Then her crying became uncontrollable again. "To think of him lying there! I can't. It's too much to bear." After a moment she composed herself. "If I had the pig I would perform a ritual here despite what they say. Then I could come each day and feel better."

Cordero found himself sympathizing with her more than he usually did with victims he encountered on a case. Maybe it was the slipper held together with twine. He reached into his pocket and pulled out a crumpled five dollar note.

"Will this help? For the offering, I mean."

The woman looked at him. He smiled and pushed his hand closer toward her. She grabbed the note, rose and ran up the path back to her house.

• • •

Carter and Estefana were approaching the outskirts of Beko on the road from Bocali. They passed a flimsy stall on the side of the road in a small break in the forest. "Can we go back, please, Estefana?" Carter asked. "I think I saw some papaya or something and I'm still a little hungry."

"Of course, *mana*," replied Estefana and she stopped the SUV and reversed carefully back to the stall, pulling into the clearing alongside it. The stall itself was empty but behind it stood a hut where the stall owner lived. Carter slid out of the SUV and closed the door behind her. A group of very young children were playing off to the side. They stopped to stare at her—arms and legs covered in mud, hair matted. They seemed both surprised and curious but unsure which feeling to act on.

"*Bondia*," Estefana called as she stepped out of the SUV and walked toward the stall. No one answered. "*Bondia!*" she called more loudly.

Two men emerged from the trees, one carrying a machete. Both were covered in dust and grime, neither looked welcoming. They stopped and stared from the side of the stall opposite the children.

There was a stirring from inside the hut and a woman burst through the doorway. She seemed too fat for a Timorese, which the goiter around her neck suggested was the result of an illness. She waddled across the clearing toward the stall wiping her hands on the dirty yellow T-shirt that covered her huge breasts.

Three boys, teenagers, came and stood beside the men.

"*Deskulpa*," the woman apologised as she fumbled a latch to enter the stall. "*Deskulpa, mana.*"

Carter walked up alongside Estefana. Two more teenagers and another man were now standing silently behind them and more boys were coming through the trees. Nobody spoke. Nobody smiled.

Carter pointed to the papayas hanging in a string bag on the side of the stall, held up two fingers, and the woman took out two of the biggest papayas and placed them on what passed for a counter. Three more cheerless teenage boys arrived to their right. The papayas were plump and inviting. Carter asked the price, in English, without thinking. The woman held up all fingers. "You're kidding me," said Carter but she reached into the pocket of her jeans, produced a ten dollar note and held it up to the stall owner. The woman shook her head vigorously. "What, more?" protested Carter.

"She doesn't have change, *mana*," Estefana said. "She wants a ten *centavo* coin."

"Oh sorry," said Carter. She put her hand back into her pocket and brought out a bunch of coins. She placed them on the counter and searched for a ten *centavo* or two fives. Four more teenaged boys had lined up and were leering at the strangers.

Estefana was becoming suspicious of the circle now forming around them. Carter seemed not to have noticed. Estefana caught the stall owner's face darken as her eyes flit from one group of men and boys to another.

"I think we should leave, *mana*," Estefana said but Carter was ignoring her. "Now!" she insisted.

Carter caught the concern in her voice and pushed the coins toward the stall owner. Estefana picked up the papayas, held them aloft for the onlookers to see and walked slowly to the SUV trying not to look panicked or afraid.

When they were both inside the SUV, Estefana locked the doors. "They're scared, *mana*. And that could mean trouble," she explained. She began to back the SUV out onto the road.

That's when the first rock hit.

It put a thin crack in the passenger's window next to Carter and she jumped with a start.

"What the—!" she began.

"Hold on, *mana*!" Estefana said. The SUV skidded backward. She hit the brake and shifted gears. Another rock clanged against the passenger's door. Carter braced herself with a hand against the dash.

Three rocks pinged off the driver's door. Then another chipped the windshield to the right of Estefana's vision. The boys were coming forward yelling across each other and making it impossible to hear what any one of them was saying. They were picking up rocks and hurling them or firing them from slingshots.

The SUV stalled.

Two teenagers scrambled onto the bonnet. A back window shattered. Estefana worked the ignition but again the SUV stalled. A man ran forward with a machete raised above his head as if to take a swipe at the vehicle. But Estefana managed to start it on the next attempt. She jerked the SUV forward trying to swing the boys onto the ground. They both flew off when she steered abruptly toward the road. Rocks hit like popcorn bursting. She pressed her foot to the floor kicking a spray of dust and gravel onto their attackers and fishtailed back in the direction of Bocali.

• • •

The ride to Uma Daiso took thirty minutes but when Cordero arrived the parents of Luana Ruiz—the eleven months old girl who'd been taken four months earlier—had nothing to say and told him to leave. The Ruiz house was in a depression on the edge of Uma Daiso and as Cordero rode back onto the main road he noticed a string of prefabricated houses on a hillock overlooking it. He pulled up to examine them. They were typical government dwellings built for former soldiers who had fought in the guerilla campaign against the Indonesians. It was unusual to see them this far west because most of the guerillas had operated out of the mountains on the eastern side of the island. But the *Falintil*, the military wing of the resistance, had members from all over Timor and if some of them were from Cova Lima and had decided to come back here, the government was obliged to provide them with the same benefits due every veteran. That included a house and a pension. And that, Cordero considered, financed a lifestyle that just might have allowed one or more of the people living on the hillock to be resting on their porch spying on their neighbours when Luana was taken.

Cordero worked the throttle and rode up a dirt track to the first of the veterans' houses. No one was home. The same was true of the second house and the third. Cordero was about to head to Fanasi when he noticed a man standing in the doorway of the fourth house, curious about a motorcycle near his home. Cordero drew closer, removed his helmet, and introduced himself as Investigator Vincintino Cordero of the Timor-Leste police.

"Have you found it, *maun*?" the man demanded. He was about fifty years of age, short, strongly built, proud, and by the look his demeanor not easily impressed or pushed around.

"Found what, *senyor*?" asked Cordero.

"My motorcycle," the man said. "I reported it stolen Monday night. Isn't that why you are here? News about my bike?"

"Well no, I'm sorry to say," Cordero replied. "I am here investigating the disappearance of Luana Ruiz. The baby in that house down there."

"That was months ago," the man said. "My bike was stolen days ago. How do you expect to find a baby if you can't find a motorcycle?"

"There are many motorcycles in Timor-Leste, *senyor*," Cordero pointed out.

"There are many babies too," replied the veteran.

Cordero considered how to turn the conversation to the more urgent issue. "Where was your bike stolen, *senyor*? Perhaps it was the same thief who stole the girl," he suggested.

"My bike was stolen in Suai!" the man protested. "From the home of a friend near the beach. He had to give me a lift back here after I reported it to the police. The theft had nothing to do with that baby going missing."

"Monday night, you say?"

"That's what I said. Do you read police reports?"

"I am not stationed in Suai, *senyor*. I have been sent from Dili to look into the abduction of children in Cova Lima. I only arrived on Monday night."

"And what have you learned about the abductions since then?" the veteran asked, sarcasm in his voice.

"Not much," admitted Cordero. "It's an unusual series of crimes, many things similar about each of the babies taken but nothing instructive." He ran a hand through his hair. "People seem reluctant to talk."

"That's because they're afraid," said the veteran. "They're scared of things they can't see, can't pick up and hold or make any sense of."

"Not you?" ventured Cordero.

"Not me," the veteran agreed.

Again there was silence as the veteran came down to inspect Cordero's motorcycle.

"Yamaha. Not bad," the veteran said. "But mine's a Kawasaki. They're better."

"They are," Cordero thought it wise to agree. "But this is all they gave me to ride. What's your name?"

"Ivando. Ivando Machado."

The veteran squatted down, examining the engine. "I saw things that will interest you," he said, his gaze on the motorcycle's gearing. "About that girl. And I'm not afraid to talk."

"That would be helpful. Can you tell me what you saw, Ivando?" Cordero said, trying not to sound too eager.

"No," the man said and stood. "You find my bike. Then I'll talk. It's red. A Kawasaki 250cc Cruiser. Less than a year old. It has a *Falintil* flag here," he added pointing to the side of the petrol tank. "Then people know it belongs to a veteran. But it must have been taken before the thief noticed the flag. It was dark. Find it. Bring it back. Then I will tell you what I know."

• • •

"What was that about?" Carter exclaimed as they drove away from Beko.

"People are not normally like that. Especially toward foreigners. They were angry and frightened," replied Estefana.

"We were buying papayas damn it," declared Carter looking back through the shattered rear window.

"We were strangers, *mana*."

They spoke little for the next twenty minutes but as they approached Lotarai, where Estefana had taken the report on the abduction of six-month-old Julieta da Silva, normal conversation resumed. "I was stationed up the road from Lotarai relieving a police officer whose mother had died in Los Palos," Estefana was explaining. "That's way over to the east of Timor-Leste, *mana*. She had no husband, brothers or brothers-in-law left alive and accordingly the officer, Nando Castro—that is his name—had to go and organise everything. He was gone almost two weeks."

"Your report was the most thorough of the lot, Estefana," Carter reminded her. "I doubt that we will find out more but I want to talk to the boy who was minding Julieta. Julio, right? He may be more open about things than the adults seem to be around here."

They found the da Silva house near the centre of the village. As Estefana had mentioned in Suai, this was a poor village. Carter noticed a few houses, like the da Silva's, were cement brick but in need of repair; most were wood slab with tin or thatched roofs. The village had two general stores—one of which was boarded up—a crude eatery, and several dilapidated government offices. Dogs and cats, their ribs showing, roamed the streets in search of scraps. Most of the children playing around the houses were naked or dressed in rags. Carter recognized the too-light brown hair, the pot bellies and runny noses that indicated health issues of several varieties but malnutrition as their root cause. When she saw the same in Native American communities she would feel angry. Here she could only feel powerless.

The de Silva house was cement brick. At the front stood its most impressive feature: a blue tiled above-ground tomb just inside the wire fence. A small bunch of fresh flowers had recently been placed on top of the tomb. Estefana became aware of Carter's curiosity. "The colour suggests her mother, or his, *mana*," she explained. "The dead are always with us."

Esmeralda da Silva greeted them with a blank expression and said her husband, Miguel, had gone to Suai four weeks earlier in search of a job. There was no paid work for men in the village, she explained, only on the projects in Suai. She had stayed with the seven children, of whom Julio was the third oldest. Julio was in school but school would be over for the day very soon. They were welcome to wait outside. She said no more and closed the door.

They sat in the SUV with the doors open, brushing away flies but hoping for a breeze to cool them down. Estefana asked Carter if she would like anything from the store but Carter declined the offer. "Those papayas cost us dearly," she grinned. "I don't know about you but I'm going to eat one." They managed to finish both and waited in silence lulled by the peacefulness of the village. Carter was remembering Estefana's report again, how Julio had run off with a friend for what he said was about twenty minutes and she was bothered by how he would have guessed that time. If the twenty minutes were a product of his imagination, what other things might be as well?

Eventually three children came running toward the house laughing as they pushed and shoved each other competing to kick an empty plastic water bottle. Estefana recognized Julio. "That's him, *mana*, the one on the left with the longer hair."

She stepped out from the SUV. "*Botarde alin*," Estefana said to the children.

"*Botarde*," they sang in unison.

Estefana asked Julio if he remembered her and if they could have a talk again. The boy nodded enthusiastically. The other two children stood enthralled by Julio's apparent importance. With them as witnesses, he knew he'd be the centre of attention at school the next day and so he puffed out his chest. Estefana introduced Carter as her American colleague. Even better, Julio imagined, and he turned proudly to his friends. Now they could see that he was of importance to a foreigner as well.

Julio gave Estefana the same account of his movements the day his sister had been snatched as he had given her the first time. He had been told to mind Julieta, had seen a friend, and run off to play with him because the friend had found a ball. When he returned, Julieta was gone.

"Ask him how long he had been gone and how he calculated the time," Carter told Estefana.

"Ten minutes," Julio answered. "I saw a clock."

"The first time I asked you it was twenty minutes. Remember?" said Estefana, attuned to the point of Carter's question, and Julio's chest sank a little.

"Where did you see the clock?" Estefana asked.

Julio hesitated. "In there," he said pointing to his house.

"I didn't see a clock in there when I was talking to your mother," Estefana said.

"There was one there that day," insisted Julio. "It was hanging on the door."

"No-one hangs a clock on a door, Julio," Estefana said. "Are you sure you saw it there?"

"Well, I thought I did."

"Ask him to read the time on your watch," Carter said.

"Julio," Estefana said. "What time is it on my watch?"

The boy looked doubtful. He looked at his two friends then back at Estefana. "Day time," he offered.

"And how would you work out ten minutes on my watch?" Estefana asked.

The boy was worried now as though he'd fallen into a trap. And in front of his friends. He started to sniffle. His lips trembled as if he was about to cry.

"It's alright Julio," Estefana said. "You are not in any trouble. We just want to know what happened that day." She sensed his humiliation at having been caught out in a lie in front of his friends. "And you are the only one who can tell us," she said more loudly in order to ensure the other children could hear. "No one else. You could help us find Julieta. But you must tell me the truth. It is very important what you say. Very important."

Julio brightened again. "You won't tell my mother?" he asked his hand over his mouth.

"No, Julio. This is between us," Estefana reassured him.

"I was sitting outside the house. Here, on the road. A woman gave me ten *centavos* and said I could go and spend it on sweets in the store. She said I could eat them all myself, and, if my mum asked, to say I was with a friend." He noticed the surprise in the eyes of the police officer. "We never have sweets in our house," he said by way of an excuse.

Chapter 15

"You shouldn't have gone there," Cordero snapped after they told him about Beko.

"*You* shouldn't have split us up," countered Carter.

Cordero pushed his hands deep into his trouser pockets. "I shouldn't have left you on your own," he conceded.

"No—you should have thought the whole thing through more carefully," she corrected him.

He sat down on one of the beds in their room in the nuns' house. Estefana stood quietly in the corner of the room. Cordero stared at the floor. "You don't think much of my policing, do you?" he said to Carter.

"What makes you say that?" she asked, surprised.

"You're always telling me to hurry up, stay focused, questioning my training. And now this."

"I could say you make a better gin and tonic than you do a policeman," Carter sniffed, letting the comment sink in. "But I won't."

"You just did," complained Cordero.

"No I didn't. I offered a proposition not a statement," Carter replied. "These things happen and we were fine," she added knowing she'd won the argument. With that settled, she reported what they had learned from the boy, Julio da Silva.

"And you believe him?" Cordero asked.

"Yes, I do," insisted Carter. "The facial expressions are hard to fake at that age."

"Well it's circumstantial but the strongest lead we have," Cordero said. "Did the boy describe the woman?"

"Not in any helpful way," regretted Carter. "We asked him to compare the woman to Estefana in the hope that would make it easier for him. He said she was older than Estefana but then he calculated Estefana's age at sixteen. At first he said the woman was bigger but it was unclear if he meant taller or fatter and we couldn't get a straight answer. His arms went out in an attempt to measure what he meant but then they came back in and went up and out again."

Carter paced the room. "The only definite thing he knew was that her hair was the same colour as Estefana's and the same texture but cut short. That might have been because the woman kept it in a bun. As for the clothes she was wearing, he thought a blue top and a black skirt. That was it but at least he was consistent about it." She paused, thinking. "But I get the feeling people are holding back, as though they are edgy about something. Not Julio. He was only afraid of getting another whack from his mother for doing something wrong. But people generally seem tense and frightened."

Estefana looked at Cordero. "Well, many of them are very traditional," he said. "Being interviewed by police officers, especially ones they don't know, can be intimidating. You being a foreigner wouldn't help either, if I can say that."

"May I make a comment?" Estefana asked.

Cordero looked at her but Carter said: "Yes, of course."

"If Julio was right about the blue top and black dress that may be important. That is not the kind of thing most women around here wear. Older ones wear traditional dress. Younger ones mostly wear jeans and T-shirts." Estefana paused, checked Cordero and Carter and decided to offer her opinion without being asked for it. "I think a blue top and black dress would be worn by a woman with a paying job. It would be like a uniform. There is a school near here, at Obago, where the uniform is a yellow top and brown shorts for boys, a brown dress for girls. The teachers dress in similar colours."

Carter considered that. Cordero prepared three glasses of gin and tonic, the one for Estefana filled with the same amount of gin as the others. Estefana didn't resist. He handed the drinks to the women.

"Okay, that's interesting," said Carter. She sipped her gin and looked over her glass at Cordero. "Because something you said yesterday has been playing on my mind."

"Really? What was it?" he asked.

"You said what sticks in people's minds are the things that aren't familiar. Everyday, usual kind of things? They don't stick. Think about it. We've been asking people if they saw anything that was *unusual*—unfamiliar people, unfamiliar vehicles. What if the person or persons doing the abducting were known to the victims' families, were a common sight in the neighbourhood—drove a vehicle that regularly visited each of the villages? None of it stuck in people's minds because they think only a complete outsider would steal a baby."

Or a demon, Cordero was thinking. He drained his glass in two swallows and considered the idea. Estefana sipped her gin and tonic, her eyes on Carter.

"What if we focus on jobs, services or organisations common to the villages where a child has been taken?" Carter asked.

"You mean like a church?" said Cordero. "There's a church in or near virtually every one of those villages we've been to."

"Okay. Or a school. Or an agricultural extension office. Do they have them here? Or, dare I say, a police post. We then narrow these down into ones where it'd be usual for people to move from site to site without anyone questioning their movements. Then, when we know what we're looking at," she continued, "we go back to Suai and look up staff rosters, vehicle movements and that sort of thing in those operations."

Cordero had been nodding as he followed her line of reasoning. "Okay," he said. "But if we are dealing with a government employee, that person would be hard pressed to steal a baby and take it across the border to Indonesia without raising questions about their absence from work. They'd have to have one or more accomplices who don't have regular jobs. Or they'd have to have someone in the loop who could juggle timesheets and such."

"Okay," Carter agreed. "But it's a start. And if we get the person who snatches the babies that should lead to the person who traffics them."

They fell silent. Carter was pacing again, slowly at first but then in a more agitated fashion.

"It's progress," Cordero offered.

"But not much," Carter countered swivelling the glass in her hand. "We're not doing enough. Back home we'd be working this case day and night. All night if necessary. Not drinking gin and waiting for clues to fall into our laps. It worries me."

"Back in *your* home, maybe," said Cordero. "With computer files, police files, the internet to check and hours of CCTV to watch. But this is Timor. You're in the Third World—actually, Fourth World. Here patience and low expectations are job requirements for the police."

"Low expectations!" said Carter, her voice rising. "We have a missing girl!"

"I know that."

"If they couldn't get her across the border and they know the police are after them she could be dead by now, Cordero! Suffocated, strangled, throat slashed!"

"You don't need to—" but she cut him off again.

"I think I do need to! Believe me, I've seen it all. When these bastards feel threatened, they'll just get rid of the kid as quickly as they can to save their own necks."

"Don't you think I know that?" he protested. "But emotion isn't going to help. We have to work through this step by step however long that takes or we risk missing crucial bits of information that could unlock the case. And as unfortunate as it is, we have to do that with all the obstacles and limitations we face here and on Timor time."

"Timor time! How long did it take to shake off the Portuguese? Five hundred—" but she was interrupted by a knock on the door and the young nun told them dinner was ready.

Carter and Cordero exchanged frosty glances and left the room. Estefana finished her gin and tonic with a big swallow, gasped at the amount of alcohol she'd consumed, and followed them out trying to maintain her composure.

Dinner proved to be a relative feast given the haphazard way they'd been eating lately. It was *Caril*—a mild Timorese chicken curry cooked with potatoes, roast capsicum and coconut paste, together with rice steamed with diced taro and shrimp paste, and a simple salad of freshly picked onions and tomatoes. Something special to mark their visit, Sister Theresa explained as she popped her head in to greet them. Before long, the food had lifted their mood.

"I thought you said we wouldn't get spicy food in the villages, Estefana," said Carter. Estefana looked apologetic, realised the tease and could only smile broadly with her mouth full of food.

Cordero ate heartily but kept up a running account of his meeting with the veteran, Ivando Machado, in Uma Daiso and how the man had said he had information but wanted his stolen motorcycle found before he'd share it.

"What information?" Carter prompted.

"He wouldn't say. Just said, 'Find my motorcycle first'. God knows how I'm supposed to do that?"

"Then why didn't you press him on what he knew?" she asked, agitated again.

"He was a veteran," Cordero answered. "You don't put pressure on veterans."

She started to argue but he was insistent and she let it go. They decided one more day was needed checking the villages to identify the services provided in common. Carter appeared relaxed about the suggestion they split up again—because there'd be no interviewing, she explained. Cordero had checked the SUV for damage from the incident in Beko before they had argued over drinks. There was the shattered back window, a few chips and cracks in others, and scattered scratches and dents but it was perfectly okay to drive. Carter and Estefana would take it again and Cordero the motorcycle. Their efforts would take them most of the day and of necessity they would have to spend another night at the nuns' house before heading back to Suai early Saturday morning. After they had finished the meal, they went back to their rooms. It had been a long, tiring day. Cordero offered to make another gin and tonic but he was displaying good manners rather than enthusiasm and Carter and Estefana declined. Cordero left them to take what passed for a shower while Carter and Estefana prepared for bed.

"Can I ask you a question, *mana*?" Estefana said as Carter made herself as comfortable as she could on the thin mattress.

"Yes, Estefana, of course," Carter replied.

"I only ever hear you called Carter. Do you only have the one name? I have many," she said without waiting and listed them off with pride. "I am Estefana Emilia Mariana dos Carvalho Castro."

"They're lovely names," Carter said. "It must be hard to remember them all."

"Oh no," said Estefana. "Each name links me to a grandmother or grandfather. When I get married the priest will call me by all my names and the people present will know where I came from and who I am related to."

"Marry your boyfriend in Dili?" Carter asked.

"Yes *mana*. Josinto Centavo Veddo. One day I would like to work in Dili. Then we could marry. I would become Estefana Emilia Mariana dos Carvalho Veddo. I would drop the Castro for Veddo, you see. Don't you think that is a wonderful name?"

"Certainly is impressive," agreed Carter.

They lay in the dark a few moments.

"Sara," said Carter finally. "My first name is Sara but everyone has always simply called me Carter because that's what they called my father."

"Sara is a strong name, *mana*," Estefana said. "She was Abraham's wife and the mother of Isaac. It is a beautiful name which means 'princess'. The nuns taught us these things in school. Perhaps you should use it more, *mana*."

"Perhaps," agreed Carter.

Silence again.

"Do you like *Senyor* Cordero, *mana*?" Estefana asked presently.

"Like?" asked Carter, surprised by the question. "What do you mean?"

"I shouldn't have asked, *mana*," Estefana said embarrassed. "I am sorry. I talk too much."

"No, that's alright," Carter said. "Good night now. We can talk more tomorrow."

"I would like that, *mana*," Estefana said and was soon asleep.

Chapter 16

Cordero's cell rang as they were sitting down to breakfast. After the caller identified him or herself—neither Carter nor Estefana could tell which it was—Cordero stood, stretched the ache from his motorcycle ride the previous day, and walked outside with the cell pressed firmly against his ear. His only contribution to the conversation seemed to be '*Uh-huh*' repeated over and over. He was being told that his sister Ana had burst her appendix around midnight and developed severe peritonitis. She was being treated with antibiotics before a surgeon was to perform an emergency appendectomy, that afternoon. Her condition was critical. Cordero had to head back to Dili.

"I am the senior member of the family now," he explained to Carter, his face lined in worry. "I must be with her when she undergoes surgery and ensure her kids are okay—whatever happens."

"That's terrible. You told me she'd been sick. We'll be fine," said Carter. Estefana looked unsettled but nodded her agreement.

"I shouldn't leave you again," said Cordero torn between responsibilities.

"It's too late for that now," said Carter. "Go. It'll be okay. But how will you get there? And how long do you think you'll be gone?"

"I'll take the motorcycle," he said. "It'll be quicker." He checked his watch—it had just gone seven o'clock. "I should make Dili by twelve, one at the latest. She won't have been operated on by then. You two keep the SUV. If everything goes well I should get back early tomorrow morning. I'll aim to meet you in Suai. We can keep in touch by cell."

He took two spoonfuls of the food in front of him and excused himself to pack quickly, settle the account for their stay with Sister Theresa, and be off. Less than ten minutes later Carter heard him kick start the bike and roar out of the churchyard heading north.

"Well then, it's you and me," Carter said to Estefana.

"Yes, *mana*," she replied.

"What's this?" Carter asked, examining her breakfast for the first time.

"It's called *Bibingka, mana*. It is rice mixed with eggs and coconut milk and baked into a sweet cake in banana leaves."

"Two nice meals in a row," observed Carter. "This could become habit forming." She savoured the serving but quickly. "Could you ask the nuns for some food for lunch again?"

"Of course," said Estefana rising from the table.

"Good. I'll throw a few things in a bag and meet you at the vehicle. We've a lot of ground to cover. Let's get away as soon as we can." Carter turned back to Estefana. "Oh and can you check the map. Our first stop is going to be that veteran Cordero mentioned—at Uma Daiso was it? I want to know what he knows."

"But *mana*—"

"Remember what I told you? If they don't say you can't do it, then you're free to do it. Come on. Let's not waste any more time."

• • •

Cordero took the most direct route to Dili, through Bobonaro then Atsabe and north past the turn off to Ermera and on to the coast road for the last twenty-minute run into the city. He had made the journey with only one quick stop to refuel at Letefoho, and arrived at the hospital just before noon feeling fatigued in muscles he'd forgotten he had. He parked the bike, took off his helmet and worked circulation back into his legs. He walked quickly into the reception area checking his cell as he went. There were two calls in the log, both from Dr Brooks. He would call him back after he had checked on Ana.

The nurse on duty at the reception desk stared into her computer. "Ana Feliciano," she punched the letters of the name slowly onto her keyboard using one finger. Cordero struggled to control his impatience. "I'm sorry, *maun*, there is no Ana Feliciano," she said.

Could she have dropped her late husband's name, he wondered. "Try Cordero. Ana Cordero."

There was more one-fingered tapping. "Ah, yes. Here it is. Ana Feliciano Cordero," the nurse said. "She was filed under 'C'. Let me see." The nurse read the file with no urgency. "Hmm. It says she has recently been given sedatives in preparation for surgery. Dr. Montoya will perform the operation. You can't see *Mana* Ana now but you may just catch Dr. Montoya in the refreshment room. I think he will be having lunch. You know how these Cubans are with their routines."

Dr Carlos Montoya was one of the few remaining Cuban doctors in Timor-Leste, a remnant of the team of front-line medical staff Havana had sent to the newly-independent country to help build its health system. Several, like Montoya, had stayed on because their skills were in short supply and they preferred the relatively privileged conditions they enjoyed in Timor-Leste over the austerity back home. Montoya was a specialist surgeon with a reputation for arrogance but a record of doing things properly. Cordero had occasion to deal with him in the course of some of his cases. At the mention of Montoya's name he felt a little of his anxiety lift.

"Thank you," he said to the nurse. "I'll check the refreshment room."

Cordero hurried down the corridor to a room where doctors, nurses, and ancillary staff were lining up for lunch. He skirted the queue and searched the room, noticing Montoya sitting by himself next to a window. He was reading something while he ate. Cordero approached him as courteously as he could.

"Excuse me Doctor," he said. "We have met in my work with the police. My name is Vincintino Cordero. I understand you are operating on my sister, Ana Feliciano Cordero—an appendectomy—after lunch. I came immediately I heard from the south coast. I was wondering how she is doing."

Dr Montoya put his fork on the table, closed the file of papers in front of him and stared at his plate, annoyed at having been disturbed during lunch.

"She was in a bad way. Her appendicitis should have been diagnosed earlier. A burst appendix producing peritonitis can be deadly." Montoya had delivered his diagnosis with accompanying reprimand staring at his rice and beans. "I ordered a course of antibiotics this morning." He looked directly at Cordero. "I don't expect any problems with the appendectomy and she should make a complete recovery. However, I suggest you check with the nurse," he said emphasising the appropriate channel of communication, "*after* I have completed the operation."

"Thank you Doctor, I will," said Cordero relieved. "I am sorry to have interrupted your lunch. Thank you again."

Cordero left feeling more at ease. There was the surgery and possible complications arising from the fact that the condition hadn't been treated earlier. But Montoya wasn't panicking and consequently Cordero told himself neither should he. At that point, he remembered the calls from Brooks. He walked out the front of the hospital and called him.

"Tino, my dear chap. Where have you been?" asked Brooks who sounded as though he too was at lunch.

"I had to come back to Dili urgently," Cordero said. "My sister's appendix burst and she is due for emergency surgery this afternoon."

"Who's operating?" Brooks asked sounding concerned.

"Montoya. The Cuban," said Cordero.

"Thank God. He's a good surgeon. A bit difficult at times but a good surgeon. Ana should be fine with him on the case."

"Yes, I just managed to speak to him. He seemed to think it was a straightforward operation," Cordero said.

"Quite. Except this is Timor-Leste," Brooks added and then regretted the scepticism. "Anyhow," he said changing the subject, "I have something that may interest you."

"Again?" asked Cordero not bothering to disguise his impatience.

"Yes, dear boy, again. I performed an autopsy on the crocodile and you'll never guess what I found inside its stomach. The missing arm no less! It was in reasonable shape given it had been swallowed by a crocodile. I imagine its digestive system slowed down as it was dying. I cleaned the thing as best I could. And *voilà*. Guess what it showed?"

Brooks left Cordero hanging. He liked these little games.

"I have no idea, Howard. What did it show?" said Cordero playing along reluctantly.

"A tattoo, dear boy. A tattoo," said Brooks. "But not just any old tattoo. I think it might be one of those gang tattoos." Brooks gave Cordero a moment to consider the implications of that. "I told Buzzi but your police superintendent said I shouldn't concern you with it, that you were busy enough on that child abduction case. But I thought you might be interested. If it is a gang tattoo, it may help to identify our body on the beach."

"It's possible," agreed Cordero.

"Since you are in Dili, are you likely to pop in to your office?" But Brooks didn't wait for a reply. "I'll email you the photographs I took. I'll send them on the cell as well but they will be clearer on your email. Cast a careful eye over them."

"I need to wait on the outcome of Ana's operation this afternoon. I can go to the office. Do that. Email me what you have. Can you do it in the next thirty minutes?"

There was a pause at the other end and Cordero could hear tapping.

"Already sent, dear boy. The photos will be waiting for you when you get to your office. I'll send them to your cell later today after I've had lunch."

• • •

Cordero rode straight to his office, parked the bike and walked into a room he shared with two other investigators who looked up from their computer screens.

"Tino!" cried Lucas Rama Savoy, the comedian of the duo. "Haven't seen you for a week. We hear you've picked up a sexy American girlfriend. Showing her the ins and outs of Timor. Is that right?"

His colleague Manuel Fonseca was grinning broadly.

"You're damned right it's right," said Cordero. "And I'll tell you what else. This girl wants all the ins and outs. Insisted on me. Wouldn't be seen dead with the likes of you two."

Lucas had no reply to that. Manuel's grin broke into laughter. "What's her name?" he asked.

"Candy," Cordero said. "You know, it's American for 'real sweet'. But that's all I'm going to say."

Cordero sat and logged on. It took a few minutes for the screen to light up. It always did.

"Anything happening while I've been away, Lucas?" he asked without interest.

"Someone shot the President, bombed the US Embassy and robbed the Wells Fargo office," Lucas said not looking up from his terminal. "Usual stuff."

Cordero wasn't bothering to listen. When his screen came alive, he checked his emails. There, at the top, was one from Brooks with the subject line 'Enjoy' and containing three attached photographs. The first showed a near full-length arm, its top close to the shoulder area horribly mangled as it was ripped off the torso by the crocodile. What appeared to be a tattoo could just be made out on the forearm. The second photograph provided a closer view of the tattoo. Only part of the design was clear—what appeared to be the bottom half of three lines enclosed in a circle— the colour had faded, possibly from the age of the tattoo, possibly from the digestive juices of the crocodile. The third photograph was a close up of the lines. None of the photographs made any sense to Cordero.

"What are you looking at that has you so intrigued, Tino?" asked Manuel.

"Flights to Bali. Candy and I are thinking of eloping," he said and pressed the keys to print out the three photographs in colour.

"You guys keep your heads down, work hard, and one day you might get a break with a good-looking American girl, like me." He reached across, grabbed the printouts and stood to leave. "But I doubt it," he added as he walked through the door.

Before he left the building he decided to check in on Jacobsen and give her an update on the investigation into the child abductions. He followed the corridor to the first door marked INTERPOL. Officer Furaha Oodanta was sitting in her plastic chair by her small metal desk staring into her computer. She looked like she hadn't moved an inch since the day he'd taken Carter in to meet Jacobsen.

"*Botarde, mana,*" said Cordero. "Is Director Jacobsen here?"

"No sir," replied Oodanta. "She has gone to lunch."

"Okay. Can you give her a message for me, please? Tell her I dropped by. I had to return to Dili as my sister is having emergency surgery. I'm told she will be fine and I'll be returning to Suai first thing tomorrow morning. We think we have a lead in the case but it is too soon to say any more. She doesn't need to call. I'll be in touch when I can."

Officer Oodanta stared at him. "Could you write that, sir?" she appealed.

He sighed. "Of course," he said. He scribbled the note, left it with Oodanta and walked back to his motorcycle.

It only took ten minutes to reach police headquarters on the other side of the city even though the traffic was heavy by Dili's standards. He'd taken a short cut down a dirt lane lined with make-do stores all selling the same kind of second-hand clothes beneath billboards of bright young Chinese and Indonesians advertising cell phones, designer sunglasses, and baby formula— the very things occupants of this neighbourhood could least afford. A tangle of overhead electrical wires criss-crossed the length of the lane offering further evidence of the impromptu nature of the area. He turned left into the back entrance of the police building and parked the motorcycle. He went in through a side door, up a flight of stairs, and entered a room marked '*Forsa-Tareta Espesial*'— 'Special Task Force'.

"*Botarde, maun*. Where's Pepe?" he asked a young officer idly turning the pages of a newspaper.

"Where he always is, *maun*," the man said and indicated a pair of shoes sticking out atop a desk behind a full-length screen beside the window.

Alberto 'Pepe' Marcelino was a man whose height seemed less than his width. Because of his bulk, Pepe was disinclined to move from a seated position except to get food or to leave for home where he'd find more food. People who knew Pepe often said that he grew at his desk like a vine but no one in Dili knew more than he about gang related crime—a long-standing problem since before Timor-Leste became independent. Many gangs had past or present political affiliations; others were engaged in crime pure and simple.

"Pepe, *maun, botarde*," said Cordero peering around the screen. "I want you to look at some printouts. They're from photographs of a guy found on a beach near Suai earlier this week. Well, they're of his arm. A crocodile had swallowed it. You can just make out a tattoo. I think it might be a gang tag. What do you think?"

Pepe sat up in his chair. He had been asleep. It took him a moment to digest what Cordero had said.

"Hey, Tino," he said. "You know how many Timorese have tattoos? About as many as have dicks. What's special about this one?"

"Just take a look for me, will you?"

Pepe took the printouts from Cordero. "Looks like a big arm. Large guy. You say a crocodile ate him? Must have been one hell of a crocodile."

"Ate his arm, Pepe. Tore it off and swallowed it. But then the crocodile turned up dead itself and the arm was extracted."

"Wow. Things get stranger and stranger in this country, Tino," Pepe said shaking his head. "Let me have another look."

Pepe looked at the three printouts again and focused on the last of them.

"I need to check some files, Tino. Is this urgent?"

"Yeah. It is. I'm on my way back to Suai," said Cordero. "Soon."

"Okay. Can you give me thirty minutes? Get yourself lunch. Better idea, get me lunch. That new Indian restaurant on the corner does a nice beef vindaloo."

Cordero checked his watch. The surgery would only have just begun, there was no way to hurry Pepe, and Cordero himself hadn't had anything to eat since the breakfast he'd barely touched. "Right. I'll be back in thirty minutes with your lunch," he said and headed for the door.

Chapter 17

Estefana had asked the whereabouts of the home of Ivando Machado as they entered the centre of Uma Daiso. They drove up the dirt track to the fourth of the new houses as they'd been directed and Estefana cut the engine. "How will we do this, *mana*?" she asked. "He is a veteran."

"The same way we question every other witness, Estefana," Carter replied taking off her sunglasses. "You start to make exceptions and you'll run into trouble."

They left the SUV and walked up the steps onto Machado's porch. Before they could knock on the door it opened and the veteran peered at them from the doorframe. Estefana introduced herself, then Carter, and explained the reason for their visit.

"I told that other one I'd tell him what I know when he brings back my motorcycle," Machado grunted. He began to close the door but Carter put her foot in the jam. He glared at the foot, then at her, and made another attempt to slam the door shut. She grabbed the door with her left hand and held it firmly open.

"Tell him we need to know what he knows *now*," she said to Estefana. "Tell him every minute counts."

Machado could hardly contain his anger. He peered menacingly at Carter. "I lost my motorcycle," he said through gritted teeth.

"And Luana Ruiz lost much more than that," said Carter through Estefana but holding his glare.

"I'm a veteran," Machado shouted. "Show me respect."

Carter was quick to reply. "I'll show you respect when you earn it by doing the right thing by that child."

Machado's left fist clenched, his nostrils flared, but he seemed speechless. Carter stood her ground, refusing to be intimidated by him. He tried to slam the door again but Carter stopped it from closing as she had before.

"*Senyor*, a child's life is at stake," Estefana said.

The veteran turned to her then back to Carter. She kept her eyes locked on his. He looked around and then back. Carter hadn't moved, hadn't even blinked.

"Please *senyor*," Estefana pleaded.

Machado turned to her again, took a deep breath, shook his head, and raised his arms as if giving up. "What is it about women these days?" he said. "Wait here."

He went inside his house leaving the door ajar, came back with three bottles of beer and gestured for them to sit down on the porch. He opened the bottles, handed them one each, and took two sips in quick succession from his own. Then he lit a clove cigarette and its sweet scent perfumed the air.

"You said you are from Suai and she's from Amercia?" Machado asked Estefana.

"That's right *senyor*. And we are both police officers."

The veteran merely nodded. "I was a *Falintil* guerrilla," he began squinting out over his yard. "I joined in 1988 after they killed my father during a raid on our village." He spat. "His crime was to protest against an Indonesian officer who had kicked an old woman to the ground. He was thirty-nine and I was seventeen years old." Machado took another sip of his beer then sucked in the smoke from his cigarette. Estefana looked at Carter who was sipping her beer.

"We lived north of Labaro." He turned to Estefana. "You know it?" he asked but continued on regardless. "About two hours from here. But I was sent to the mountains near Viqueque where most of the *Falintil* were hiding. Eleven years in that place, living in caves, eating whatever the villagers could give us when they weren't frightened of the Indonesians coming and taking what little food they had or killing people as a warning. Not eating when the villagers had nothing to give us. I didn't see much action. We were short of everything—weapons, ammunition, uniforms, boots. And if we did conduct an ambush, the Indonesians would extract revenge on the villagers, especially on women and children. I hated what they did to women and children. That's why I'm talking to you."

The guerillas' main task, Machado told them, had been to just stay alive in the mountains. That told other Timorese that the Indonesian occupation remained opposed, would always be opposed, and that *Falintil* would never surrender. They didn't need to win battles to get that message across, didn't need to kill many Indonesian soldiers, just needed to be out there. Free. Defiant. That was enough.

Just before the referendum on independence, he and some other guerillas were moved south, toward the town of Viqueque. They were there to reassure the villagers that they could vote in safety. But that was a lie. Machado and the others were under strict orders to take no action. Whatever provocations the Indonesians or their militia allies might create, they had to stay out of it. Had they reacted and fought back, defending the villagers, the Indonesians would have used that as a pretext to call off the vote. For this reason they hid and watched but could do no more.

There were two others with him assigned to a position near Ossu: Ernesto Lopez—who they called 'Che' after the hero of the Cuban revolution, Ernesto 'Che' Guevara—and Virgilio Amaral. Che was reliable, strong and he feared nothing and no one. Virgilio, on the other hand, was crazy. He had joined when he was only fourteen. Just after the invasion. Virgilio had witnessed his family being killed—mother, father, brothers and sister—as suspected terrorists. Virgilio's extended family had also been killed or starved to death. How he'd survived Machado couldn't say but Virgilio had and he stayed alive as a guerilla for over twenty years—years spent hiding, scavenging food like an animal, living constantly on the run.

As he related his story Machado placed his bottle of beer on the step below him and rubbed a hand across his face.

"It was a day I can never forget," he said. "Two weeks before the referendum. It's burned into my memory," he repeated, shaking his head. "We had received news of atrocities near Suai, in Bobonaro, Ermera, around Los Palos, even in Dili. But up 'til that day we had seen nothing ourselves."

That morning the three of them decided to patrol a ridge overlooking a river on which there was a small village of perhaps sixty people. He didn't know the name of the village but the river was called *Halai Makaas*, which meant 'strong running'. They'd stopped mid-morning for a short rest under trees just below the top of the ridge. Che was talking about the village they could see below them: children playing, men tending gardens of maize, cassava and sweet potato, the women sweeping their yards or washing clothes. It was, Che had said, a scene that could represent the whole of Timor-Leste, its beauty and tranquility, all in the one place, all at the one time.

Machado picked up his bottle again and drank the rest of the beer. He wiped his mouth and glanced this time at Carter.

"They came out of the forest on the other side of the river," he said. "Eight of them. Heavily armed with Pindad assault rifles and a few M-16s all supplied by the Indonesian military. Some had machetes hanging from their belts. They were Timorese pro-Indonesian militia but with an Indonesian officer in the rear. They crossed the river and entered the village. A dog was barking at them as they approached and the man in front shot it dead with a pistol. Women rushed to collect their children and shield them from the intruders and men came running from their gardens. The man who shot the dog gunned down two farmers as they ran into the village and then ordered everyone else to gather in the centre of the huts."

Machado placed his empty beer bottle down on the ground and stared at it a moment.

"There was a lot of shouting, wailing, screaming," he said. "The militiamen went from hut to hut dragging out any stragglers, terrified children, old people. They threw them into the centre of the village. Kicked them, butted them with their rifles. We had Kalashnikovs and about ten rounds each. We had a clear line of fire. We could have taken all of the militiamen in seconds. But we did nothing. Che was the hardest to control. I had to point my rifle at him and repeat the orders we were given. Virgilio seemed to be reliving the killing of his family. He was paralysed with terror."

His shoulders slumped as he continued.

"When the villagers had been herded together, the Indonesian came forward. He inspected the younger girls, took their faces in his hand and made them look up at him. And his actions told what he was thinking. If their mothers tried to protect the girls he would knock the women away, kick them, spit on them as they lay on the ground. I'm sure this man was from *Kopassus*— the Indonesian special forces. He wore a pistol in a holster on his hip but he never took it out. He didn't have to. He was clearly directing the operation and money or drugs would have been all he needed to control the others."

Machado gazed out across the yard again.

"Eventually the Indonesian came and stood beside the Timorese militia leader—the one who'd shot the dog and the two villagers. *Kobra* I heard him called by the Indonesian," he said.

"*Kobra*?" asked Estefana to check she'd heard correctly.

"Yes, *Kobra*. It means 'cobra'—you know, the snake—in Bahasa. Meant to scare people, I guess, by suggesting a ruthless killer."

The Indonesian and this *Kobra* spoke together for a few moments. Then the Indonesian went back into the crowd and pulled out one young girl. Machado guessed her age at twelve. Her mother tried to stop him and this *Kobra* came and struck her down with a savage blow from his machete. She bled out on the ground where she fell. The Indonesian dragged the girl to a hut and soon Machado and the other two could hear her screaming.

Kobra then gave orders to his men. Four of them spread out around the villagers while another two began burning all the huts except where the Indonesian was raping the girl. There was more crying and screaming and *Kobra* shouted at the people to shut up. But they weren't listening because everything they owned, everything they valued was being destroyed. He shouted again but they took no notice. The villagers began running to the huts to put out the fires. *Kobra's* men gunned them down. Then they turned their guns on the rest of the villagers and shot them all.

When it was finished, *Kobra* walked back and forth through the bodies. Any wounded, he struck with his machete. The Indonesian reappeared hitching up his trousers and smiling. Pleased with himself and the job the militia had done, Machado figured. Then he heard *Kobra* call out to the man.

"'Tengassi!'" he said. "I will never forget that name. Tengassi. The wind had changed direction and we could hear what they were saying. This Tengassi grinned and said to *Kobra*: 'I broke her in for you. You know what to do when you're finished.'"

Machado grimaced, a vacant look in his eyes, took another cigarette from his pocket but didn't light it.

"While *Kobra* had his way with the girl, the others searched the bodies for the little they might have on them. Tengassi ordered four of the dead be hung upside down from trees to add to the warning this massacre was meant to convey. After about fifteen minutes they left."

Machado, Che and Virgilio made their way down into what was left of the village, took the bodies down from the trees.

"I found the body of the girl—she had been cut open with *Kobra's* machete and was covered in blood. I buried her," he said. "Che, the good Communist that he was, affixed a cross to her grave. Virgilio simply wept and wept. We counted fifty dead and couldn't bury them all. So we left, supporting Virgilio between us to report the massacre to our regional commander."

Machado wiped his eyes and coughed away his emotion.

"On the way we vowed that when the referendum was over and Timor was free we would find this *Kobra* and kill him. It would be a *festa da cabezas*, Che had said. You know, what the Portuguese call a festival of beheading. We couldn't do anything about the Indonesian. He would return to his country and probably be given a medal. But we could take care of *Kobra* for the sake of those who had been killed. It has always haunted me that we didn't."

"Why didn't you go after him and kill him?" Estefana asked at Carter's prompting.

Machado glanced sideways at her. "Strange question for a police officer to ask," he said then looked straight ahead again.

They kept their plans quiet until independence came three years later, he explained. But by then Che had developed cancer and was dying. Machado and Virgilio had moved back to the Suai area. They brought Che back and nursed him as best they could because what was left of his family was too poor to take care of him. Mostly it was Machado who nursed him and that became a full-time occupation. Virgilio seemed to be losing his mind. Che died in 2006. It was not an easy death and in its own way it brought back the cruelty of what they had witnessed more than the anger at what they had seen. Machado started to wonder what would be gained by extracting revenge. Timor's new leaders kept talking about the need for Timorese to leave the past behind and learn to live with each other no matter what some people may have done. Machado could see sense in that, or at least convinced himself that he could.

Carter took the last sip of her beer and waited. The veteran fell silent. "Tell him that is a terrible thing he witnessed," she told Estefana. "And a terrible situation that he was placed in. I can't begin to imagine the pain it must have caused him. But he told Cordero he had information relevant to the investigation into the abduction of Luana. I don't see any connection."

Machado looked directly at Carter after Estefana had finished the translation.

"He was there," he said.

"There? Who? Where?" Estefana asked.

"*Kobra*. I saw him down near that house the day the baby was taken. A woman who I've never seen before went into the house and came out with a bundle in her arms. I didn't know what it was. I took no notice of her. *Kobra*—that's who I was watching. He put the bundle in his van and drove off."

"Are you sure it was him?" Carter asked. "A lot of years have passed since the referendum and it was on the other side of the country that you first saw him."

"It was him," Machado insisted. "I wasn't sure at first but then I recognized the militia tattoo on his arm when he took the bundle from the woman and placed it in his van. There's no mistake. I remember seeing it on the same spot on his arm when he used his machete that day. The three columns. That was their symbol. The *Coluna Negra*."

Carter shielded her eyes and stared toward the far-off Ruiz house. Machado drew the implication. "Field glasses," he said. "Keep them by the door. It's an old habit I can't quite shake."

"The woman this *Kobra* was with that day. Do you remember anything about her?" Carter asked.

"No. I was watching *Kobra*."

"Nothing at all? Her age. How she was dressed?"

"No," Machado said.

"Had she driven here?"

"Yes. She left in a car."

"What do you remember about her car?"

"Not much," Machado answered. "It was blue I think. Yes blue. I don't remember the make."

"What about the van you say this *Kobra* was driving?"

"I remember it was small. Old. It had me thinking the bastard hadn't done all that well for selling himself out to the enemy."

Chapter 18

The vindaloo was good, very good, and Cordero brought another serving for Pepe.

"What do I owe you, *maun*?" asked Pepe, removing the lid from the container, closing his eyes, and enjoying the sweet, sharp aroma.

"Just an answer to my question," said Cordero.

Pepe laid Cordero's three printouts on his desk alongside the container of food and took the first forkful of vindaloo. "Well, I'd say the tattoo is three black columns in a circle," he said munching a mouthful of curry.

"Yeah? And?"

"Ever heard of the *Coluna Negra*? The Black Columns. Originally they were Dutch Timorese recruited by the Japanese to terrify people when they occupied the island during the Second World War. Those columns are meant to represent strength and the circle that they're in unity or some shit. Look here."

Pepe placed another photograph on his desk alongside the printouts. It was a clearer image of three black columns enclosed in a circle just like the partial tattoo on the printouts.

"That's the full tattoo," said Pepe. "Nice detail, huh?"

"Right. Okay we know what it is and what it means. Does that tell us anything about the guy with the tattoo who turned up dead?" Cordero asked.

"Well," said Pepe swallowing another mouthful of curry as he spoke. "This photograph is from a member of a pro-Indonesian gang called '*Coluna Negra*'. Original, huh? Set up in early 1999 but using the old name because of its reputation. They were trained, funded and controlled by the Indon Army to terrorise people into voting against independence. Most of the members were from West Timor but some were from here. Almost all of them went to West Timor to avoid prosecution after independence. This guy" —Pepe placed a fat finger on the photograph— "was garroted by some villagers before he could get away. Hence we have the photo. I haven't heard anything about this gang being active since the Indons left."

Pepe shoveled more vindaloo into his mouth.

"Do you have a list of the members of this gang?"

"I can give you three or four names of the most prominent leaders. That's all. But the gang numbered anywhere from sixty to one hundred people. Many of them came and went depending on which way the wind was blowing. You know what these guys are like. Even the names we have are probably fake," said Pepe, working his way to the bottom of the container of curry. "But I'll get Felix here to run you off a copy. Feliciano!"

• • •

There had been four names on the list—Eurico Fiar, Murilo Wasai, *Kobra* and *Momem Forte*. The last two were clearly *noms de guerre*. Cordero folded the list and put it in his pants pocket. By the time he had ridden back to the hospital Ana's surgery had been completed and she had been moved to the recovery ward where she was sedated. He sought out Dr Montoya and found him giving instructions to a nurse in the corridor outside an operating theatre. When the doctor had finished and the nurse was leaving, Cordero asked about his sister.

"The surgery went well," said Montoya, folding bits of paper back down on a clipboard, "as I said it would. She should make a complete recovery. But I want to keep her here for another three or four days just to make sure. If you have any other questions, direct them to the nurse on reception. I am very busy."

And with that, the Cuban was gone to scrub for another operation.

Cordero breathed a sigh of relief. The nurse at the reception desk checked her computer and told him it would be another hour before he could see his sister. He walked outside the hospital into the glare of the afternoon sun and stretched the tension from his neck and shoulders. He rang one of his sister's neighbours to check that her kids were being taken care of. They were. Then he sat on the steps of the hospital, took out the list of 'Coluna Negra' members and read the names again.

His thoughts were interrupted by a pickup truck screeching to a halt at the foot of the steps. In front were two young men wearing baseball caps. In the back Cordero could see what looked like a red Kawasaki 250cc Cruiser and another young man holding a girl in his arms. The youth in the front passenger seat leapt out and helped his friend to carry the girl, who was screaming in pain, up the steps past Cordero and into the hospital. Then the pickup driver drove to the visitors' parking area and cut the engine.

Cordero walked across to the truck and examined the bike. There were scratches on the fuel tank but the Falintil flag was clearly visible on the side. He walked to where the driver sat listening to music on headphones. Cordero tapped on the window. The youth wound it down, reluctantly.

"Nice bike," said Cordero. "Yours?"

"What's it to you, maun?" the youth said, over the music from his headphones.

Cordero took out his badge and put it directly in front of the young man's face. He sat up, took off his headphones.

"It belongs to that girl, maun. She came off it in Lecidere. Going too fast around a guy on a pushbike. We saw her skid off. We just brought her here, maun. I think she broke her arm or her leg or something, she was screaming real bad."

"What's her name?" asked Cordero.

"I don't know, maun. Never seen her before."

"What's your name? Cordero asked.

"Eduardo. Eduardo Romes."

"Show me your licence."

The youth took a wallet from his pocket and handed the licence to Cordero. "Eduardo Avelino Romes, nineteen years old, from Bidau in Dili. Well Eduardo, you ever see this bike before?"

"First time, *maun*. Honest."

Cordero took the keys out of the truck's ignition. "Wait here," he said and walked back to the hospital.

The nurse said that Nazaria de Oliveira had been taken into 'Emergency'. Looked like a fractured leg, she said, adding that for all the screaming it might have been both legs and both arms. Cordero found her lying on a bed with a nurse about to inject a painkiller. Nazaria was yelping and howling.

"Just hold that a minute," Cordero said to the nurse, showing her his police badge. "Nazaria." She kept screaming. "Nazaria!" Cordero said raising his voice. "Look at me and stop screaming. Stop!"

The girl went quiet. "It hurts," she moaned. She was thin, wearing a short black skirt, a thin red bandeau across her breasts, and what remained of heavy dark make-up streaked down her cheeks from tears. Her hair had been braided, her fingernails painted bright red. A party girl or at least a girl off to a party on a Friday night.

"I know it hurts, Nazaria. And as soon as you tell me what I need to know this nurse here will give you something to stop the pain. But first you have to answer my questions. Okay?"

The girl nodded, holding back tears.

"Who gave you the bike, Nazaria?"

"No one gave it to me. It's mine."

"How old are you? Seventeen. Eighteen maybe? You can't afford a bike like that. Who gave it to you?"

"I'm nineteen and I told you. *It's mine*," she insisted and started to sob again.

"Do you want that pain killer, Nazaria? I can wait all night but there won't be much left of that pretty little leg of yours if it isn't treated soon. Likely amputation by the looks of it," he suggested to the nurse with a wink.

Cordero could see the girl thinking hard, could almost hear the wheels turning in her head as she weighed up the trouble she

might be in against the pain in her leg and his bluff that it might
have to be cut off.

"Izzy," she mumbled.

"Izzy? Someone called Izzy gave you the bike? Is that Izzy as
in Isaiah?"

"I don't know. I only know him as Izzy."

"Just Izzy?"

"Alright Izzy Pinto!" she screamed, and closed her eyes tight
with the pain.

"Where does Izzy Pinto live, Nazaria?" Cordero pressed her.

"I don't know," she said and opened her eyes.

"I think you do Nazaria," Cordero said. "And I can wait."

She lay there, clutching the sheet tightly on both sides of the
bed, decided that didn't help ease the pain and conceded. "All
right. Somewhere near Suai. I need that pain killer now!"

"Just a few more questions," said Cordero. Nazaria started
whimpering again.

"How often does Izzy come to Dili?"

"I don't know," she sobbed. "Maybe every two weeks. To see me."

"Where does Izzy stay when he's in Dili?"

"My place, of course," she said. "He's my boyfriend."

"OK. I can get your address from the hospital. How long have
you known him?"

"I need the pain killers!" she grimaced. "I don't know. Maybe
two months."

"Why did he give you the bike. And when?"

"He loves me, that's why," she said. "Izzy gives me lots of things."

"I bet he does. When did he give you the bike?"

"Tuesday morning, after we'd had se—after we'd eaten
breakfast."

"And where is Izzy now?"

"He went back to Suai. He has a job there."

"What does he do?"

"How should I know? But he makes a lot of money and comes
to see me in Dili whenever he can. I told you—he loves me. Haven't
I answered enough questions?"

Cordero motioned to the nurse to attend to the patient.

"Am I under arrest?" asked Nazaria as Cordero was leaving the room.

"Not this time, Nazaria. But I'd choose my friends more carefully if I were you. Izzy will soon be under arrest for stealing a motorcycle."

Chapter 19

"What do you mean you questioned the veteran?" Cordero fumed. "That wasn't part of the plan."

"Well you're the one who doesn't follow procedure," Carter tried by way of a deflection.

"Don't put this back on me! If you'd let me take his motorcycle back and *then* talk to him I might've managed to get a lot more information out of him."

"But you didn't have any motorcycle to give back to him when you left us," she said getting angry now. "And time is running out, Cordero. At least now we have an idea of who the accomplice might be."

As she recounted what she'd learned from the veteran, Cordero had to concede she had a point. He sipped the coffee she had brought for herself on her way from the guest house but had offered to him to cushion the news of her questioning Machado. It was just after eight o'clock on Saturday morning. "How's your sister anyhow?" she asked to restore the peace between them.

"She's out of danger and doing fine," Cordero said, now slumped into a chair in a back room at the police station in Suai where they'd met up. "I saw her for a few minutes in the hospital last night. She was very tired but comfortable enough and glad it was all over. A neighbour is taking care of the kids 'til Ana is able to go back home," Cordero added.

"Well that's good then," said Carter, pleased she'd manage to swing the conversation away from who did what. "The motorcycle? What's the story?"

"Turned up at the hospital while I was waiting for Ana to come to after her operation." He yawned. "The rider was a flighty girl who went too fast, came off and broke her leg." He took another sip of the coffee. "Gave me the name of the guy who handed her the bike. Said he does a run from Suai to Dili about every two weeks." He looked at her and raised his eyebrows. "Curious wouldn't you say? You don't normally steal a bike, ride a hundred miles and hand the thing over just to impress a girl you've only known a couple of months. Even though she was cute," he added, knowing this would annoy her. "I'll take the bike back and see if there's any more the veteran can tell us. I'll also see if he wants to press charges. Eventually I'll check out the bike thief."

"It's a baby we're after Cordero," Carter reminded him.

Cordero drained the coffee, ignoring the comment. "This *Kobra* was on a list of members of a militia group called 'Coluna Negra'—the 'Black Column'—that a colleague who heads up a gang investigation team gave me. And their insignia matches a tattoo on the arm of the guy they took from the crocodile." He noticed her face light up. He paused for a second, teasing with the information that had come his way. When he was satisfied he'd won a point he told her about the call from Brooks and his conversation with Pepe.

"Interesting," was all she conceded to his disappointment as she sat and laid out a pen and pad on the table. "The veteran told us about the 'Coluna Negra' and recognizing its symbol tattooed on this *Kobra's* arm. It could be the guy on the beach. But we don't know who killed him, how he fits into the abduction racket, or more importantly where Luana Ruiz might be."

"He wore boots," Cordero said.

"What?"

"The guy on the beach, remember? He wore boots not sandals. Either he worked construction or maybe, just maybe, he needed them when he was trudging through the forest to the border with a baby in his arms." He waited but she didn't react. "Did you search the villages as we'd agreed?" he asked and stared forlornly into the bottom of the coffee cup.

"Yeah and we might have narrowed the search for the abductor down a bit," she said as Estefana came into the room. As usual Estefana was neatly dressed but wore her hair down today, a bright pink hairclip making a ponytail of it at the back.

"*Bondia, maun,*" she said to Cordero, looking eager to start work.

"*Bondia,*" he replied and noticed the folders under her arm. "What have you there?"

"We did a lot of driving yesterday," Carter said resuming her account. "We didn't get to every village but we did go back to," she looked at the pad in front of her, "Metidade, Bocali, Leho, etcetera. There are churches everywhere, of course, but priests are men and nuns are highly visible in their habits and generally constrained in what they do by the fellow nuns around them." She leant back in her chair, remembered its cheap plastic construction, and lent back over the table. "We're not worried about the church connection. We found agricultural extension officers spread around that area, but they're men as well. As are road crews. There is a literacy outreach program employing men and women but in the last six months it hasn't been active anywhere near more than half of the villages where children have gone missing."

Carter paused, picked up the coffee cup, remembered Cordero had drunk it all and put it down again. "But in or near every village there is a neo-natal clinic, usually open one day a week with quite a few of the staff moving to different locations from one day to the next. All of the staff are women, both young and middle-aged. There is no uniform but typically they dress in a simple blouse and business skirt for handling the babies." She tapped the desk to emphasise her next point. "And a neo-natal clinic is the perfect place to shop for babies."

Carter pointed to the folders Estefana was carrying. "When we made it back here yesterday we contacted the local office of the Ministry of Health for employment records for neo-natal clinics in the area. A number of women have worked villages where children have been abducted but only three have been in continuous employment in the last twelve months." Carter looked again at the pad and read the names out: Manuela Ramos, Barita

Budiwati and Fernanda Xavier. "We requested files on each of them—their education, marital status, addresses and what not—which Estefana has just picked up. We were just about to go through them and check them against possible police records."

Cordero looked interested. "One of these women matches orders for children from the Indonesian side against the babies coming into the neo-natal clinics, finds out where the babies live, gets to know the routines of each household, and takes the kid without raising any suspicions about why she was in the village or what she was doing. Is that your theory?" he asked.

"You got a better one?" said Carter. Cordero shook his head. "Then she hands the baby over to someone—maybe this *Kobra* character—who takes it across the border, probably through a taboo forest where they are unlikely to be seen, to whatever network is operating in Indonesia," Carter added.

Cordero was nodding now. "Could be," he said. "Why don't you two check those employment records and I'll run those names through police records." He reached for the pad Carter had brought in, tore a fresh page and scribbled the names on it. "I'm checking the records for our bike thief anyway. We could meet back here in thirty minutes."

She sat up straight again. Cordero left the room and Estefana sat down with her folders next to Carter.

"We could be getting close, *mana*," Estefana said holding back her excitement.

"Let's hope that's the case, Estefana. With a bit of luck we may still find Elisanda Soares. Show me what you've come up with."

• • •

On his way to the room which held computerised and hardcopy police records, Cordero encountered a flustered Superintendent Basilio Modesto. "*Bondia, maun*," Cordero offered.

"Nothing good about it," Buzzi grumbled. He'd gotten the gist of the elders' meeting from a tried-and-true method: he'd paid for information from one of the men who was there. None of it was good. The elders were planning a rally on Sunday morning and he suspected they were intending to march someplace or other. The destination hadn't been decided—or else he hadn't paid enough to be told. Maybe they'd head for the hospital where Brooks was keeping the crocodile's body, maybe a project site they were particularly incensed about, maybe even police headquarters. Buzzi had stopped at Cordero's approach, scratched his head and seemed unable to decide where to look. "I've brought more than thirty officers into Suai but I have no idea where to assign them," he said shifting from one foot to the other. "I know the elders blame us for that damn crocodile. And Brooks cutting it open won't help. Apart from that I'm in the dark."

"Well that's—" Cordero began but Buzzi cut him off.

"I've decided to go to Fatuloro and talk to villagers. Some of the elders seem intent on rallying more supporters over those babies going missing. Talk of spirit revenge or similar nonsense. If you ask me it's a cover for complaints over compensation for land they've lost to the developers. But it's up to me to stop it all linking up into something big." Buzzi sounded as though he was still trying to convince himself of the good sense of what he had decided to do.

"Go to Beko and Rotia" Cordero suggested. "The most recent beatings of suspect villagers have been around there."

"The most recent abduction has been in Fatuloro! I don't want the beatings craze catching on there. It's too close to Suai."

Buzzi was red-faced, his feet and hands twitching. He focused on Cordero. "Where have you been?" he asked. "Any progress?"

"I had to go to Dili yesterday to see my sister. Burst appendix. Needed an emergency operation. Rode back early this morning."

"She alright now?" Buzzi asked without seeming to care about the answer.

"Yeah. Fine. I recovered a motorcycle that was stolen from a veteran out at Uma Daiso. Brought it back. The American is looking into women who worked in neo-natal clinics around Fatuloro, Metidade, and the rest. She thinks one of them could have done the snatching."

Buzzi seemed disinterested in details. "Try for a breakthrough on the abduction case as soon as you can. Find that missing baby! Call if there are any developments."

With that, the superintendent charged down the corridor. "Oh, one more thing," Cordero called after him. "Did Brooks show you the photographs of the arm he took out of the crocodile? The dead guy's? On the forearm was a tattoo."

Buzzi stopped. Turned. "Yeah. What are you getting at?"

"I checked the photos in Dili. Seems the tattoo might indicate the guy was a member of a pro-Indonesian militia called 'Coluna Negra'. And we think we might know who he was."

Buzzi walked back to Cordero and looked up directly into his eyes. "Do you understand what's going on, Tino? There's a whole lot of trouble about to erupt in Suai. We have hot-headed villagers coming down from the mountains to join up with angry elders and God knows what could happen. Forget about the crocodile's kill, forget about damned stolen motorcycles and focus on those stolen babies. I need you to focus Tino, you hear me? Focus!"

• ••

Cordero was checking the computerized police records when Jacobsen rang. "I hear you were in Dili," she said without pleasantries. "I also hear you have a lead on the abductions. Tell me."

He eased back from the terminal. "Early days but we have reason to believe a middle-aged woman, familiar in the communities, perhaps a government employee, may be involved."

Jacobsen waited. "That's it?" she asked not hiding her disappointment.

"We may have identified an accomplice but we're not sure at this stage," he said.

"The Prime Minister was on the phone to me again this morning, Tino. He's getting calls about unrest down there and he's scared and angry. Very angry. He's putting the screws on us as if it's INTERPOL's role to solve local crimes and settle community problems. I explained what our role is in this country but he wouldn't listen. Threatened to wind down our operations if we didn't give him something he could work with. You have to do better than tell me you're looking for a middle-aged woman who *may or may not* work for the government and *might or might not* have an accomplice."

"We're doing our best—" he began.

"Well your best isn't good enough, my friend. Find that baby. Or find who took her and give us something to stop the locals taking matters into their own hands. And fast. What about Modesto?" she continued without taking a breath. "Are you helping him deal with the local unrest? Is he listening?"

"I've made suggestions, yes. He seems to have taken my advice to go up to the mountains and reassure villagers. He's going up today."

"Well that's good," said Jacobsen. "But hardly enough."

She hung up. *Typical Dutch insensitivity*, Cordero told himself as he closed his cell. He went back to the computer files before turning his attention to the older paper files. There was no reference to two of the names on Carter's list in either set of files: Manuela Ramos and Fernanda Xavier. There was an old paper record on file concerning the other woman—Barita Budiwati. Cordero knew that it was an Indonesian name which meant the woman herself or her husband was Indonesian or that her father at least was Indonesian and the mother possibly Timorese.

Five years earlier, Barita Budiwati was involved in a dispute at the border as she was returning to Timor-Leste from Indonesia. It may have been something to do with her passport or her lack of one, a problem with what she was attempting to bring back into Timor-Leste, or even an offence of some kind she had caused to immigration officials. The record wasn't clear, which didn't surprise Cordero. Police records often weren't. What was clear was the minor nature of the incident and the fact that no conviction had been recorded.

More importantly, Barita Budiwati had reason to travel to Indonesia and presumably had connections there, connections that could come in handy if one was dealing in human trafficking across the border.

Cordero made a note against her name on Carter's list. Then he looked up Izzy—and cross-checked Isaiah—Pinto on the computer. There was one entry.

Pinto had been arrested, charged and convicted of drug trafficking two years earlier. The report was matter-of-fact and gave no insights into the young man other than a birth date, by which Pinto would now by twenty-four years of age, and a residential address on the western outskirts of Suai. The name of the arresting officer was Silvano Moudino who Cordero knew as an experienced, no nonsense senior officer and who he'd seen in the foyer of the police station not fifteen minutes earlier trying to work through Buzzi's scrawled notes about where to assign people over the weekend.

Cordero printed out a copy of the Pinto record and walked out to find Moudino. He was standing in the foyer, frowning over bits of paper and ordering a huddle of junior officers to keep quiet. "Silvano. *Bondia*. Could I ask you a quick question when you have a moment?" Cordero said.

"Hey Tino. *Bondia, maun*," said Moudino looking up from the collection of notes in his hands. "Sure, *maun*. I need a break anyway. Where you want to go?"

"Away from this noise would be fine," Cordero suggested.

"Okay." Moudino turned to the other officers and bellowed: "You people who know your assignments—get out of here now. The rest take a break but be back in ten minutes. That's ten minutes and no more or I'll come for you and I won't be happy."

Cordero and Moudino walked out of the building and over to the shade of a nearby fig tree. Moudino lit a cigarette. "This is crazy stuff, *maun*. Buzzi has everyone falling over each other but for what? He thinks there's a big protest today or tomorrow and wants a heavy police presence on the streets. He doesn't have any idea where the protest is, how big it's going to be or what form it's going to take. I doubt he even knows there is going to be a protest. You know how nervous he can get." He took a long drag on his cigarette. "Police work? Guess work more like it!" He blew out the smoke from his lungs. "Anyhow, good to see you Tino. What can I do for you?"

Cordero showed him the police report on Izzy Pinto. Moudino read it and chuckled. "Izzy. Yeah. Nasty piece of work that boy. Real nasty." He took another puff on his cigarette.

"This report is two years old," Cordero began. "I believe Pinto stole a motorcycle off a veteran about a week ago and I'm told he does a run to Dili about every two weeks. The theft of the bike leads me to think he's still involved in criminal activities and the regular run to Dili makes me suspect it's running drugs or contraband in or out of the capital. I'm looking at kids being trafficked across the border. If this Izzy is into smuggling, his connections could be interesting to look into. But if it's true that he's active, I'm wondering why it's been two years with no further charges or police reports." Cordero tapped the printout. "You think this guy went straight and then all of a sudden decides to steal a motorcycle for the fun of it?"

Moudino laughed at that. "Hardly," he said. Cordero looked at him as Moudino took another drag on his cigarette. "This kid is a serial offender. Drugs, thefts, assault, probably a rape or two truth be known. But Buzzi gave an order—off the record, of course—that he wasn't to be touched. Said he was an important informant and his activities allowed us access to more important criminals."

Moudino tossed his cigarette to the ground, stomped on it, then picked up the butt. "I've developed a real thing about people who toss their cigarette butts down and walk away, you know, Tino? I believe there's even a government decree making it an offence. I pull people up on it all the time. Could spend my whole day doing it." He put the butt in his pocket and adjusted the pistol he carried loosely on his hip to impress the junior officers. His eyes narrowed as he focused on the question Cordero had asked.

"I caught Izzy in the middle of a robbery about a year ago. Nurse. Rosaria Surito, although it's Rosaria Narciso now. She married about six months ago. She invited me to the wedding," Moudino said and looked pleased with himself. "For catching

Izzy, I guess. Truth is I couldn't help but catch him really. Ran out of the house and flew straight across the bonnet of my car. Must've been high or drunk. Anyway, I bring him in, see. Buzzi hears about it and next thing he's standing over my desk yelling: 'Give him to me. Give me the stuff he stole. I'll take care of it.' And that's the last I heard. Until the order to leave him alone, that is."

"And does that bear out? That Pinto supplies good information?" Cordero asked.

"You'd have to ask Buzzi," Moudino shrugged. "Nothing to do with me anymore."

• • •

Estefana read Carter the contents of her folders. Manuela Ramos was thirty-six years of age, married with five children—all under ten. She had a certificate in midwifery from the national teaching hospital in Dili, lived in Fatuloro and had worked in the neo-natal program for fourteen months. She had a number of citations in her record for excellent service. Prior to becoming a qualified midwife, Ramos had been a nurse's aide on-and-off due to the birth of her children for a span of eight years.

Fernanda Xavier was twenty-four, married with no children. She was completing her nursing qualifications through Suai hospital and was being sponsored by a Portuguese NGO. Her progress reports were exemplary. She lived with her husband in Suai and, when working in the villages, stayed with relatives outside Fatuloro. She had trainee status in the neo-natal program where she had been working for the past twelve months.

Finally, Estefana read the entry for Barita Budiwati. She was forty-two, unmarried, childless and lived in Bocali. There were no details of her qualifications other than an entry which read 'Qualified midwife'. She had been with the neo-natal program for thirteen months. Prior to that the record only showed 'Midwife, Maliana' with no details as to how long she had worked there or for whom.

"That's the one to start with," Carter commented.

Estefana nodded. "She is the one with the most mystery about her, *mana*," she agreed. "The others seem to be well-settled and from their qualifications maybe more committed." She paused, looked through the file on Budiwati again. "There is a street address, *mana*, but no phone number. We could drive back there. It would take maybe three hours from here. Or we could first find someone to ring in Bocali and ask if this woman is there. No point in driving three hours if she isn't."

"That's true," Carter replied. "But if she's our culprit we don't want to alert her if she's there. And if she isn't there I'd like to see her place, find out about her movements from neighbours too. There's nothing more we can do here. Let's find Cordero."

They found him coming into the building with Moudino and told him what they had in mind. Cordero nodded. "She's the only one in police reports," he said. "Incident on the border five years ago. Nothing major but shows she's been to Indonesia, maybe goes across on a regular basis." He thanked Moudino who was heading back to the mayhem at the front of the office with his head in his notes. Cordero pocketed the printout on Izzy Pinto. "Jacobsen rang me a while ago," he said.

"Any developments?" asked Carter.

"Yeah," he said. "She's more pissed than usual. Wants that missing baby found without delay."

"What do you expect a management type to say?" Carter replied.

"I'll go with you and take that bike back," Cordero told her. "If we leave now we can be back well before dark."

Chapter 20

Barita Budiwati wasn't home. According to her neighbour she hadn't been home in days.

"The last time I saw her was over a week ago," said the woman who lived diagonally opposite in the same kind of run-down cement block house. The only obvious difference between the two houses was that Budiwati's was surrounded by a wall topped with slivers of glass cemented into the concrete. The message seemed clear: 'Keep out'. "But I'm not here all the time," the neighbour was saying. "I work for the literacy program. At times I can be gone for days and days. She may have come back while I was away."

Cordero, Carter and Estefana were in the street with the neighbour, staring at Barita Budiwati's house. The woman was about thirty years of age and willing enough to tell them what she knew.

Cordero was blinking and stifling yawns as he shook off a short spell of disturbed sleep in the backseat of their vehicle on the way to Bocali. Estefana had driven. The motorcycle Cordero would return to the veteran as they headed back to Suai was strapped to the back of the SUV. Roosters were crowing in the grounds of several houses and off through the trees a church bell rang the midday Angelus. "Did she usually go away for a week at a time?" asked Estefana interpreting for Carter.

"No, not usually. A day or two at most," the woman said. A small girl in pigtails played peek-a-boo with the strangers from behind the neighbour's back. Only Carter noticed her. "The dog stopped barking on Friday. I noticed that," the woman continued. "Maybe someone had come to feed it. It could have been her, I

178

don't know. But it was barking non-stop again yesterday. Can you do something about that? It's annoying."

"Did she have a cell phone?" Estefana asked, ignoring the appeal.

"Yes, I've seen her talking into it," the woman said but she had no idea what the number was.

"And a vehicle? Could you describe her vehicle?" It was an SUV, like theirs but smaller, older, light blue in colour. Carter, Cordero and Estefana shared a thought at the mention of the colour. The Ministry of Health was meant to pay Budiwati a mileage allowance for the use of the car in her neo-natal work because funding for new staff vehicles had not come through. The woman didn't know the registration number but she said the passenger's front side had been scraped in a collision with a truck last year.

"Did Barita have many visitors?"

"No," the woman said running a hand unconsciously across the young girl's braided hair. "None that I ever saw. She kept very much to herself."

"Family?"

"Not that I know of."

"Did she bring any children or babies to the house?" asked Estefana at Carter's prompting.

"Not that I saw. Why are you asking me these things?"

"We just need to find her and talk to her," Estefana said. "What kind of person is she?"

"Well, like I said, very private. I've had maybe four, five conversations with her the whole time she's lived there."

"How long is that?"

"About twelve months."

The little girl was smiling at Carter. Carter returned a smile and moved slightly as if to grab her and she ducked back again giggling to hide behind her mother.

"What did you talk about?" Estefana asked, at the suggestion of Carter who was listening carefully while toying with the child.

"Nothing really."

"Keep pressing her," urged Carter.

"Try to think, it's important," Estefana said.

The woman frowned. Stroked her daughter on the back. "We talked about the price of gasoline, I remember that," she said trying hard to remember. "And tyres. Yes, that's right. She had needed two new tyres a few months ago and she complained about the cost. She was angry that she hadn't received any money for the use of her car. Really angry."

"Nothing else?"

"Not that I can remember."

"What does she generally wear when she goes to work?" Estefana asked.

"Blouse, skirt. Nothing unusual."

"Can you remember the colour of her clothing?"

"Colour? Not really." She thought for a moment and frowned. "But now that I think of it, I never saw her wear anything too bright, you know like yellow or pink. Nothing that would make her look pretty."

Or make her stand out, Carter was thinking.

"Does she have friends in Bocali? Anyone who might know where she has gone?"

"I don't think she does," the woman said. She looked down the street. "But maybe you should talk to *Senyor* Amerudi. He's over there," she said pointing to a small wooden structure about fifty yards from Barita Budiwati's house. "He's at that kiosk day and night. Never seems to leave. It's his life. His wife is deceased, you see. If anyone knows about people's movements in this street, it'll be him."

They thanked the woman and headed down to the kiosk. The girl in pigtails waved goodbye to Carter from behind her mother's skirt. A few stray dogs and cats crossed their path in the midday heat but most people had either gone home for lunch or were stretched out under the shade of trees while children played nearby. Carter and Estefana had not eaten since breakfast, Cordero since he had left Dili after consuming a stale croissant and an apple at his home before five o'clock that morning. They were hungry. A café or food kiosk would be hard to find in a tiny village like Bocali and they resigned themselves to make do with whatever could be purchased at the farmer's market they had passed coming in. Cordero sent Estefana on that mission. "I'll take over the interpreting," he said wiping a hand across his face.

Senyor Antonio Amerudi appeared very old. He squinted up from a newspaper into the glare that shrouded the new customers, only to realise they were there to ask questions rather than spend money. He removed his glasses and lowered bushy grey eyebrows over pale brown eyes while they explained who they were and what their purpose was. If the old man couldn't make any money from them at least he could be distracted from the tedium of his day by their questions.

Cordero asked him if he knew Barita Budiwati. The old man scratched his head through the white mane that covered his scalp, adjusted the old army fatigues he wore just to keep the young ones guessing about his past and how handy he might be still, and slumped back on a stiff wooden stool behind the counter of his ramshackle kiosk. He was in no hurry to answer.

"Occasionally she buys cigarettes here," he told Cordero who in turn translated for Carter. "But I've never seen her smoke," he added and raised an eyebrow.

"You think there's someone else? A man perhaps?"

"I'm not paid to think," the man huffed. "And I don't get money for my thoughts. But usually a woman who buys cigarettes and doesn't smoke them herself—"and he raised his hands and grinned in a gesture that the reason was obvious.

"You ever see her with a man?"

"No," the old man said.

"Have you seen anything of her in the last week?" Cordero asked.

"She came early on Friday morning. Very early. I was just opening up," the man said. "Didn't stay long. The dog was whimpering. She fed it. Grabbed a few things from the house and left. Ignored me. I haven't seen her since."

"Do you know what she took?"

"My eyes aren't as good as they used to be and the house is a long way off from here. So no, I don't," he said. Then he turned a mischievous face to Carter, smiled and added: "And although I'm widowed and available now I don't pry on women. Make sure you translate that!"

"Do you know where she went or might have gone?"

"How would I? I never leave this spot and she, well she's hardly the type to confide in me. She's Indonesian, you know," he said as though that was sufficient explanation.

"What was she driving on Sunday?"

"That vehicle of hers."

"The SUV?"

"If that's what it's called."

"Did you ever see her drive anything else?" Cordero asked.

"You mean like the vehicle owned by whoever smoked the cigarettes?" the man teased Cordero.

"Yes," Cordero said. "You catch on fast."

"I wouldn't have lived this long if I didn't. Can you guess how old I am?"

"Seventy," Cordero answered, knowing the man's real age would be much higher.

"Eighty-five!" the old man said in a guttural bark. "Eighty-five years old—or young," he said smiling again at Carter. "But what was it you wanted to know? Oh, yes. Does she drive another vehicle. Well yes, I have seen her drive another one," he said and scratched his chin while he retrieved the memory. "A small van. Don't ask me the make. I'm not interested in such things. It's white—or was once. Quite old. Battered."

"'Small and old' was how the veteran described the van *Kobra* drived," Carter pointed out to Cordero after he had translated what the old man had said.

"How do you mean, 'battered'?"

"General wear on these roads. Crumpled up a bit in front like it hit another vehicle or a tree or a buffalo maybe! You know, nothing more."

"And how often have you seen her drive that vehicle?"

"Few times."

"When?"

"Well now," he began and knitted his brow. "Couple of months ago. Couple before that. Maybe once late last year. Not often. Just now and then."

"And you don't know who owns this van, where it comes from?"

"How would I know?"

"When you saw her on Friday morning, she was coming out of the house, right?" Cordero asked and the man nodded. "Did she appear to be going away for a while? Carrying a lot of stuff, for instance?"

"She seemed the same as always. Focused, no nonsense." He looked down the street at Barita Budiwati's house. "Didn't seem to be packing anything more than usual in that, what did you call it, an SV?"

"SUV," Cordero corrected.

"SUV then. Didn't seem to be packing that for a long trip, that's for sure. What's this all about anyway?"

"Police matters. That's all I can say."

"Has it anything to do with the devil talk around here?"

"Why do you say that?" Cordero asked, and stopped translating for Carter.

"Well, they say that sorcerers or devils are taking children. Taking them to Suai and, you know, burying them in different places."

"How did this idea start?" Cordero pressed him.

"With several of the older women a few months ago because babies were being taken from around here. They like to believe in devils and demons, maybe because many of them are scary themselves." The old man snickered. "Then they started egging on the elders. Telling them *real* men would do something. Take action. You know how nagging and annoying old women can be." He looked straight into Cordero's eyes. "I'm sure you know that. And you know talk like that has led to men being beaten. Maybe even killed." He paused for a moment. "What may interest you is that the talk has gotten even louder recently and people from Suai have come through stirring things up."

"How?"

"People are saying that the land spirits have been disturbed by all the change, all the building, going on down there in Suai and must be appeased with human sacrifices," he said.

"And what has this to do with Barita Budiwati?"

"You tell me," said the old man. "I know she worked with babies around these villages. I know I haven't seen her in a while. And I know police officers are asking me a lot of questions about her."

"What's the old man saying?" Carter asked Cordero.

"Nothing important," he said. "He's complaining about government services around here."

The old man had no idea what they were saying in English and just smiled at Carter. Cordero thanked him, as did she with a nod of her head. Cordero turned to head back to Budiwati's house.

"I think it's time we had a look inside," he said.

"You bet," agreed Carter. "But first—" She smiled at *Senyor* Amerudi, pointed to a small bag of sweets on the wall behind where he sat and produced a dollar bill from her pocket.

"I didn't know you had a sweet tooth," Cordero said as Carter pocketed her change.

"I don't. But I bet the little girl with that woman we just talked to does," she said.

Carter took off back down the road ahead of Cordero to test her assumption. When the little girl saw her returning, her eyes lit up though she continued to half-hide behind her mother. Carter handed her the bag and the girl took it sheepishly. When she realised what was inside, she took Carter's hand and, bending slightly, pressed it to her forehead as a gesture of respect. No words were said but a big grin spread across the girl's face, her eyes brightened, and she tore off into the house clutching the bag of sweets to her chest like something very valuable that she'd sworn to keep secret.

• • •

Estefana caught up with them outside the house. She had managed to buy bananas, mangos and rice cooked in banana leaves which she placed in their vehicle to eat after they had taken a look through Budiwati's house. Cordero prised open the gate but the house itself was locked. The dog at least appeared to have run off in search of food or companionship and leaving them one less thing to worry about. Cordero forced a window at the side, climbed in and unlocked the back door for the other two.

It was a simple three-room house. The largest room was a kitchen, dining and lounge room combined. It was neatly though sparsely furnished and contained nothing unusual for a house occupied by a middle-aged woman. Atop an open shelf above a stove powered by a portable gas cylinder was a metal box in which were stored letters, bills and receipts. Estefana read through them. "The letters are from the Ministry of Health and are all general in nature," she reported. "The rest are bills and receipts just like mine." On one wall of the room was a calendar but no dates were marked. On the opposite wall hung an old sepia picture of a wedding couple in what Cordero thought was traditional Indonesian dress. Budiwati's parents, he guessed.

The second room appeared to be used as a spare. It contained a few boxes of clothing, books, kitchen utensils and assorted bric-a-brac. There was nothing particularly distinctive of the personality, interests, or movements of the owner. The other room was the bedroom. In it was a single bed, a wardrobe and a chair. Above the bed was a religious picture. "*Nain Feto*," said Estafana. "Our Lady. The Virgin Mary." The wardrobe contained four blue blouses and two black skirts plus jeans, towels, sleeping attire, two pairs of flat-soled shoes and underwear.

Next to the bed was a paperback book entitled '*Menjadi Wanita Paling Bahagia*'. "'Be the Happiest Woman,'" Cordero said for Carter's benefit. "It's Bahasa. A popular Indonesian book with women, I gather."

Carter examined the cover, and flicked through the pages in case a note, a cell number, anything at all had been placed there. But nothing had. She scanned the room then looked at Cordero.

"Okay she reads romantic fiction and she may be Catholic," she said. "That's it. There's nothing else in this entire house that gives any insight into this woman at all."

To the side of the back door stood an improvised bathroom, laundry and toilet. Nothing in them gave any indication about the occupant of the house. "Look for the trash," Carter instructed Estefana and the two of them scoured the back of the house for a bin of any kind. Estefana found a bucket behind the laundry tub. It contained used noodle containers, food scraps, plastic wrapping and a small medicinal bottle the label of which had been removed and its contents drained. Carter picked up the bottle gingerly using a kerchief out of habit. She smelt it but the bottle was odourless, rinsed clean. "Any idea what this may have contained?" she asked carefully passing the bottle first to Estefana and then to Cordero. Estefana shook her head. Cordero sniffed the bottle and did the same. "Well, let's keep it and find out," said Carter who pocketed the bottle wrapped in her kerchief.

• • •

"We know there was nothing extravagant about her," began Cordero. "We know that she kept to herself, was almost secretive about it, seems to have been fairly organised, even regimented, and could possibly have had a man in her life in some capacity but one she would rather not make public or even perhaps admit to."

"And we know that a lack of money concerned her," added Carter. "You know, the cost of gas and tyres for a start. That could be a motive for stealing and selling babies."

They were sitting in their vehicle, doors ajar in a vain attempt to combat the heat, quickly devouring the fruit and rice Estefana had bought. "Anything she needed for the babies—diapers, bottles, that kind of thing—she could have taken when she needed it from her work. And explained the stuff away as work-related. That would look far less suspicious than a single woman keeping such things in her own home," Cordero said wiping his mouth on his sleeve. "Let's head back to Fatuloro. See if we can find the other two women on your list. Maybe they can tell us more about our mysterious Barita Budiwati."

Carter nodded as she finished the last of her rice and collected the remains of her lunch in a paper bag for disposal. "Anything about the house or the woman you'd like to add, Estefana?" she asked.

She brushed her uniform down before answering. "It would only take this woman a few minutes to pack up and leave that house and nothing she might leave behind would seem to have any value," Estefana said. She frowned. "It seems to me like she is waiting for life to begin. She is waiting to have nice things and do interesting things like the woman in the book, you know—the happiest woman. Her house tells me she is just marking time."

Carter glanced across at Cordero. "That could be another motive for stealing babies. Make enough to get out of town and start what she dreams of as a real life."

• • •

They arrived back in Fatuloro early afternoon and went straight to the house on the other side of the village where Fernanda Xavier stayed when she was working in the area. The house belonged to her aunt and uncle. They told Cordero that Fernanda had three days off work and had gone back to Suai to be with her husband. Neither of them recalled the name Barita Budiwati or could remember Fernanda talking about a middle-aged Indonesian nurse she worked with. In fact, they said, she mainly talked about the younger nurses and their troubled love lives which gave her great amusement and led them to believe that young Timorese had too much freedom these days. To their knowledge Fernanda had never been to the village of Bocali. Her clinics were further west of Fatuloro. She had never mentioned anything specific about the babies who had disappeared but expressed sadness for the parents and anger at what was happening. They thanked the couple and moved on to the next address on the list.

Cordero noticed Manuela Ramos pulling up to her house at the same time they arrived. She was returning from visiting a sick baby in Metidade. As they both exited their vehicles Cordero introduced himself and his companions, explained they needed to ask a few questions about her colleague and she invited them to sit on her porch, went inside and was soon back with cups, saucers and a pot of tea.

Manuela Ramos was a large, middle aged woman. She was dressed in a kaftan covered in big, bright orange and yellow flowers. Her hair sprung out of her head in an Afro style and she wore thick, green-rimmed glasses. *Definitely conspicuous*, Carter was thinking to herself, *and clearly not a suspect if for that reason alone.*

"I don't know her well," Manuela said of Budiwati. "There are over a dozen nurses working this part of the district and they come and go. Most of us are assigned clinics in particular villages that we go to each week. Barita I know volunteered to do relief work. Most nurses don't like that because you don't know from one week to the next where you'll be working and there's a lot of driving involved." She filled their cups with tea and took a sip of her own. "Besides, with relief work the mothers know who you are but don't get to know you well on a personal basis because you're moving around too much."

The clinics, she said, mainly dealt with newborns and babies up the age of 18 months, occasionally two years. All the details of a baby in a clinic would be available to a nurse working there: their age, weight, family connections, any known health issues. And with the high number of children being born to Timorese women, even a small village clinic could have twenty or more babies registered at any one time. Things were often a little disorderly as a result.

"Do you know if Barita has friends, family, a boyfriend, in this area?" Cordero asked.

"No I don't. And if she had I wouldn't know anyway. She was very private," he translated for Carter.

"Were any of the other nurses close to her?"

"Not that I know. Like I said, she kept to herself." Manuela took another sip of tea. "I think there was some trauma in her life. Maybe to do with her parents. I heard that they both died in prison in Indonesia a few years back."

"What were they in prison for? Do you know?"

"What is anyone in prison for in Indonesia? If they want to put you away they say you are either a drug dealer or a Communist—either will do."

"How did she seem to be with the babies? Did she take more interest in certain of them than she did in others?" Cordero asked on Carter's urging.

Manuela finished her tea. "I didn't work with her very much, as I said. There were never any complaints about her, I know that, and from what I saw of her I would say she knew her job and did it well. Would you like more tea?"

They declined the offer, finished what was in their cups, and then Carter produced the bottle she had taken from Budiwati's house and showed it to Manuela. The woman looked at the bottle closely and nodded her head.

"Tincture of opium," she said and noticed their bewilderment. "You might know it as laudanum. The Ministry of Health has banned its use but you can get it without too much trouble. A couple of the younger nurses use it to keep the babies quiet. Is that Barita's?"

"We found it in her house, yes."

"I'm surprised she would need it. She was very experienced working with babies. I never saw one cry in her arms."

Manuela's children appeared from the back of the house and the two youngest wrapped their arms around their mother. "They tell me they love me but really they're just hungry," she said. The three police officers rose to leave. They thanked Manuela for her time and the tea and started toward their vehicle.

"When you find Barita ask her about the money," Manuela called after them.

Cordero stopped and turned to her. "What money?'

"She borrowed twenty dollars from the clinic's spare cash Friday last week. Said she needed to get gasoline to drive to Suai and that she would repay the money on Monday. But I haven't seen her since."

"Do you know where in Suai she was going? Or why?"

"All I know is that she took twenty dollars and it hasn't come back," Manuela said herding her children into the house. "Twenty dollars is a lot of money out here."

Chapter 21

Cordero turned off to Uma Daiso on their way back to Suai. It was late afternoon but there was time to drop off the stolen motorcycle and get back into town for dinner. "I don't want to waste time getting back to Suai but this shouldn't take too long," he said to Carter and Estefana as he drove up to the home of Ivando Machado. "And getting it back just might jog his memory a little more."

The veteran guerrilla fighter appeared in his doorway when he heard Cordero pull to a stop. "I've brought your bike back," he called out to Machado who stood watching, expressionless. Cordero cut the engine and exited the vehicle.

Machado ambled across his small porch and down the steps to meet his visitor. He glanced at the two women in the SUV and then over to Cordero. "Those two again," he said to Cordero.

Machado went to the back of the vehicle where Cordero had strapped on the motorcycle and ran a hand along the machine. Cordero thought he saw relief on the veteran's face but couldn't be sure. "Wait a minute," he said and he unfastened the motorcycle and with Machado's help stood it on the ground.

"A bit of damage," Machado said examining the Kawasaki closely.

"The rider was a young woman," Cordero told him. "Couldn't handle the power. Lost control and came off at a busy intersection. I found her in the hospital."

"She okay?"

"Broken leg and damaged pride," replied Cordero.

"She the thief?"

"No, the thief's occasional girlfriend."

"Where was this?"

"Dili."

"You found my bike there and you brought it back here," Machado said. "Fast work. Good work. If only all police were that good." Machado glanced again at Carter and Estefana then squatted and took a closer look at the damage to the bike. "I can live with this, provided it runs okay," he said, running a hand along the gas tank.

"I rode it back from Dili and it went fine," said Cordero.

Machado nodded. "I can touch up any damage myself. You know who stole it then?"

"Young guy called Izzy Pinto," said Cordero. "Lives on the outskirts of Saui. I'll be paying him a visit in the next day or two."

"Why bother?" asked Machado looking up at Cordero. "My motorcycle's back. I've never heard of Izzy Pinto and putting him in jail won't make me feel any better. Likely make a worse thief out of him."

"Stealing bikes is a crime, Ivando," Cordero said. "And besides, I suspect that isn't all he gets up to. I'm curious about the rest." Machado rose and the two men stood looking down at the Kawasaki for a moment, saying nothing. Then Cordero prompted the veteran. "You spoke to my colleagues."

"They didn't give me much choice," Machado said. "That foreigner is very determined."

"Oh, she is that," agreed Cordero. "Can I show you something?"

Machado nodded, took a cigarette from his shirt pocket, and lit it in cupped hands. "What about those two?" the veteran asked, poking a finger over his shoulder toward Carter and Estefana.

"Oh, they'll be okay. I'll just let them know I'll be busy for a little while."

Cordero walked back to the SUV and told Carter and Estefana he wanted a few minutes alone with the veteran. Carter said they'd drive down to the village and take a look around. Estefana got in behind the wheel and they were soon gone.

"A body was found on a beach in Suai last week. You may

have heard," Cordero told Machado when he'd come back to the veteran.

"Everbody heard," said Machado. "Big news. A crocodile killed it."

"Well no. A crocodile found the body and tried to eat it. But the man had been killed by a *rama ambon* and the body dumped on the beach." Cordero paused. "The crocodile was shot by a policeman and later washed up dead. It was cut open and they found the man's arm in its stomach. It had a tattoo with three columns enclosed in a circle."

He reached for his cell phone and found the images Brooks had sent him. He showed them to the veteran. "That what you were talking about when you mentioned the militia insignia to my colleagues?"

Machado took the cell and examined the photos carefully, moving the cell this way and that to avoid the glare. "Yeah. That's the tattoo. That's what I saw."

"Then the body on the beach was likely this *Kobra* you were telling those two police women about," Cordero said. "The woman he was with that day. Do you remember anything more about her?"

Machado shook his head.

Cordero pocketed his cell. "You mentioned to my colleagues the other two resistance fighters who were with you. One you said seemed to go a little crazy."

"Virgilio Amaral," Machado agreed.

"Is there any chance Virgilio might have killed this *Kobra*? You know, recognized him same as you did after all these years and decided to carry out the vow you all made. The vow to kill this man."

Machado considered that. "Last I heard Virgilio was living somewhere in Suai," he said. "If you could call it living. Didn't want anything to do with me anymore. Refused veteran's housing I heard. May even have refused to take a veteran's pension. I was told he lived on the streets. Had gone to pieces. Didn't take care of himself. Wore army fatigues like a guerilla. Grew his hair and his beard long. Ranted about things to anyone who'd listen. Made little sense. Ate food scraps. Crazy, like I said."

"But crazy enough to kill *Kobra*?" Cordero asked.

Again Machado considered the question as though it pained him, as though to answer was a betrayal.

Finally he looked Cordero in the eye, held his gaze for a time and stood with a grim expression on his face. "Maybe," was all he said and he stomped out his cigarette, walked away from the policeman into the house, and closed the door.

Cordero stared at the motorcycle and scratched the back of his neck. He turned slowly and made his way down the road to find the others.

• • •

Carter and Estefana had driven toward Luana Ruiz's house, parked on the side off the road, looked around but found nothing useful to their investigation. They decided to check out the market while they waited for Cordero. "Somebody might know something," Carter said. "We should ask around."

The market had been a small affair and was finishing for the day but several women remained seated on the ground hoping to sell what was left of the produce from their gardens and another had not yet packed her rack of second-hand clothes. Old men continued gambling on a ball being tossed around in a huge wooden bowl where slots had been scooped out and numbered. Children milled around in groups of twos and threes playing at their own games. On the other side of the road a man sat on a stool outside a house sharpening a knife with a stone. Two others stood beside him and both looked up and paid close attention to the strangers.

Estefana asked several people if they knew anything about the abduction of Luana but none did. The same response came from the woman selling the second-hand clothes. Estefana took a cursory look at the offerings by way of thanks. The men started yelling and cheering as the ball was tossed around the bowl. Estefana spied a pair of glittering pink hot pants and turned to share a giggle with Carter. But Carter wasn't there. Estefana peeked through the rack of clothes then gazed around the market but there was no sign of her companion. She looked to the houses behind the market and then up and down the length of roadway. No Carter.

"*Mana*," she called. "*Mana* Carter!" There was no response.

Estefana went from one woman to another in the market asking if they had seen a *feto malae*—a foreign woman—but they answered her with a shake of their heads or blank stares. She asked the men who were gambling. They brushed her question aside and told her to go away and leave them alone. She looked across the road toward the man sharpening his knife. He and his companions had gone.

Estefana ran back to the SUV. Carter wasn't there either and there was no sign that she had returned to get something and left again. She jumped in behind the wheel and drove past the market. No sign of Carter. She made a sharp U-turn and headed back for Cordero. She found him ambling down the road in the direction of the Ruiz house.

"*Maun!*" she called from the SUV. "*Mana* Carter is gone!"

"Gone? What do you mean 'gone'?" he asked.

"She was with me in the market but now I can't find her," said Estefana rushing out the words. "I've looked everywhere, *maun*."

Cordero climbed in. "Quick. Drive down to where you last saw her."

Estefana U-turned again and headed down to the market. "We were there," she said pulling to a sudden stop and pointing at the woman selling clothes. "Looking at those dresses and things. I turned and she was gone." Cordero surveyed the market and roadway. "Over there," Estefana pointed, "was a group of men. One was sharpening a knife. When I looked for *mana* they were gone."

"Come on!" Cordero said.

He jumped out and ran to where Estefana had indicated. A woman was standing in the doorway of the house. Cordero asked her where the men had gone. She gestured toward the forest at the back of the house. Had she seen a woman with them? "Yes," she said and walked back inside.

Cordero hurried around the house to a track leading off through banana trees and on through the forest. Estefana was right behind him.

"Do you think they would harm her?" she asked as he parted the leaves the better to see the track ahead.

"You were in Beko. They're looking for scapegoats and scared of strangers. They'll mix the two. And there's nothing more strange around here than a foreigner. If they think she's a demon—" but he didn't finish his answer and rushed on.

They ran on until the track divided at a large teak tree, its trunk eight feet around, and Cordero stopped. "You take that way," he said to Estefana waving a hand to the left of the tree. "Be careful. Shout if you see them."

Estefana headed off. Cordero continued to the right. He'd gone a hundred yards when a clearing appeared up ahead. Two men were standing with their backs to him. As he drew closer he saw that they were facing another man hunched over, clutching a knife. There was blood on the knife and on the man's hand. There was blood on his lower legs. All three men were surrounding something which Cordero could not make out.

"*Polisia!*" he cried. "*Para!*"

He pushed the two men aside. Both began protesting but Cordero ignored them. The men had been looking at a woman slumped on the ground. Her back was to him. She had brown hair the length of Carter's and a blue blouse like—damn, he couldn't recall what colour top Carter had been wearing. He put a hand out to the man with the knife to keep him at bay and bent to touch the woman. She turned and looked up. There were specks of blood on her face and her eyes flared in anger.

On the ground lay a piglet, its throat cut.

"What do you want?" the woman shouted at him. "We have to kill the piglet for a ceremony this evening. Do you think we can afford buffalos around here?"

Cordero felt his heart settle back into his chest. "Why are you killing a piglet here?" he asked, trying to hide his awkwardness.

"Her little girl loves that piglet," the man with the knife said. "Do you think we'd kill it near the house in front of her?"

Estefana, who'd heard the commotion, caught up with Cordero and ran to a stop. She froze when she saw the blood but then noticed the dead piglet. "Come on," Cordero said to her and they ran back the way they'd come. When the SUV came into sight, Estefana spotted Carter leaning against the driver's door.

"Where have you been?" Carter called out to them.

"Where have we been? Where have *you* been?" Cordero demanded.

"A little girl caught my eye and motioned me to follow her," Carter explained. "I called out to you, Estefana, but you mustn't have heard me over those men playing roulette or whatever it was. The girl led me to the back of her house where chickens had just hatched. She was sweet. She wanted me to have a chicken and it took me ages to convince her that I couldn't take one with me." She stared at them and hesitated. "Why are you looking at me like that?" she asked.

Chapter 22

They went on to Suai, Cordero driving, Carter next to him, Estefana in the back but leaning forward between the front seats to be part of the conversation. Cordero gave them an account of what more he had learned from Machado. The body on the beach had a tattoo the same as the one the veteran had noticed on the arm of the man outside the home of Luana Ruiz. If this *Kobra* had led a pro-Indonesian militia around Viqueque during the lead-up to the independence referendum, that could explain why he had settled in Suai where there was less chance of being recognised and why he wasn't working for a regular employer who might have checked his background. Clearly *Kobra* had a brutal past. Stealing babies would mean nothing to him. Neither would killing them if the need arose.

What Machado had told Carter and Estefana about the Indonesian special forces officer, Tengassi, might also be critical. A special forces officer in Indonesia, even a former one, would have all sorts of connections—to police, immigration officials, border control officers, civil servants, counterfeiters, and a variety of professional criminals—and could organise smuggling operations without too much difficulty. Even getting false adoption papers, medical certificates, travel documents and the rest would create no insurmountable problem for such a man.

"Looks like the pieces are starting to fall into place," said Carter. "But who is this *Kobra*? We need to find out where he lived. In or around Suai it seems but where exactly?" Carter added, turning to face Cordero. "Any ideas?"

"Machado seemed to think that his former comrade Virgilio might have been crazy enough to kill him," Cordero said. "If we find Virgilio we should be able find where *Kobra* lived. In the meantime there could be something on this *Kobra* in the files. Estefana can check as soon as we get in. I'll get in touch with Pepe Marcelino in Dili. I'll tell him what we now know about this *Kobra* and he may be able to dig up more information. I can get him on the case first thing tomorrow."

"What about tonight?" asked Carter.

Cordero remembered their clashes over procedure, urgency and expectations. He didn't want to re-ignite them now.

"Yes, even better," he said.

Cordero would also call a friend in Viqueque to see if the police there had anything on the '*Coluna Negra*' militia in general or *Kobra* in particular. "How will we find Virgilio?" Estefana asked.

"Machado says he lives on the streets in Suai. Must be in his late fifties, early sixties. Long hair and beard. Scrounges for food apparently. Wears army fatigues and talks gibberish all the time," Cordero answered. "Shouldn't be hard to find."

"I have seen a number of people who fit that description in Suai," said Estefana.

"Then we check them all," said Cordero.

"Barita Budiwati might be staying at *Kobra's* place," said Carter. "And she may have the baby with her. Manuela Ramos said she'd taken money for gas to drive to Suai and she hasn't come back."

"That's right," said Cordero. "We can ask Buzzi to tell his officers to look out for an old blue SUV around Suai. Of course it may be garaged or disguised." He paused. "Then there's the man's van. Old, small, in poor shape, maybe white. I know you are going to tell me that matches a lot of vans in Suai as well Estefana but police can be on the look out for it all the same."

It was getting dark now and they were only a few miles from the outskirts of Suai. Cordero overtook a construction truck and blew the horn to clear a path through slower motorcycles carrying three and four riders apiece. "This Tengassi," Carter began bracing herself on to the door handle as their vehicle swerved and sped. "We need to know more about him. Where is he now? What's he doing for a living? Who are his associates? What do his bank accounts tell us? Is there anything to suggest he's been in contact with this *Kobra*? He may be a key part of the puzzle in terms of the smuggling operation across the border and delivering the babies to whoever is paying for them in the States."

"That's a job for Danique Jacobsen at INTERPOL," Cordero replied. "I'll ring her too tonight. She can get on it first thing tomorrow. Background checks, financial statements, phone records. That kind of thing."

"Good thing you ran into that veteran," said Carter in a rare hint of praise.

"Sometimes luck is on your side," replied Cordero as he drove into the streets of Suai proper and headed for the police station.

"What are you going to do about the motorcycle thief?" asked Estefana who was being buffeted around in the back.

"Right now nothing," answered Cordero. "Machado isn't keen to press charges and we have more urgent things to do." His driving reflected that.

"Izzy Pinto will keep for another day," he added.

Chapter 23

Cordero stretched and reached for his coffee which had gone cold on the desk. He had spent hours the night before on the phone, caught a few hours of sleep slumped across his desk, and wasted more time in the early hours going over files that Estefana had managed to locate in the police station in Suai where they had spent the night. "The fact that there is nothing here, nothing on this *Kobra*, is curious in itself, isn't it?" asked Carter who had only caught a couple more hours sleep than he had. "I mean if this guy was a war criminal you would think the authorities would want to keep an eye on him."

"Maybe they couldn't," yawned Cordero. "As Pepe said, records of all kinds were destroyed by the Indonesians before they pulled out. Birth records, marriage records, land titles, everything. This is a country without a written past. Unless you were living on a government handout, well, even then I suppose, anyone over thirty, forty years of age and without family connections could change their identity multiple times and pass themselves off as anyone they wanted."

"Maybe he was protected," offered Estefana, unable to stifle a yawn of her own. She had stayed with them through the night rather than return to her mother's home.

Cordero and Carter both glanced at her. "Protected by whom?" asked Cordero.

"I don't know, *maun*. Didn't you say that Izzy Pinto was being protected?"

Cordero scratched the stubble on his chin. "Yes I did. And what I heard from my friend in Viqueque was curious: no record

in police files of any activity by a militia gang called 'Coluna Negra'.
No massacre recorded. Nothing. Either our veteran is telling a lie,
although I can't see why he would, or there could be some kind of
cover-up. But who would cover up that sort of thing and why?"

"Let's see what INTERPOL turns up on Tengassi," suggested
Carter. "Maybe there's something that could prove the missing
piece in the puzzle. In the meantime I think we start looking
for"—she consulted her notes on the desk—"Virgilio Amaral."

• • •

Cordero almost collided with officer Silvano Moudino as he
headed for the washroom to run water over his face. "Hey Tino,"
Moudino said. "You seen Buzzi?"

"Not this morning. Why? I thought he'd gone to Fatuloro to
reassure the villagers."

Moudino let out a laugh. "He cut the trip short. It was a
disaster apparently. Buzzi told one of the other officers that he
took a priest along with him to address the crowd from the back
of a truck. The priest just spouted platitudes and held aloft his
Bible like Moses with his staff." He laughed again. "Only nobody
parted the way. Then Buzzi gets up and starts saying the police
will get to the bottom of all those abductions but he was shouted
down. They pelted him with clumps of dirt and banana peels. I'm
told he came back last night looking like he'd spent the day in a
rubbish bin." With a satisfied grin Moudino thrust his hands in
his pockets.

"That why you're looking for him now?"

"No. No. Not at all. The elders were holding some kind of rally
at the church after Mass this morning. Lots of people from all
over turned up, apparently. Angry about the crocodile they say
we killed. Angry about the abductions. Angry about the projects
encroaching on their land. Anyway Buzzi sent a half dozen
officers up there with tear gas. Can you believe it? Tear gas! Talk
about playing with fire. Anyway one of the younger officers fired
a tear gas canister onto his foot he was that frightened. That sent

everyone into a panic as you can imagine. I'm told a couple of officers broke ranks and ran. One dropped his riot gun. A kid picked it up and fired it into the air as a joke, and now all hell's broken loose. This is all in the last ten minutes, Tino. It could get worse. I'm trying to find Buzzi to see what he wants to do now."

With that Moudino was off again. Cordero shook his head, wiped a hand across the back of his neck and was about to enter the washroom when a shout came down the corridor from the duty officer. "They're headed this way! Everyone to the front of the building! Arm yourselves. Assemble outside. Quickly!"

Moudino came running back. "What I told you, Tino," he said as he rushed past.

"What the hell—" Carter began to say as Cordero shot back into the room. "Could be a riot," he said. "You'd better report out front," he told Estefana. "I'll take Carter someplace safe until this blows over. She's too conspicuous to be in the middle of this. Take care of yourself. Good luck."

Cordero poked his head back out the door and into the corridor. Police officers were scrambling over each other to grab what equipment they could and race outside. "Come. Now!" Cordero called back to Carter. He led her to the back door, peered out, took her by the arm and raced her across to a wire fence at the back of the police building. They could hear the commotion out front, someone shouting orders into a bullhorn and a mob howling, screaming, back. "Can you climb?" Cordero asked Carter and without an answer put his hands under her backside and almost threw her over the fence. He scrambled up the wire mesh, dropped behind her and pointed to a disused shed on the other side of the road. "We should be okay over there," he said as he grabbed her arm again and hurried off. "Nothing to attract their interest. Come on."

He forced open a door at the front. When they were inside he slammed it shut and boarded the door with scrap iron stacked against the back wall. He wiped dust off a small window that looked across to the police compound. "You okay?" he asked and Carter nodded adjusting her clothing.

"My fanny pack!" she said.

It was the only thing she'd said since they'd left Estefana and it took him completely by surprise. The word 'fanny' in the English he'd learned growing up in Australia referred to female genitalia and he had no idea why she'd be bringing the subject up now. Here. With him!

"Your what?"

"My fanny pack!" she repeated. "You know, money bag, personal items. It must've come off when you tossed me over the fence. I'm going back to get it."

"Hold on!" he said. "You can't go out there. I told you, you stand out too much. Those people are angry and they could turn on you."

"I need my gear back," she insisted. "I can't afford to lose it. I'm going."

Cordero grabbed her shoulder and pulled her back. "Wait. I'll go," he said. He rummaged around the shed, found a stretch of burlap and an empty beer can.

"What are you doing?" Carter demanded.

"The best way to go unnoticed is to make yourself conspicuous—but as someone they're not going to take much interest in," he said as he tied burlap around his waist and rubbed dust through his hair. Before Carter could respond, he was out the door and walking unsteadily like a drunkard, the beer can shielding his face. A few youths collecting rocks to hurl at the police saw him and one pointed in his direction. But the others had better things to do in an all-out brawl with the police than hassle what they saw as a homeless drunkard and went back to collecting rocks. Cordero reached the fence, stumbled around until he found the bag in the grass and shoved it inside his shirt. Then he staggered back to the shed careful to keep the pace and unsteady steps of the character he pretended to be.

As Cordero cleaned himself off, Carter took the bag, checked it and cinched it firmly around her waist. "Thank goodness," she said. "What the hell is this all about?"

Cordero scanned the scene outside buying time:

Thinking…

Considering options…

Weighing up instructions, responsibilities….

"Well?" she insisted.

Cordero pulled up two fruit crates. He positioned one for Carter in the centre of the shed and placed the other to the side of the window to enable him to keep an eye on the mob across the street. She stood her ground in front of him until he began to talk. "The government has invested a lot of time and money developing this town into a major industrial site," he said in a rush. "Remember me telling you about the gas and oil off-shore? Well to develop it means building refinery plants, a new port, and all of those things mean new highways, new airfield, you name it but all of it big, bigger than anything people around here have ever seen, and most of it on taboo land or land owned by traditional farmers. Lot of foreign money and foreign expertise behind it too."

He peeked out the window again. Over a hundred people had amassed at the police station. They were shouting at police officers along the front of the building. The more reckless youths were throwing rocks in an attempt to break windows. The officers dodged and ducked but stood their ground and did not panic or retaliate. Cordero noticed Buzzi had appeared behind the officers and taken charge of the bullhorn. For now the police were holding their line and the crowd a critical distance.

"That's angered many people," Cordero continued. "Some feel their whole way of life is under threat, particularly elders who no longer have a say in what's being done or how," he said turning back to Carter, who was sitting now and leaning forward on her crate. "Others feel that they haven't been properly compensated for the land they've had to sell. A few just don't like change. In a situation like that, people start interpreting things in ways that seem to make sense to them and rumours spread." He wiped a hand across his face. He'd reached the hard part. "The rumour around here is that those babies are being stolen by demons who sacrifice them in order to placate spirits disturbed when forests are cut down, the rivers are bridged, and buildings are put up on sacred land." He checked out the window to avoid her glare. "That rumour mainly circulated in the villages outside Suai. Many of the people we talked to mentioned it," he said, lowering his voice as he did.

"What did you just mumble?" she asked.

"I said many of the people we questioned mentioned that rumour."

Carter's eyes narrowed. "They what?" she scowled. "Why wasn't I told any of this?"

"I'm getting to that," said Cordero. "On top of everything else you have the crocodile being shot by a police officer. It was a sacred totem. That pissed a lot of people off. And it threatened to unite fearful villagers and angry Suai residents in a push against the developments." Cordero glanced up at her. "Hence," he added gesturing out the window with a thumb.

"Why didn't you tell me this stuff about the babies before?" Carter demanded.

"I was told not to. By Jacobsen. I answer to her on this assignment, don't forget. She's under pressure from the government to keep any unrest quiet. Stop news of it spreading, turning people against the government and scaring off foreign investors." He looked out the window to avoid the look of anger building in her face. "She didn't want you getting mixed up in the demon thing. You know, as a foreigner. And she didn't want you alerting your embassy about this stuff in any reports you wrote or talking to reporters and making matters worse."

"What reports? My embassy couldn't give a rat's ass about what I'm doing here. I'm here as a gesture. And reporters! We're in Timor for fuck's sake. What did you call it? Fourth World. Do you see any network film crews out there?" She stood, stamped her foot and turned away from him.

"Well, you know how politicians and bureaucrats think," Cordero said.

"Yeah. And police officers," she replied turning back sharply toward him. "Fellow officers on a case together. I know how they *should* think and now I know how you *do* think."

"I'm sorry," said Cordero, turning to face her again. "I should have told you."

"You're damn right," she spat. Carter paced to the back of the shed, her arms folded tightly across her chest. "Did Estefana know this? About keeping me in the dark?"

"Yes," Cordero admitted. "But I gave her strict orders not to tell you anything about it." He turned his sights back to the police station. "She wasn't happy about that."

"I bet she wasn't! She's smarter than you, that's for sure." She paced back and forth a moment. "And when she and you were translating conversations with victims' parents and witnesses you were holding things back?"

"I don't know what good that information about demons would have done," Cordero said. "It's nonsense."

Carter moved toward the window. "Take another look out there and you'll see what nonsense can lead to!" she said.

"Hey, get back down!" he said and pulled her away from the window. For a moment he thought she was going to hit him.

They were silent then. Cordero focused on what was going on outside the police station. There was no sign of tear gas being used and no sound of gunfire, which suggested Buzzi and the police believed the situation was manageable. But the shouting and rock throwing had not stopped and the ranks of the protesters were growing. Buzzi was trying to control things with his bullhorn, calling for 'Calm!' and 'Order!' and offering reassurance to anyone with a mind to listen.

Cordero stole a peek back at Carter. She was chewing at a fingernail. All at once she spun on her heel. "The sacrifice thing," she said. "Tell me about it."

"That comes from old folklore that big constructions require human sacrifices if they're not to collapse due to floods, typhoons or whatever."

"How would a demon rumour connecting abductions and sacrifices have started?"

Cordero considered the question. "Well, first a baby disappears. There's no obvious reason. And no obvious culprit. As a result the idea starts that something unseen and unknown must be involved. Like a demon. Because the disappearance has to be explained somehow or else people are powerless to do anything to protect themselves. Why would a demon take a baby? The only obvious thing that's happened is all the construction activity going on. The two must be connected—at least that's the general conclusion. If people beat up somebody they suspect is a demon, they reclaim a sense of control." He looked across at her and assumed a plaintive tone. "These ideas are just ways traditional people have of making sense of the world."

"I don't mean that," said Carter. "I mean what triggers the rumour?"

"Triggers it? I don't know. Someone in the community stands out for one reason or another—their looks, their behaviour—and draws attention, becomes the scapegoat. That's why you needed to be protected. You're a foreigner. You stand out. That's probably what happened in Beko."

She threw her arms in the air in frustration. "Thanks for letting me know that little detail."

"Well you weren't supposed to go to Beko," Cordero said.

"Don't start that again," she ordered, a finger pointed directly at his face. The mob grew louder. Cordero could see Carter's lips moving but couldn't make out what she was saying. The noise died. "—given us some idea of what we should be looking for, or where, or when," she was saying and sat down heavily on the fruit crate again. "I *do* know about this kind of stuff, you know Cordero. In the Navajo and Hopi reservations where I work they're called 'skinwalkers'. Whenever something happens that people don't understand they explain it away as the work of a 'skinwalker'—witchcraft. They claim to have seen a 'skinwalker' take on the appearance of a person or an animal to fool people. But you can work back from what people thought they saw to what they actually did see." She blew out a deep breath. "God, it would have helped to know that we're dealing with this kind of thing. Might have changed the whole direction of our questioning."

"That's why I was looking closely at the clothes of the dead man," Cordero said. "You know, in Brooks' rooms the first day here. When you thought I was distracted. The clothes were black, like demons are said to wear. Might have been what he was wearing if he took the stolen kids through the forest to the border. And then there were the boots like you'd wear in rough forest terrain."

"Well it's a bit late to be sharing all that now," she said.

"And that's why I split us up—to protect you from being seen as a threat by jittery people in the more remote villages." But she was ignoring him now and his excuses didn't seem to be helping matters.

The sound of the bullhorn came in waves as Buzzi directed it to one side of the mob and then the other. Cordero waited. Carter was silent for a long time. Finally he said: "I never did ask you about your family." He glanced back at her trying to look remorseful.

"What makes you think I would have told you?" she responded.

"Fellow officers on a case together?" he said, attempting a grin.

"Yeah, right," she said and turned her back on him.

After a few minutes he tried again. "Funny how this job gets you into sticky situations like this. Why did you become a police officer anyway? And why the FBI?"

She turned and looked at him. "I know what you are trying to do Cordero. You're trying to avoid talking about how you might've compromised this investigation."

He raised his shoulders to indicate he didn't know what else to do and went back to the scene out the window. The stand-off outside continued but he noticed two army troop transports pull up within view of the mob but a block from the police station. Apparently Buzzi had called for backup but kept the soldiers at bay to stop things escalating. In an emergency soldiers could be tougher than police because they didn't stay long in the communities to which they were posted and had less reason to worry about what people thought of them. As a result, people feared them more than they did the police. "We should be okay now," he said. "The cavalry has arrived." He paused, caught her eyes and looked directly into them. "I really am sorry, Carter. I should have ignored Jacobsen and confided in you." He lowered his head but raised it again. "But you know you don't exactly let people into your world in a way that inspires confidence either." And he turned back to the window.

She was furious but rather than say any more she resumed her pacing. Her role in this investigation was difficult enough but to have been kept out of the loop of what was going on made it virtually impossible. In fact her whole presence in the country was an impossible situation. She didn't speak the language or know the customs. She wasn't even sure where she was right now on a map. She looked across at the back of his head, his hair speckled with dust from the fanny pack recovery mission. It made her think. He didn't have to do that for her. He didn't even have to be in here with her when he could be standing shoulder to shoulder at the police headquarters with people he knew, people he actually liked. She felt a mixture of anger and vulnerability. He was clever, Cordero, could twist words to his advantage, but maybe there was also something in what he had said. She'd built a wall around herself—she knew that only too well—but in this environment it wouldn't protect her and might only hinder her efforts. If she wanted him to meet her half-way maybe she should be prepared to go that far herself.

The army trucks revved their motors to make their presence felt. No soldiers appeared but the mob's attention was now split between the police and the tougher troops likely about to spring from the trucks. The yelling and the rock throwing began to ease off.

"Why did *you* become a police officer?" she asked.

"Police investigator," he corrected, his back to her.

"Okay. Police *investigator* then," she snapped.

"When I decided I should come back and do what I could for my country I thought 'Do what?' Then it occurred to me. After twenty-five years of Indonesian rule, the whole of Timor-Leste had become a crime scene. I thought I'd join the police. It's my contribution. Same as Estefana, I guess."

She said nothing for a few minutes. Back and forth she went again. He kept his eyes on the mob. "That statue you showed me," Carter began and stopped her pacing. He had to re-connect the dots to follow what she was talking about.

"Yes?" he said, a little unsure.

She took a newspaper clipping from the wallet she kept in her fanny pack and handed it to him. He unfolded it carefully unsure where this was leading. It showed a picture of a young girl cradling the head of a man who lay prostrate on the ground in a pose similar to that of the statue of Sebastião Gomes they had driven past their first day together in Dili. Under the photo ran a headline: 'Daughter comforts dying father'.

"We were in a supermarket carpark," Carter began before he had a chance to read any more. Her back was turned to him. "A car had pulled up and two men shot him with a 12-guage sawn off shotgun. Point blank. He bled to death in my arms." Cordero could hear the pain in her voice. "I was fourteen."

"Why did they shoot him?" Cordero asked but there was a loud disturbance outside. Cordero jerked his head back to the window to see a dozen youths storming toward the shed. He rose, looked around for a club of some kind to use as they came through the door. He reached for an iron pipe just as the noise seemed to circle them and was gone. He checked the window. A few younger boys were running toward them but they were skirting the shed as well and taking off to avoid the soldiers.

Cordero straightened, folded the clipping and handed it back. "I'm sorry," he said and looked out of the window again to avoid eye contact.

"Don't be. It wasn't you who did it," Carter replied.

The crowd had started to break up. The women drifted off, then the older men, and finally the youths, emptying rocks from their pockets as they went. It wasn't just the threat of the soldiers: several of the elders had arrived with the carcass of the crocodile dangling off the back of a flatbed truck. Either they'd taken it from Brooks' rooms or more likely he'd had the good sense to surrender it. The elders were calling everyone to follow them to the beach to conduct a ritual burial for the crocodile near where it had been found. The demonstration, protest, riot—whatever it had been—was breaking up.

"It's over now," Cordero said watching events unfold out the window. "Peacefully, thank heavens."

In the confusion to leave the police station, some people had knocked into a street vendor pushing a large hand cart piled high with coconuts. The cart was thrown onto its side and the coconuts spilled out and had rolled across the road. The vendor, a dwarf, was trying now to collect his load as best he could but he was slow and clumsy and the coconuts had attracted a few paupers searching the rubbish in the street. "Hold on a minute," Cordero said with a start. "Over there on the side of the police station. See that man in the jungle fatigues? The one chasing coconuts." Carter bent down to follow his gaze. "Long hair, long beard. Does that look like a veteran who lives on the streets to you? Come on," Cordero said. "I think we've found Virgilio Amaral."

Chapter 24

Cordero coaxed Virgilio Amaral into the shed with the promise of something for his lunch more appetizing than a coconut. The man's hair was filthy, his clothes little more than rags and the smell of him suggested he hadn't washed in days, maybe weeks. His eyes were dark pools and wary.

Cordero sat Virgilio on the fruit crate he'd set up for Carter and gestured her to the one beside the small window. Cordero himself stood in front of the old veteran.

"Where's the food, *maun*?" Virgilio asked looking at Cordero and around him to Carter. "I see no food here."

"Soon Virgilio," promised Cordero. "Soon. First I have questions for you. This is my friend *Mana* Carter," he said pointing to Carter. "She is here to help."

Virgilio stood, agitated and turned toward the door but Cordero eased him back down. The man crossed his arms tightly across his chest, trembled, closed his eyes and started to hum.

"Virgilio," Cordero said. He didn't reply. "Virgilio!"

The man's eyes turned wild beneath the long hair that covered his head and he glared directly at Cordero. He was breathing hard through his nose. His whole body shook.

"Have you always lived in Suai, Virgilio?" he asked.

"Yes," the man answered and pointed his bearded chin upward.

"But you were once in the *Falintil*. You were a guerrilla fighter in the mountains. Is that not true?"

"Yes. No. Yes. I was," and he nodded in an exaggerated way, trembling again.

"Do you remember those days, Virgilio?" Cordero asked and placed a hand on the man's shoulder to calm him down.

"Yes. No. No!" His body twitched again.

"Concentrate, Virgilio," Cordero said. "Remember when you were fighting in the mountains."

Virgilio shut his eyes tight and creased his brow. He began to sway back and forward on the fruit crate. He rubbed his hands firmly on his trousers, breathing hard. He raised his head and pointed his beard upward once more.

"Yes. I was there. In the mountains," Virgilio agreed. He nodded rapidly.

"Where was that, Virgilio?"

"Where? Where? It was—" but he stopped abruptly, opened his eyes and then shut them again. He said nothing more.

"Was it in Viqueque?" Cordero waited. "Was it in Viqueque, Virgilio?" he repeated.

"Yes. That's where. Viqueque. Viqueque. Viqueque!"

"And do you remember any of the fighters you were there with?" Cordero asked.

"Fighters? Yes. No. Fighters? Yes. There was Avo...Ava... Avelino. And Lamberto Tutti but he was shot dead. There was Adriana. Yes. I remember her. She was a pretty girl from, from, from...very pretty! Where's the food you promised me?"

"Do you remember Ivando Machado and Ernesto Lopez—the one you called 'Che'?"

"Che?" He stood, looked around the shed and called. "Che!"

"Che's not here, Virgilio. Sit down. Do you remember Che and Ivando?"

Virgilio nodded.

"Do you remember just before the vote on independence you were on patrol above the river *Halai Makaas*? Along a ridgeline. With Che and Ivando?"

"*Halai Makaas*? No." More twitching.

"Villagers were killed, Virgilio. A lot of villagers. You, Che and Ivando witnessed it. They were shot by the militia."

"No!" he cried and trembled.

"What did you see, Virgilio."

"No! No!" he cried again and put his hands to his ears.

Cordero squatted in front of the man. He touched him gently on the knee. "It's okay, Virgilio. We are here to help." He paused a moment. "Tell us what you saw, Virgilio, that day on the ridge above *Halai Makaas*."

The man hugged his chest with his arms and again swayed back and forth. Then he stood and simulated firing a machine gun at targets only he could see in his mind.

"That's right, Virgilio. It was a massacre," said Cordero as the man slumped back on his fruit crate and his face twisted in pain. "And do you remember seeing a man named *Kobra*, leading the men who did the killing?"

Virgilio looked up, fear and hate in his eyes. He mumbled something but didn't speak and then spat and ground his spittle into the earthen floor of the shed.

"You vowed to kill this man, Virgilio. You and Che and Ivando conducting a *festa da cabezas*. Do you remember?"

"Yes. Kill him!" A far-off look came into his eyes.

"And years later you came to live in Suai. Why was that?"

Virgilio refocused directly on Cordero. "Ivando told me Che was sick and that I had to come here and help him," he said in a voice like a child's.

"And like a good comrade you did. And then you stayed. And recently you saw this man *Kobra* again, didn't you?"

Virgilio became agitated. Again he stood and simulated firing a gun and using a knife to cut somebody's throat. "You recognized him from the tattoo, didn't you Virgilio?" The man nodded. "And you decided to carry out your vow to kill him."

The man looked up, breathing heavily. Cordero waited. "I needed a weapon to kill him with," Virgilio began. "Kill him properly dead. I found the wood to make a bow and the nails to sharpen into arrows," he said. He smiled proudly. "I learned how in the mountains."

"And then you killed this man, right?"

"I *will* kill him. I promised Che. I will, I will. *Festa da cabezas*."

"But he is dead, Virgilio," Cordero said. "He was lying dead on the beach and nearly eaten by that crocodile they were protesting about over there at the police station."

"What crocodile? Dead. No. Che is dead. I will kill *Kobra*. I promised." And he struggled to control another twitch.

Cordero had been translating the essence of Virgilio's answers for Carter. He looked over at her now, confused.

"You shot the *rama ambon* into the chest of *Kobra*, Virgilio," he said turning back. "And then you dumped his body on the beach. Isn't that right?"

"Right? No. But I will kill him. After lunch. Where is the food you promised?"

Cordero ran a hand through his hair and looked at Carter. "Ask him where his weapon is now," she said.

"Where is this *rama ambon* you made, Virgilio?" Cordero asked him.

Virgilio looked around the shed, confused. "He has it!"

"Who, Virgilio?"

"Izzy."

Cordero lent in close to Virgilio's face. "Izzy? Izzy who?"

"My friend Izzy. Izzy Pinto. He took it from me," Virgilio said. "I tried to take it back but he hit me." He made a motion like a blow with a clenched fist to the side of his head. "But I'll get it back and then I will kill that man. Finish it! Kill him dead!"

"How do you know Izzy Pinto?" Cordero asked.

"Izzy is my friend," he said smiling at Cordero as though he should have known that. "He gives me food. Money sometimes. I do jobs for him and he gives me food and money."

"What kinds of jobs do you do for Izzy?"

"He tells me to pick things up. Take them to him."

"What things?"

"Things. Things that are his."

"You mean like packages?"

"Yes. Packages. That's what Izzy calls them too. Packages. He tells me: 'Go to the dock' or 'Wait for this man in Suai' and I get a package and take it to Izzy."

Cordero stood upright. Virgilio was looking from him to Carter. He was growing irritated and suddenly he stood. "Where is my lunch? My lunch! My lunch!" he demanded.

"In a minute, Virgilio. In a minute," Cordero said easing him down. "When did Izzy take your *rama ambon*?"

"When? I don't know. A week ago. Yes a week ago because after he hit me he bought me a fish to eat. It was a Friday. Good Catholics don't eat meat on a Friday, you know. The Pope told us. It was Pope John, no Paul, no—"

"How many arrows did you make?"

"John Paul. No Pope Pius, Pope—"

"How many arrows, Virgilio?"

"He say 'If Catholic don't eat fish on Friday'. The Pope."

"How many arrows?"

"Arrows? How many? One, two, three. Of course." He began to whisper as though bringing Cordero into a conspiracy. "Three I made. Must have three. One you miss. Two you kill. Three you can defend yourself if they come. We learned that in the mountains. One you miss, two—"

"When you get your *rama ambon* back, Virgilio, how will you find *Kobra*?" Cordero interrupted.

"Where is the food, *maun*? You promised me!"

"In a minute. Answer my question. How will you find *Kobra*."

"I will go to his house. How else would I find him?"

"You know where he lives?"

"I went to his house," he said then stamped his foot on the ground. "With Izzy. No more questions 'til I get my lunch. My lunch!"

Cordero asked Carter to head to a restaurant down the road from the police station and get some take-away food. "It'll be okay now. The crowd's moved away. When you get to the restaurant just point to whatever they have," he said. "I'll stay with our friend to make sure he doesn't take off."

"Why was Izzy at *Kobra's* house?" Cordero asked as Carter slipped out the door.

"Packages. It is always about packages."

"What's in the packages?"

"How should I know? They never show me. Where is my lunch?"

"Why did Izzy take the *rama ambon* from you?"

"He said I was a crazy man and could kill someone. But I'll kill that man, you'll see!"

Virgilio fell silent and Cordero began pacing the shed. Carter came back a few minutes later. Cordero was thinking through what Virgilio had told him, while the veteran sat, eyes closed, humming to himself.

"Here's your food, Virgilio," Cordero said taking a container from Carter. Virgilio reached for it. "But first you must tell me where this *Kobra* lives."

"Are you going to kill him too?" Virgilio asked and twitched again.

"No, I'll leave that to you. But you must tell me where he lives and then you can eat."

Virgilio looked at the container Cordero held and smelled its contents. Then he looked up. "In the forest," he said.

"What forest, where? And how do I get there?" Cordero asked, teasing the container before Virgilio's nose.

"What forest?" Virgilio asked, staring at the container.

"Concentrate Virgilio," Cordero encouraged him. "Yes, what forest and how do I get there?"

"Izzy drives toward Tilomar. Half way. A side road runs north before the bridge. Up the side road a little he turns again onto a track through the trees. *Kobra* is at the end."

Cordero handed him the container of food and Virgilio filled his mouth like he hadn't eaten for days. He stopped chewing and grabbed Cordero's arm. "But don't take this woman to that man's place," he said looking at Carter with a pained expression. "I have seen what *Kobra* does to women."

Chapter 25

Cordero and Carter found their vehicle untouched by the mob outside the police station. Only a few people were there now gathering up children who had run off during the excitement. Around the entrance to the building police officers were sharing cigarettes and slapping each other on the back for a job well done. Carter looked out for Estefana but she wasn't to be seen. She let it go and hopped into the passenger's seat as Cordero drove out onto the road to Tilomar.

"If that crazy Virgilio was making sense," Cordero said, "we should be at the place in twenty minutes."

Carter tried Estefana on her cell but there was no response. She looked across at Cordero.

"I hope Estefana's okay," she said. "Was he making sense?"

"Virgilio? Well he certainly was hungry enough. That food focused his mind," Cordero replied, laughing. "The directions he gave were the clearest thing he said. Probably made to memorize them by Pinto." He glanced at her. "What was in that container?"

Carter shrugged. "I don't know. I just pointed to a whole lot of stuff and when they put it in the container I covered it all in chili sauce." Her thoughts shifted. "Do you think there is a chance? That we'll find that baby, I mean."

"Well Barita Budiwati is still missing," he said, pushing the vehicle to the limits the road would allow. "We know that much. If Barita and *Kobra* were in the abduction business she was probably the one who found the babies and he was probably the one who took them across the border. He knows the territory and she has the contacts. Barita has to be somewhere and *Kobra's* place is as

219

good a bet as any since she has no family or friends that anyone knows about. If she's hiding out, she may have the baby because she couldn't get it out of the country without *Kobra's* help. She may not even know he's dead."

Cordero edged a microlet off the road and almost ploughed into the back of a truck laden with bags of rice as he sped around a blind corner. Carter clung to the strap of her seatbelt as their vehicle careened from one side of the road to the other around motorcycles and potholes. The minutes added up. She noticed the determination in Cordero's face and decided she admired that about him.

"We're halfway to Tilomar," he said. "Look ahead. That could be the bridge Virgilio was talking about. If there is a side road off it going north—yes, there it is."

He hit the brakes, throwing Carter forward in her seat, backed up and took the side road. He had to slow because it was a low-lying road and boggy at first. Once through the mud they climbed a hillock. From the top they could see a thick clump of eucalypt trees two hundred yards along the ridge. "Keep your eye out for a side road. It'll be on your side but it won't be much more than a track."

Carter noticed a trail heading off into the trees. "There!" she called, pointing. Cordero took the turn, the vehicle skidding on tufts of grass and bouncing over rocks. They drove another five minutes until a hut appeared in a clearing. "This must be it," he said and pulled to a stop at the front.

"In back! Over there!" Carter said pointing again. "Light blue SUV. Barita's!"

"You take the front door. I'll go round back," said Cordero and was on the ground and running down the side of the hut as she left the vehicle.

Carter approached the front door conscious she had no weapon and did not speak Tetun. "*Polisia!*" she tried, remembering that word at least and knocked violently on the door. "*Polisia!* Barita!" There was no response. She tried the door. It didn't budge. "Barita!"

Cordero found the back door locked. He looked around, noticed a pile of logs that had been cut to fuel a stove, grabbed one and smashed the lock. The door swung open. A nauseating smell of death assailed him.

He covered his mouth and nose and entered. A woman's body lay against the front door. A trail of blood suggested she had crawled from the centre of the front room, collapsed and died, jamming the door shut. He brushed away flies, slid the body to the side and opened the door to Carter who immediately recoiled from the smell.

There could be little doubt that the body was that of Barita Budiwati. It was then they heard the whimper of a baby. Carter stepped over Barita and the pool of dried blood and rushed toward the sound. Cordero stayed by the body. The whimper turned into a cry and Carter re-appeared with a baby in her arms.

She was a plump little thing with wisps of black hair and chocolate-coloured skin. She would have been pretty but her eyes were shut tight in sunken sockets and her lips were parched.

"She's badly dehydrated," she said. "Get filtered water from the vehicle, hurry!"

Cordero hurried to their vehicle and came back with a small plastic bottle. He watched Carter administer the water in small sips against the baby's voracious thirst. "Salt! Is there any salt?" she asked and Cordero scoured what passed for a kitchen. He found the salt and handed it to her. Carter fed a pinch into the bottle, shook it, administered more sips. "We must get her to hospital quickly. I don't know how long she has been left like this but I'd say days." She looked at Cordero. "She hasn't long."

"Put her in the vehicle," he said.

Carter left the hut with the baby. Cordero made a quick inspection of the scene. Barita Budiwati had been killed by an arrow shot into her chest. He knelt down next to the body and examined the arrow, a sharpened nail like the one that had killed *Kobra* and no doubt from the same *rama ambon*.

The woman had been facing her killer when the fatal arrow was shot. It suggested she was not taken by surprise, and probably knew who did it. Nothing in the hut seemed disturbed. Some dollar bills lay on the table in plain sight, along with car keys and a purse unopened. This was an execution not a robbery gone wrong or the result of a heated argument.

There were papers, bills and receipts in a box in the corner of the room. They were for utilities, repairs to the van, a sim card for the cell phone. The name Norberto dos Ries appeared on several. That, he assumed, was the name *Kobra* had assumed when he moved to Suai. Cordero slipped one receipt into his pocket, replaced the rest where they had been, jammed the back door shut as best he could and closed the front door behind him.

• • •

They had rung the hospital to prepare for the baby's arrival and had called the police station for a motorcycle escort to avoid traffic delays if the crowd was making its way back from the beach after the ritual for the crocodile. They arrived on dusk. Buzzi was waiting at the Emergency Department when they pulled in, Estefana behind him with several other officers.

"Excellent," Buzzi said, playing with a toothpick in the corner of his mouth as he watched Carter hand the baby over to hospital staff. As the baby was rushed to an intensive care unit Buzzi turned to Cordero. "Out on the road to Tilomar, is that right? And a woman found dead in the house? How was she killed? Any idea what happened? Who did it?"

Too many questions too fast. "Easy Buzzi," Cordero pleaded. "It's been a long day."

"Of course, of course. Me too," Buzzi said. "Tell me over dinner. I insist on buying for you and the American for an excellent job. Finding that baby will take heat out of the superstitious nonsense about human sacrifices." He dismissed all but two of his officers. One he ordered to arrange a guard on the baby. "No one sees her apart from doctors and nurses. No details given out. I don't want a new disturbance in Suai by onlookers or people clambering to see if she's their daughter." The second officer was told to send a team to the hut where Barita Budiwati's body had been found, and seal the scene until what passed for a forensics team could be mustered in the morning when rosters and workloads would return to normal after the day's chaotic events.

Carter had walked over to Estefana and was explaining the day's events. She was talking, gesturing, Estefana was smiling. "We've done well today, Tino," Buzzi whispered to Cordero. "I requested troop trucks be driven up to the station and rev their motors. Insisted the covers be kept over the back of the trucks," he giggled. "There were no troops. They're out on an exercise in Bobonaro. But it fooled that mob. They're angry still, of course, and hold us responsible for the crocodile but it bought us time. As have you, Tino. Well done. Leave the rest to us locals. You know, the dead woman, the crocodile's kill. Leave it all to us. Take a break," he said and slapped Cordero on the back. "You can fill me in on the details over a beer."

• • •

Estefana's mother, Fabiola, had invited Carter to dinner in order to meet her daughter's new friend. Now they could celebrate finding the baby as well. Carter, who had excused herself from Buzzi's celebratory dinner, was reluctant to leave the hospital but Estefana was insistent and pointed out that there was nothing either of them could do but leave the baby in the care of the doctors and nurses.

Carter went back to the guest house and showered. She relished the chance to wash her hair for the first time in days. After she'd dried herself she dressed in a pale-yellow blouse and slacks. Tonight, for the first time in days, she also brushed out her hair now that it felt soft and sleek once more. Estefana's younger brother, Rafaelo, came for her on his motorcycle and doubled her back to the house, the wind blowing through her hair as they went. It felt good. She could feel the tension of the week lift as she swayed this way and that atop the motorcycle.

A table had been set on the porch of Fabiola's house as was customary. The over-crowding typical of Timorese households, often with only blankets to separate sleeping spaces from living and cooking areas, was not something to inflict on guests, especially foreign guests. Next to where they were seated on the porch was a mandarin tree and its fragrance wafted lightly through the warm air.

Fabiola greeted Carter with a big, warm smile. She looked to be in her fifties, had a round friendly face unlike Estefana's lean fine-featured one but their eyes were the same, intelligent and sparkling with life. She was dressed in a simple pink cotton dress with big yellow and blue flowers and wore a small silver crucifix around her neck. Her hair was held back by a purple headband. Carter sat down at the table on Fabiola's invitation. Estefana, out of uniform now and in a pretty orange dress and bright red earrings, appeared briefly from the kitchen, said 'Hello' and placed two cans of warm beer on the table. Either warm beer was the norm in this house or there was no refrigerator.

"Estefana has told me a great deal about you," Fabiola began. "It is a pleasure to meet you."

"Thank you very much. You speak very good English," Carter observed.

"After my husband died, the Filipina nuns at Estefana's school were kind enough to offer me a job cooking for them. I took English language classes between cleaning up after lunch and preparing their dinner and I kept up talking English with Estefana when she left school hoping she would not lose the language. I speak moderately well."

"Better than moderately well, I'd say," said Carter sipping her beer.

The sound of laughter and thumping from children playing in the house reached the porch. Crickets were chirping in the yard and Fabiola slapped at a mosquito on her neck. "Este!" she called. "Este! Bring the spray for mosquitoes, please."

"Yes *amaa*," Estefana said and soon appeared with the spray before disappearing again.

"I didn't know you called her 'Este' for short. I like that," Carter said spraying her arms and ankles. "Your daughter is very nice. Not to mention a very good policewoman. We wouldn't have found the baby without her."

"She tells me the baby would not have been found without you," Fabiola said.

"Perhaps it's best considered a joint effort," Carter said and smiled. "She is a good policewoman though."

"I know," said Fabiola. "She could go a long way in the police force. She would like to be transferred to Dili." Fabiola bent toward Carter and whispered, "She has a boyfriend there." Then she sat back again. "But it will take a long time to get a transfer. There's a lot of activity in Suai now with all the projects and foreign workers. Police are needed here. And male officers, of course, are more likely to have their requests for a transfer met ahead of female officers."

Don't I know it, Carter was thinking.

Estefana appeared carrying a large platter. "It's a special Timorese dish, *mana*," she told Carter. "We call it *Ikan Pepes*. Fish steamed in banana leaves then grilled in lime juice, curry paste, tamarind, chili peppers, and saffron powder." The aroma was inviting, especially to Carter who couldn't remember when she had eaten last. But Estefana had more to bring—fried rice, fresh pawpaw salad—and Fabiola made no move to start eating. Carter sat stoically, tortured by the sight and smell of the food.

"You said your husband had died?" Carter asked to get her mind off the food. "Do you mind me asking what happened?"

"Not at all," Fabiola said. "I will tell you about my Aniceto. But first, when you were in Dili, did you notice an island called Atauro?"

"Yes, I did," said Carter. "It was a long way off and very hazy."

"It usually is hazy. Until recently Atauro was one of the remotest places on earth I've been told. Perhaps for that reason when the Indonesians were here they used it as a prison. It was where they tortured people. People who they thought worked for the resistance." She tittered. "Well, I can tell you that was most people in Timor. Some were fighters, some supported the fighters, others were merely protesters working for our independence but peacefully." Her tone turned serious again. "My husband was one of the latter. But that was enough for the Indonesian military to send him to that place. He was there three years. Afterwards he was never the same. It was the beatings and the conditions he was forced to live in. He died a few years after independence. The doctor said it was heart failure."

She sipped from her can of beer. Carter made no comment. "This is a habit I picked up from Aniceto," Fabiola continued raising the can. "Drinking beer. We would often have one together sitting outside on summer nights." She was quiet a moment, wistful. "I was angry with him at first, you know. For his political activities. But mostly for his dying and leaving me with the children to raise on my own. But now I see my children growing up in a free Timor-Leste and I am proud of my husband for what he did and grateful that he had the courage to stand up for what he believed in. I remember one of the nuns quoting your Reverend Martin Luther King." She sat up straight as though giving a presentation. "'If a man has not discovered something that he will die for, he isn't fit to live.'" She relaxed again and took another sip of her beer. "That's how I think of my Aniceto now. But tell me about your own family. You must be missing them."

"I have no family," Carter said. "My father is dead and my—" she started to say and ran a hand through her hair.

"Yes?"

"My mother left us when I was five years old. He remarried and had another daughter. My half-sister. I never liked my stepmother, I'm afraid."

"You say your mother left?"

"Walked out. Apparently my father didn't make enough money for her liking," Carter said, brow creased. "It happens in America. Here in Timor you seem much more family-oriented, less self-centred."

"Oh yes," agreed Fabiola. "We are that. It is how we survived during the Indonesian times. Sharing food, watching out for each other. It has its disadvantages. You see we are related to many, many others and there are responsibilities toward each of them. When my husband and I married, he became responsible not only for me and our children but, after my father died of tuberculosis, for my six sisters who had not yet married, and for two other sisters and their children because their husbands had also been killed during the Indonesian times. That is a big burden. It is the same for most Timorese—all of these people to whom we are obligated. That is why few are interested in better jobs or higher salaries. The more you earn, the more that is expected of you by your kin. The foreigners think we are lazy. We are not. We just do not want to be working harder and harder for the benefit of all those relatives."

Estefana came with bowl of salsa made with a variety of fresh chilies. This time she sat next to her mother and gestured for Carter to serve herself.

"I would not be too hard on your mother," Fabiola continued. "We do not always understand why people do what they do or what consequences flow from it."

"But to leave your child?" Carter protested.

"I hear children in America leave their parents all the time," said Fabiola. "When the parents get old they are put away and not visited. Here we respect the old. They live with us until they die. And after they die we honour them regularly." She scooped fish and rice on to her plate after Carter had served herself. "Of course, that is another responsibility we have," she added and grinned in Estefana's direction. "Tell me about your father and your sister."

Carter seemed choked for words. Fabiola saw the tears well in her yes. "Never mind, my dear. I'm just a meddling old woman who asks too many questions."

Carter regained composure. "Not at all," she sniffled. Then she laughed the emotion away and they started eating.

"Spicy enough for you, *mana*?" Estefana asked.

"Delicious," Carter replied.

They were soon hearing stories of Estefana's antics as a child, comparing descriptions of Arizona and Timor, laughing, drinking more beer. After the meal Estefana cleared the dishes and came back with a bundle wrapped in paper. She seemed excited. "*Mana*," she said, "we have a gift for you," and she handed Carter the bundle. Carter looked at Estefana then Fabiola.

"Thank you," she said. "What is it?"

"You must open it, *mana*," said Estefana.

Carter did and withdrew a length of woven cloth like a shawl but longer and in brightly coloured bands of yellow, pink and blue with a pattern of delicate triangles and squares woven down the middle band in red. It was a beautiful piece of handicraft.

"It's a *tais*, *mana*," explained Estefana taking the weaving off her and placing it around Carter's shoulders. "When a Timorese person gives you one of these it means you have become part of their family," she said and kissed Carter gently on both cheeks.

Tears welled in Carter's eyes and Estefana stood back embarrassed.

"I'm sorry, *mana*—" Estefana began to say.

"No, no, please," said Carter wiping her eyes. "It's amazing. Very pretty. Thank you."

"You are part of our family now, *mana*," said Fabiola touching Carter's thigh softly. "Please regard this as your home away from home."

Chapter 26

Early next morning Cordero found Carter asleep in a chair outside the intensive care unit at the hospital. After the dinner she had declined a lift back to the guest house and walked instead, enjoying the warm, peaceful night. Without consciously planning it she found herself outside the hospital and decided to check on the baby. There were no new developments but she thought she'd stay close, had found the chair and nodded off after the busy day and one too many beers at Estefana's house.

Police were searching the hut where the baby was found and the body of Barita Budiwati was lying on a slab in Brooks' rooms. The autopsy would confirm that the arrow that had killed her was the same design, using the same type of nail, as the arrow that had killed the man on the beach—now believed to be the former militia leader *Kobra*. Despite Carter's skepticism about reporters in Timor-Leste, a couple of young students working freelance for outlets in Dili were filing stories on the recovery of Elisanda Soares and trying to tie it to the bigger issue of stolen babies in the area. Buzzi was heading to another elders' meeting determined to gain access this time and deliver the news of the girl's recovery and the discovery of her abductors. He had instructed officers around Fatuloro to call similar meetings in villages where babies had been taken.

Cordero placed the coffee he had bought himself on the floor next to Carter's chair. He'd get another later. He watched her sleeping and gently removed a strand of hair causing her eyelid to twitch. He checked his watch. It had just gone eight o'clock. He had slept in. His cell phone rang. It was Jacobsen and he asked her to hold while he walked outside blinking into the dazzling sunlight.

"You heard the news," he said working his jaw in an effort to fully awaken.

"Yes. Well done," the old warmth had returned to her voice. "Needless to say the PM is very pleased. There might even be a citation in this for you, Tino."

"Yeah, right," he said. "Ask him to turn it into a cash bonus and see what he says about it."

"But that's not all the good news I have for you."

He rubbed the back of his neck. Waited.

"This Indonesian, Tengassi," she began. "Seems he was a high-ranking officer in the Indonesian security forces. Nasty fellow." Cordero was longing for coffee. "Saw ten months duty in East Timor running militia operations prior to the referendum. Then back to Jakarta for a while before a posting in Ambon. Earned a reputation there for cruelty to separatists. On to West Papua. Responsible for at least two massacres there connected with questionable dealings in gold."

"Where did you get this information?" Cordero asked. "And this fast?"

"I'm getting to that Tino," Jacobsen replied. "Don't rush me this early on a Monday morning." He could hear the sound of papers being shuffled. "Political changes in Jakarta saw Tengassi's faction in the security services fall out of favour. That's why we were given this information so readily. He's been on a watch list for the past year or more. His opportunities for corruption are drying up fast. And that's why he may have turned his attention to making easy money by smuggling babies to rich Americans. He still has powerful connections in high places. Probably holds dirt on others. That's why nobody has moved against him yet. And that's how he could arrange to get kids out of the country. But his options are narrowing and fast now by all accounts."

Cordero was pacing up and down outside the hospital. He noticed through the doorway that Carter had stirred and discovered the coffee. "Here's where it gets really interesting,"

Jacobsen was saying. "Not only has Tengassi been making calls to various officials in Indonesia who are involved in adoption and migration services, he's also been making calls to a cell phone in Suai around the time of each baby's disappearance. Again, this information came from the people keeping an eye on him in Indonesia but they hadn't joined the dots. The cell in Suai is owned by a Rosaria Surito. She may be the key person at the Timor-Leste end of the operation and those people who've turned up dead accomplices working for her."

Cordero had stopped pacing. Where had he heard that name? Rosaria Surito. Was she on the list of workers in the outreach clinics around Fatuloro? No. She could be a nurse. That was it—a nurse, a nurse involved in a robbery whose name he'd heard from Silvano Moudino.

"Do you have the cell number?"

Jacobsen did and he wrote it down.

"Is that all?" he asked.

"Isn't that enough? It's only been 36 hours since you called me," she replied.

"Yes. True. Great. Thanks," he said. "Talk to you later."

He called Silvano Moudino.

"Hi *maun*," he said when Moudino answered. "Tino here."

"Hey Tino," Moudino said. "Turned out all right yesterday, *maun*. Bit of damage to the building but no injuries, no arrests. Heard you're a hero. Found that kid. Well done."

"Thanks but listen. When I was asking you about Izzy Pinto you mentioned a robbery you arrested him for. Victim was a nurse? What was the name?'

"Surito," yawned Moudino. "Rosaria Surito. Saw her again just last week. Rosaria Narciso now. Remember? She married. Pregnant I think. What's this about Tino?"

"Do you know if she's working at the hospital these days?"

"Far as I know, yeah. You need medical attention?"

"I'm fine," replied Cordero. "I'll explain later. Thanks *maun*. I owe you."

"Nothing Tino."

How likely would it be that a newly married Timorese woman would be using her maiden name on her phone account, Cordero wondered? Or would be using her maiden name on calls connected to the theft of babies anyway? He passed Carter with a curt "Back in a minute" and headed down to the nurses' station.

"Is Rosaria Narciso on duty this morning?" he asked the nurse at reception.

"Let me check," she said startled by his sudden appearance. She clicked a file on her computer and waited for it to open, in no hurry despite Cordero's finger tapping. "Yes," she said. "She's in the maternity ward this morning until lunchtime." Cordero looked left and right. "That corridor on your left," the nurse said and pointed.

He found Rosaria Narciso checking the dials on an old humidifier on the far wall of the ward. She looked to be in her late twenties, her hair in a loose bundle down her back, concentration in her eyes.

Cordero identified himself and asked if she would mind following him into the corridor to talk. "You were robbed about a year ago, is that correct?" he asked when they were outside the ward.

"Why yes. A bit late to be asking now isn't it?" she replied.

"You're right. I'm asking in connection with another case. What was taken?'

"Taken?" She thought a moment. "Well, let me see. As I recall there was a purse, earphones I had just bought, my engagement ring, cell phone. Why?"

"Did you get everything back?"

She stared at him a moment.

"Most of it."

"But not all?"

"Not the cell. The police officer said it wasn't among the items recovered."

"Do you know the name of the police officer who gave you back your property?"

"It was the police superintendent. Basilio Modesto. Such a nice man."

Cordero thanked Rosaria Narciso and headed back to Carter. She was standing now, stretching. "Morning," she said rubbing her eyes. She collected her things. He noticed the coffee cup empty beside the chair.

"Sorry. I had some quick questions to ask a nurse while she was on duty. How's the baby?" Cordero asked.

"Touch and go, I think," she replied. "Boy, do I need a shower!"

"No time," he said. "Where's Estefana?"

"Sleeping I hope but probably at her desk working. Why? What's up?"

"Call her. Tell her we'll pick her up in five minutes. Tell her to bring her service pistol if she can and not to say anything to anyone. I'll explain on the way."

Chapter 27

"Izzy Pinto is the key to this," Cordero declared as he drove them to the address west of Suai he had taken from the files. Moudino had assured him it was current. "He had a get-out-of-jail card from Buzzi," he said. "That meant for a bit of information here and there he could easily have a lot of what he was up to ignored by the police. He knew *Kobra*. They were both smuggling. That may have given him the idea to graduate from drug running to baby trafficking if there was more money in it. He had taken Virgilio Amaral's *rama ambon*, probably after a dispute with *Kobra* over payments knowing that the weapon could be traced to Virgilio who made no secret of his intention to kill *Kobra*."

He was swerving recklessly to avoid other vehicles. "He could have hidden that cell phone he'd taken from Rosaria and Buzzi would not have known it was stolen when he took everything else back to her. She mentioned it wasn't among the items returned and by then Izzy had been let loose. He then uses the cell to take instructions from Tengassi about what type of baby to steal and when. *Kobra* would have given him the contact." Cordero cleared his throat. He was lamenting his lack of morning coffee.

"To cap it off, he kills *Kobra*, takes his body to the beach in his van, dumps the body and the van, steals a motorcycle and rides to Dili to screw a girl in order to have an alibi for the time of the killing if something goes wrong. Barita Budiwati had to be gotten rid of or else she could have blown his identity." Cordero glanced across at Carter. "Sorry," he said.

"For what?" asked Carter.

"The bit about screwing the girl," he replied.

"Estefana and I are all grown up now, Cordero," she said suppressing a grin. "In case you hadn't noticed."

Cordero coughed again, adjusted his position behind the driver's wheel.

"Wouldn't Izzy be a bit young to be involved in an international baby-smuggling ring?" asked Carter.

"People grow up fast in Timor-Leste," he answered. "Look at Virgilio. He was fighting the Indonesians in the mountains at fourteen."

"Point taken," she said as he shifted into a lower gear to accelerate around a microlet crammed with people and their goods.

"What kind of information could he have given Superintendent Modesto," Estefana asked leaning from the backseat and clutching Carter's headrest.

"Good question," said Cordero. "I'm not sure. I'd say petty stuff. Drug houses. Prostitution services for the foreign workers. Vehicle thefts. Those kind of things are turned into statistics and big numbers look bad for police superintendents trying to justify their positions. That's why it would have been valuable information for Buzzi." Estefana nodded, seeing sense in that. "But I'm only guessing," Cordero added.

Izzy Pinto lived in a sparsely populated area on the outskirts of Suai where a faint smell of sewerage seeped through the ground. Cordero pulled up a hundred yards from the house and cut the engine. There was little to conceal their approach to Izzy's house beyond this point and the road appeared to be bordered by an embankment which might be difficult to climb if he managed to scamper over it. There was a motorcycle at the side of the house, its front wheel lying on the ground awaiting repair. The house was a shabby cement block structure behind a chain wire fence. No other vehicles were in his yard or in the street.

They could hear reggae music coming from the house even at this distance. Someone was home. The noise meant it would be hard to hear anyone approaching from outside. Maybe the occupant was too absorbed in the music to notice anyway.

"Okay. Who's doing what?" asked Carter.

"You two stand out because you're a foreigner and Estefana's in uniform," Cordero said. "I'll make my way around the back of the house. You get behind the wheel. That way Estefana can get out quickly with her sidearm. Give me three minutes then drive up to the house. If I haven't flushed him out, Estefana, you go to the front door but be careful. This guy's already killed twice."

Cordero slipped out of the driver's seat and Carter shuffled across to replace him. Estefana climbed over the centre console into the passenger's seat and checked her firearm. They watched as Cordero ambled down the road casually and then ducked quickly into the smoke from a smouldering fire in the vacant block next to where Izzy lived. He seemed to check the fire and poke around in the ash for a moment then clambered through an opening in the wire fence and was inside the rear of Izzy's yard.

They waited. One minute went by. Two minutes.

Carter noticed Estefana staring at the pistol in her hand. "If you're not sure about it, leave it, or it could bring you a whole lot of grief," she said.

Estefana looked across at her. "We've had training in firearms, *mana*, but I've never had to use one. I don't know that I could—"

"Shoot someone?" Carter said finishing the statement for her. "You never know until you have to and then, if you don't, you could be the one who ends up injured or worse."

They waited. Another minute went by in silence. "Here goes," Carter said to Estefana and shifted the vehicle into gear.

As she pulled up outside the house, the front door burst open and Izzy bolted out into the street. Cordero was behind him but slipped on discarded bottle lying on the porch and crashed heavily onto his side. Estefana took a breath and reached for the door handle but Carter pulled her back. "Stay here. He's mine!" she said and leapt out of the driver's seat.

Izzy took to the embankment, knowing a route that made it quickly scalable. But only wearing flip-flops he lost his footing half way up and rotated his arms in mid-air like the sails of a windmill trying to regain his balance. Carter caught up, managed to grab an ankle and slide him back down the incline. He took a wild swing at her which she blocked and countered with a swift kick to his stomach. Izzy doubled over but she saw him grab a rock after he'd tumbled onto the road and steadied himself. As she approached his fist clenched around the rock and his expression turned desperate. She poised to strike but then straightened and wagged a finger at him instead. She imagined him weighing up his chances. He met her gaze. Her eyes seemed to bore right through him. He lent forward to take her on but crumpled from a sharp, burning pain in the muscles where she'd kicked him. He blinked, dropped the rock and she helped him to his feet.

• • •

"He's stoned," said Cordero as he sat Izzy down on a chair, cuffed his hands behind his back and turned off the music. "The smell of it nearly knocked me out from the back door." He rubbed his side. "Leave the front door wide open, will you? Get a breeze through the house to clear this gunja. Estefana can you make coffee for our friend here, please, and don't spare the sugar?" He shot Carter a glance and lowered his voice. "This could work in our favour. The effects of the dope just might ease his reluctance to talk."

Izzy Pinto was unshaven, his unwashed hair in a bun at the back of his head. He had tattoos of a tiger on his back and another of a scorpion down his right arm. He wore boxer shorts and nothing more. He'd left his flip-flops at the embankment.

"Are you going to read him his rights?" asked Carter.

"This isn't the United States and he's not Al Capone," Cordero answered her.

"I take it you learned police procedures watching Dirty Harry movies," Carter said.

"Dirty Harry was fond of guns. Guns are dangerous if you act on impulse."

The sugar and strong coffee soon brought enough sense back to Izzy Pinto for him to be interrogated. Cordero sat in the chair opposite, staring into Izzy's face, Carter and Estefana stood to one side as there were only two chairs in the room. The table was covered with newspaper—the single man's idea of a tablecloth. The house was sparsely furnished: the table, the two chairs, a lounge that had seen better days, the ghetto blaster, a TV with a missing leg propped up on a cardboard box, a large poster of Bob Marley on the wall. In the only bedroom was a mattress on the floor, a video camera pointed at it, and a laptop connected to the camera.

Cordero began with the smaller offence hoping to draw Izzy slowly into the bigger one rather than scare him into silence straight off. "Tell me about the motorcycle," he said.

"What?" replied Izzy.

"The motorcycle. You know what I'm talking about," Cordero said.

"I hit a pothole, *maun*. Bent the front wheel," said Izzy. He looked puzzled. "I'm fixing it. You arresting me for that?"

"Not *that* motorcycle," said Cordero. "The red Kawasaki 250cc Cruiser."

"Don't know what you're talking about, *maun*," said Izzy.

"Yes you do, Izzy," Cordero corrected him. "I know you stole it and rode it to Dili. Nazaria de Oliveira told me." He smiled and lent in toward Izzy. "You really shouldn't give such a big bike to such a little girl, Izzy. She ended up in hospital."

There was a flicker of alarm in Izzy's expression. "Nazaria? Hospital? She okay?"

"Then you do know her," Cordero said. "Bad slip." Izzy shuffled in his seat, fidgeting, looking even more nervous. Sweat appeared on his forehead. "Where did you steal the bike?" Cordero asked.

"Where?"

"That's right. Where?"

"Don't know. Don't know what you're talking about."

"I'd say near a beach. After you'd driven a van with something you needed to dump. We can come back to that. Let's move on," said Cordero. "What's your relationship with Norberto dos Reis?"

"Who?" asked Izzy.

"Norberto dos Reis," Cordero repeated. "You know, *Kobra*, if he used that name."

"Don't know who that is," Izzy insisted.

"I think you do," said Cordero. "I have a witness who says you two worked together. Smuggling operations."

"Don't know what you're talking about," said Izzy.

"You're repeating yourself," Cordero said. "You're telling me you never saw this guy, never knew him, never visited his place north of the Tilomar road," he said.

"Yeah. That's what I'm saying," Izzy said.

"How about Barita Budiwati?" asked Cordero. "Remember her?"

"No. I don't remember any of these people because I never knew them."

"Okay. Let's try Virgilio Armaral," said Cordero.

"Who?"

"Come on Izzy, you know. People have seen you two together in Suai. You give him lifts, buy him lunch. He does odd jobs for you."

"You mean that crazy old guy in town? Yeah I know him," Izzy admitted. "Help him out once in a while. That's all."

"That's very noble, Izzy. Helping a former guerrilla fighter. Very noble," Cordero said. Izzy merely shrugged. "Did you take his *rama ambon* in return?" Cordero added.

"His what?"

"His *rama ambon*, Izzy. You know, the bow and arrow," said Cordero. "The thing you killed the man and the woman with."

It happened quickly but Cordero was alert to it. Izzy's eyes shifted ever so slightly, ever so quickly to the block next door and back.

"Officer dos Carvalho," Cordero said. "Go outside and check that fire smouldering on the adjoining block. Rake through the ashes. Look for a makeshift arrow. You know the type." He titled his head and looked Izzy in the eye. "The arrowheads are made from iron nails, Izzy. Iron doesn't burn."

Cordero lent back in his chair. Izzy's eyes shifted nervously, sweat ran down his face. Cordero let the tension build. Nothing like silence, he knew, to unnerve a suspect. "Let's go back a bit," Cordero began after a minute had passed. "A year ago you robbed a house owned by Rosaria Surito. Remember Izzy? You were caught fleeing the house by Officer Silvano Moudino. He took the property you stole but not Rosaria's cell phone. How did you hide that?"

"I don't know what you're talking about."

"There's a lot you seem to have forgotten, but this is a matter of police record."

Izzy sniffed. Rubbed his nose against a shoulder. "The police took everything. Cell too," he said.

"Everything?" asked Cordero but Izzy didn't answer.

"Superintendent Basilio Modesto let you walk on that offence. Why was that?"

"I don't know," Izzy said, trying hard not to seem startled at the mention of the name.

"You work for Modesto, don't you? An informant, is that right?"

"You're crazy, *maun*."

They could hear Estefana coming back into the house, Izzy's eyes darting nervously in her direction. She carried in her gloved hand a blackened nail that had been sharpened and barbed. She placed it on the table between Cordero and Izzy.

"Well now," began Cordero. "I'd say that's the third arrow Virgilio made, wouldn't you?" He looked up at Estefana.

"I'm not saying any more," Izzy cut in. "You can't make me."

"No I can't make you, Izzy," replied Cordero. "But that," he said, taking a pen from his pocket and poking the nail with it, "is enough to convict you for the murder of two people. The best thing you can do to help yourself now is to cooperate." He waited. "When you killed Barita, why did you leave the baby?"

"What?" asked Izzy, fixated on the nail.

"The baby in the house with the woman," said Cordero. "You went there and killed her but didn't touch the baby. Why not?"

"I don't know what you're talking about," said Izzy, this time more insistently. "I'm no baby killer."

"Time to be smart, Izzy," Cordero said. "Tell us about the baby."

Izzy looked up, confused. He lifted and dropped his shoulders in a gesture of 'no idea'.

Carter was following Estefana's translation of the interrogation carefully and watching Izzy's reactions. "The baby was in the back room," she reminded Cordero. "It might have been asleep. He might not have known it was there if he was only in the house for a few minutes."

Izzy looked across at Carter as though noticing her for the first time. The presence of an American woman was making this whole ordeal seem even more unreal to him.

"True," Cordero said in English to Carter. "But he knew it had been snatched and he would have figured Barita had it with her." He focused on Izzy again. "Did you take your instructions from the Indonesian?" he asked. "Tengassi?"

"What? Who?" said Izzy.

"Tengassi," repeated Cordero. "The Indonesian who told you what babies to steal. He called you on that cell you stole from Rosaria Surito."

"What? You're talking crazy, *maun*," Izzy said shaking his head. "Why are you asking me about babies? And Indonesians I never heard of? I told you, I didn't have that woman's cell. The police took it. Modesto took it."

Cordero looked up at Carter as he translated this, calm enough, but she could read surprise in his expression. He looked back at Izzy who was fidgeting with his cuffed hands. "I didn't have no cell," Izzy repeated.

That's when Carter noticed it.

"Ask him why Buzzi was here?" she said.

"What?" Cordero replied, glancing back up at her.

"Just ask him," she insisted. "Why was Buzzi in this place? At this very table."

Cordero looked doubtful but he put the question to him. The blood drained from Izzy's face. He shifted his gaze from Cordero to Carter and back again.

"What?" asked Izzy trying to wipe his eyes on his shoulder

"Ask him again," said Carter. "Tell him we know Buzzi was here only a few days ago. Why?"

Cordero asked the question again but Izzy fell silent, wriggling his cuffed hands, jiggling his legs.

"We have enough evidence to convict you for two murders, Izzy," Cordero pointed out. "And we know you're involved in the kidnapping and international smuggling of a dozen babies. Unless you cooperate, you'll be inside a prison for the rest of your life. I'll make sure of that. No pretty young girls in prison, you know." Izzy looked up. Jiggled some more. "The opposite in fact," Cordero added for emphasis.

Izzy sniffed. He looked from Carter to Cordero and at the nail on the table. Cordero was twirling the nail around and around before Izzy's eyes.

"I don't know anything about babies," he said. "Does this place look like I care about babies? Do I look like I care?" Izzy's voice was near hysterical now but his eyes seemed mesmerised by the nail.

"I think that part is true," Carter broke in. "The babies. He doesn't seem to have any idea what you're talking about. But put it to him again. Why was Buzzi here?"

Cordero asked a third time. Izzy's face contorted, he started to cry.

"I don't know what you're talking about—"

Carter bent across the table, picked up the end of a toothpick in a gloved hand and held it in front of Izzy's eyes.

Chapter 28

"You ever taken a close look at a toothpick?" Carter asked Cordero. They were driving back to Suai now, Izzy Pinto in back next to Estefana, watching out of the window as freedom drifted by. The arrow Estefana had retrieved from the fire was safely tucked away on her other side. Carter had a small section of toothpick wrapped securely in her pocket.

"Well I've seen Buzzi chew a few," Cordero replied. "But no, I can't say I've taken much notice of it."

"What did you say back in Fatuloro? It's the things we're familiar with that we tend to overlook," said Carter. "Maybe that's why you didn't notice it."

The sky was darkening. Black clouds folded in upon themselves, and the breeze gathered strength over *Tasi Mane*— Timor's male sea.

"Some toothpicks are turned at the end," she explained. "You break it off. Use it as a kind of stand when you want to take the rest of the pick out of your mouth and sit it on the table for a while. Like the thing you stand chopsticks on. Only smaller." She looked around at Izzy. "I noticed it on his table when Estefana put the arrow down and Izzy started staring at it. You might have noticed the sheets of newspaper he had covered the table with. They were dated the day before Budiwati was killed. I can read dates on newspapers even in Tetun." She looked across at him and grinned. "The piece of the toothpick was on top of the paper. So it hadn't been put there any earlier. Buzzi uses toothpicks. Only person I've seen here who does. I remembered him breaking off the end of his toothpick over dinner that first night I met him. He rested it on the table in that restaurant just like that as well."

"How did you come by this expertise in toothpicks?" asked Cordero.

Her smile broadened. "My dad used toothpicks too. He'd often let me break off the end for him when I was a kid. Kind of a treat."

"Strange how simple little habits can bring you down," said Cordero as he turned into the grounds of the police station in Suai. "I remember reading once about an African dictator who feared his people that much he had to be driven around in a bulletproof limousine. Trouble was he couldn't stand air conditioning. When it was really hot he'd always tell the driver to wind down the windows instead." He pulled into a parking space and turned off the engine. "No surprise really, but the rebels waited for a very hot day and shot him through an open window."

• • •

Cordero told Estefana to hand Izzy over for charging on two counts of murder and to secure the *rama ambon* arrow and the end of the toothpick in the evidence locker. Buzzi had stepped out for lunch but was due back any minute. Cordero pulled Officer Silvano Moudino aside. He glanced at Carter who nodded and made herself scarce. This was a matter solely for Timorese to deal with. Then Cordero and Moudino walked to a room at the rear of the building where Cordero explained what they had learned while they waited for Buzzi to return.

A few minutes later Buzzi came back in high spirits. They could hear him complaining in colourful language about the wind as he walked to his office. Cordero gave him a moment to settle in. Then he and Moudino entered Buzzi's room without knocking.

"What?" Buzzi looked up puzzled by their sudden appearance. He peered from one to the other of the men standing before him, read their expressions and straightened in his chair.

"We brought in Izzy Pinto," Cordero began. "He told us everything, Buzzi."

"Izzy? Izzy Pinto? He's a small-time crook. Can't be trusted. What are you talking about, Tino?" Buzzi replied trying to lighten the mood. "What's this about? What did he tell you?"

"I'm talking about you ordering the murder of Norberto dos Reis and Barita Budiwati."

Buzzi's expression turned abruptly dark.

"Tino. You're crazy. What are you talking about?" he asked.

"Izzy told us everything," Cordero said. He noticed Buzzi's jaw set firm. "You ordering him to kill Norberto because he was drawing attention to your baby smuggling operation. Then telling him he'd have to kill the woman or she could identify him as Norberto's killer."

Buzzi offered no reply.

"Told us he used a *rama ambon* on Norbeto, then dumped his body on the beach for the crocodiles. Told us where the van he used to move the body had been left. Told us how you sent him to Norbeto's place to kill the woman, and how he hit a pothole riding back on his motorcycle because he was upset at what you'd asked him to do. Confessed to everything and implicated you in the lot."

Buzzi shuffled papers, rose, walked to the front of his desk. Through the window the palm trees were pitching wildly and the pane began to rattle.

"Tino," he said and stared at the floor.

"I'm sure when we search your vehicle, your house, this office, we'll find Rosaria Surito's cell as well," said Cordero. "And, of course, we'll check your finances."

Buzzi's looked up sharply. "Cell?"

"The one you used to get the particulars of which babies to take and when. Let's try it now."

Cordero took out his own cell and punched in the number he'd got from Jacobsen. Immediately a whirring sound came from inside the cabinet in Buzzi's office. Cordero ended the call on his cell. The whirring stopped. He stared accusingly at Buzzi.

"You'll never prove anything Tino. There's no evidence. *Kobra—*"

"Is dead?" said Cordero completing the statement for him. "You knew Norberto dos Reis as *Kobra* then. That's interesting Buzzi. I never called him by that name in your company. Norberto dos Reis is the name I found on some paperwork in the place where the dead woman was found. *Kobra's* place. What did you do before independence? Work with a pro-Indonesian militia? Is that how you got mixed up with *Kobra* and the Indonesian, Tengassi? Are you responsible for the files on the '*Coluna Negra*' in Viqueque going missing? I happen to know you were posted out that way for a while. We'll check that as well."

Buzzi moved back around his desk and made to open the top drawer but Moudino stopped him, checked inside the drawer, and shook his head at Cordero.

"Cigarettes," Buzzi said. "That's all." And he took them from the drawer. "What did you expect, a gun?"

"We know Tengassi gave you details of which type of babies to take. We know Barita Budiwati found the ones that were a close enough match and abducted them. We know she then passed the babies on to *Kobra* who took them across the border. Any details you'd care to add?" asked Cordero.

"Tengassi," Buzzi said. "You'll never get him."

"Why not?" Cordero said. "Friends in high places in Jakarta?"

"Hardly," Buzzi said. "Enemies. They hate him. But he has dirt on all of them. If they bust him, they all go down as well."

"How did you get tied up with him?" Cordero asked. Buzzi didn't answer. "What was is it my friend Pepe from the gang taskforce in Dili told me recently? With the destruction of records in 1999, anyone could conceal their identity and become anyone they wanted. Is that what you did Buzzi? Hid your past as an informer for the Indonesians?" Buzzi looked grimly at Cordero. Said nothing. Then Cordero asked: "Why did you have *Kobra* killed, Buzzi?"

Buzzi produced a cynical laugh. "Greed. He was greedy." Cordero waited. "When INTERPOL became involved I wanted to shut it all down. But Tengassi wanted another kid and then another. I said no. But *Kobra* agreed. It was too much of a risk, I said. He wouldn't listen. I had to stop him. Look at what it's led to with all this superstitious shit. *Kobra's* greed and that damned crocodile. What a combination!" Buzzi looked up at the ceiling. "In a way I'm glad it's over."

"And Barita Budiwati?"

"I knew she would do whatever *Kobra* asked of her—even find babies for a bastard like Tengassi. She must have been in love with *Kobra* though I don't know why. But I never actually knew her. All I knew was that she was desperate. You know how these women can get. No family. No friends. No prospects. That's why she fell for him, I guess. With *Kobra* gone, she had nothing to live for. Besides, as you and that American came close to tracking her down, I figured she'd be the one blamed for those kids. If she was dead that would've been the end of the story. Case closed."

Buzzi humphed. He took a cigarette and rolled it through his fingers.

"What was the hold you had over Izzy?" Cordero asked. "Surely not just petty drug-running operations?"

Buzzi shook his head. "Don't go too hard on that boy," he said.

"Izzy Pinto is a killer," Cordero pointed out.

"He's not right in the head," Buzzi responded. "His father's long dead. He was a fellow I once knew. I took over fatherly responsibilities on his death. Guess not too well."

"And the babies?" he asked. "What about the babies, Buzzi?"

"They would have been better off with rich American parents than raised out there," he said, his voice raised and the hand that held the cigarette pointing to nowhere in particular. "You know what it's like Tino. No food, no proper health care, no prospects."

"And no dumpsters to wind up dead in," Cordero added. "But you didn't do it for them, did you Buzzi?"

Buzzi stared at Cordero but went silent. "Time to go Buzzi," Cordero said.

"Moudino," Buzzi said and put the cigarette to his lips. "A light please."

Moudino approached him and took out his lighter. He struck it under Buzzi's cigarette before suddenly finding himself spun to the wall with a gun to his head.

Buzzi had moved with surprising speed and agility for a man of his age and build. He had grabbed the arm Moudino had offered the lighter with, twisted him enough to expose his right hip, and slipped the pistol out of its holster.

"I know you don't carry a gun, Tino," he said to Cordero. "But I'll have your cell."

Cordero held his hands open in front of his chest. "Don't do this Buzzi," he said.

"The cell!" Buzzi demanded.

Cordero reached into his pocket and threw his cell on the desk. Buzzi ordered Cordero and Moudino to sit back-to-back on the floor. He reached into his bottom drawer and extracted a pair of handcuffs. He clipped one cuff to Cordero's right wrist and the other to Moudino's left wrist around the leg of his heavy desk. He pocketed the key along with Cordero's cell and pulled the cord to his desk phone out of the wall. He picked up Moudino's lighter and struck his cigarette.

"What tipped you off?" he asked, as he stood before the two men, the pistol pointed loosely at them. "A policeman's curiosity?" he added by way of explanation.

"You left the end of a toothpick on Izzy's table," said Cordero.

"A toothpick?"

"The American spotted it."

Buzzi shook his head. "And they say cigarettes are bad for you," he said and grinned through a cloud of smoke. He went to a filing cabinet in the corner of the room, unlocked it and lifted out a strong box, his eyes on Cordero and Moudino. He opened the box and scooped out a thick wad of notes into a large paper bag. "What better place to hide valuables than a police station?" he said and grinned again.

"You won't get away with this Buzzi," Cordero said.

"I've gotten away with far worse," Buzzi said. Then he peeked out his office door and slipped quickly down the corridor.

Chapter 29

They shouted out for help. After several minutes an officer came to check on the noise and alerted others while he released Cordero and Moudino. One of the other officers said he saw Buzzi head out the back of the station and speed away in a police car.

"He won't try for the border in a car," Cordero said. "He knows we'll notify the checkpoint."

"His only other chance is by sea," Moudino said.

Outside the wind roared in from *Tasi Mane* and lashed across the town. Trees were bending sideways, branches blew off. People scurried for cover. A woman with two small children slipped and fell, spilling her shopping. Another came to help through a whirlwind of paper and plastic rubbish, her skirt billowing as she wrapped her arms around the children. Cats were slinking into drains and dogs barking madly. The few gulls that had taken to flight were blown backwards. Windows and doors slammed shut. A man was tossed off his pushbike and blown along the street.

They took a car and headed for the port area. Cordero had instructed other officers to spread out around Suai in case Moudino's hunch was wrong and Buzzi was heading east along the coast road or north toward Fatuloro and the deserted forests bordering Indonesia. He told Carter to stay put in the police station but she took no notice of that and joined Estefana and another police officer in a car patrolling the town for Buzzi.

Out to sea, massive white-capped waves crashed onto the beach and over the end of the old pier in an explosion of froth and foam. An old cargo ship was bobbing recklessly, its rigging torn from the spars. Several canoes left too close to the water's edge had been sucked back into the sea and were being tossed about in the swell.

Cordero had just made the shoreline when he saw the police car parked awkwardly against the seawall. Far off a figure was pushing a canoe with an outboard motor through the waves. He threw open the driver's door and a gust slammed it shut on him. He tried again and managed to slip out of the vehicle. Moudino also struggled to free himself but was able to force his way out and around the vehicle to Cordero's side. Driving rain stung their eyes and the noise of the storm was deafening.

"Look there!" Moudino shouted and pointed to a man on the sand struggling to find his feet.

They pushed through a flurry of sand and rain toward the man. He was a fisherman. Blood was flowing from a deep gash across the side of his head. They helped him stand but he stumbled again and slumped heavily in the sand. "He's crazy, *maun*," they could just hear the man yelling through the howl of the wind. "He took my boat. I tried to tell him it isn't safe. I was dragging it off the beach. He hit me and took it anyway." The man touched his head and looked at the blood on his hand. "It will fill with water quickly in this storm," he shouted up at them.

Cordero could see Buzzi trying to head west toward the border. But the choppy water rendered the outboard motor useless against the swell and the wind was pushing Buzzi toward mangroves at the far end of the beach.

"Let's get him into Buzzi's car," Cordero called out to Moudino indicating the injured fisherman and the two of them helped the man back to the roadside. Cordero told Moudino to stay with the man while he went after Buzzi. "He won't get far in this storm and I expect he'll take a dumping before he crawls out in those trees down there."

"Be careful, Tino," Moudino shouted back.

Cordero drove along the seafront. Carter and Estefana passed him heading in the opposite direction and they told the officer who was driving to make a quick turn and follow. Cordero hadn't noticed them. His eyes were on Buzzi as he was thrust by wind and swell closer to the mangroves. Cordero pulled up as close as the road allowed. Leaning into the wind he made for the trees, just as Carter and Estefana pulled up and ran from their car.

"Stay here!" Cordero yelled when he saw them but was uncertain if they could hear him. He could see Buzzi was yelling as well but the sound of the wind and the sea made it impossible to hear what it was he was saying. Cordero gestured for Buzzi to paddle inward toward him, the outboard now completely water-logged. Buzzi took no notice, alternately working the pull cord on the motor and cupping water out of the canoe which was now on a dangerous tilt.

Cordero pushed further into the mangroves. He slipped on submerged roots, fell waist deep into the fetid water, and thought he caught sight of a large, serrated tail slither underneath to his right.

"Cordero!" Carter screamed after him. "Tino! Tino!"

Buzzi was only thirty yards from Cordero now but in deeper water. Cordero gestured again for him to paddle in but it was hard to see through the rain and the spray. Again a sudden swirl to Cordero's right caught his attention but he let it pass. He scaled a mangrove for a better view of Buzzi. Banknotes were blowing out of the bag Buzzi had put the money in and he lurched out frantically to catch what he could. Cordero saw the canoe yaw, capsize and the police superintendent plunge into the water.

The upturned canoe floated off to the side of a whirlpool where Buzzi had gone under. He resurfaced in a flurry of arms and legs struggling for purchase on the hull. His hands slipped on the rounded surface once, twice, until he managed to heave himself higher and get a grip. The sea lifted him and thrust him closer to the trees. Buzzi's head turned and Cordero could make out the look on his face—a mixture of relief and resignation.

Cordero even thought he caught him smile before Buzzi was gone, pulled violently from below.

Chapter 30

She'd called to say she'd be walking along the seafront on the *Avenida de Portugal*. He found her sitting on a bench staring at the statue of Sebastião Gomes. He parked his vehicle, approached and sat down next to her. He pocketed his sunglasses sensing something wasn't quite right and didn't say a thing. He lent forward and studied his hands.

"Do you know why they sent me here?" she asked, her gaze on the statue.

"Sent?" he said, surprised. "I thought you'd volunteered."

"I was sent. Gotten out of the way, actually. It was my superior's idea." He waited. "Goes back to when I shot someone." He looked at her, not quite sure how to respond. Her voice was flat. He pursed his lips and looked back at his hands.

"I'm sure you had your reasons," he said, wondering where this had come from.

"Oh I had my reasons," she said. "Only none of them were strictly legal."

He waited.

"What did you say about Dirty Harry and guns? They can be dangerous if you act on impulse. You're right there." She took a deep breath. "I was a cop in Missouri. We burst into a house where a ten-year-old girl was being held for ransom. Two ex-cons had taken her. They were stoked high on meth but just wily enough to keep us guessing for three days."

She looked down at the ground.

"Finally tracked them down. When I entered the room, I saw the girl bound, gagged, naked. One look told me she'd been raped. One of the guys, the smarter of the two, was in the room. We'd frisked him and made him sit on the floor cuffed. The other agents had left the room to deal with the second guy and get an ambulance for the girl. The bastard on the floor could see what I was thinking. 'Real juicy at that age,' he said to me and grinned. Even now I can hear his voice and see that look on his stupid face. I shot the fucker." Carter wiped away a tear. "In the thigh. Man did it feel good to see him thrashing around in agony!" She paused for a moment. "It was written up as an accidental discharge of a firearm. Everyone knew the guy was a scumbag. I received a caution. That was it. After a while my chief suggested I try out for the FBI. Said he'd bury the record of the caution and give me a glowing reference. Removed me, in other words."

She turned to face Cordero.

"It happened again in Arizona recently," she continued. "Not as bad, no shooting. But I beat the crap out of a guy who'd raped a little Navajo girl. A partner helped me cover it up. But whispers, gossip, you know, they follow you and my supervisor wanted me gone before I did even worse on his watch." She paused. "That's why I'm here."

"Why are you telling me this now?" he asked.

She sat up straight and gestured toward the statue. "Remember that newspaper clipping I showed you. It goes back to that. I'm looking to set my dad's death right somehow. You asked me why he was shot? It was over Bec—my half-sister, Rebecca. The guys who shot my dad were abducting her. She was eight years old. I've never seen or heard from her again. Every time I go through a door to rescue a kid in my head I'm thinking 'Will I find Bec there?'" She looked at him. "How do you let go of it, Tino?"

He tapped his feet and rubbed a hand across his face. "You don't," he said. "You never can. But that's grief, not anger. You have to keep the two separate. Look at this place. Think of all the killing and dying that's gone on here. Timor-Leste is a country full of tragedy. But we memorialize it. That way, it's contained as grief and doesn't consume us as anger. If we confused the two, we'd all go mad."

They sat in silence a while. "I may be ready to separate the two," Carter said. "Until I came here, met Estefana," she looked at him and smiled, "met you too, of course, I didn't realise how alone I'd become. Kind of a shell I grew myself into, I guess. Easy to feed your own grief with anger if there's no-one else in your life to pull you up and stop it." She took her gaze back to the statue and they simply sat there, together.

Children were playing soccer around the statue and a small boy kicked the ball toward their bench. Cordero sprang up to intercept it. He dribbled the ball, called "Hey" and passed it to Carter. She rose and kicked it back to the boy.

"Thanks mister," the boy said to Carter and ran back to the game.

• • •

On the way to the INTERPOL office Cordero had to drop a report on the Suai assignment into his own office. It was overdue—as usual. Carter followed him through the door. Lucas Rama Savoy and Manuel Fonseca were sitting at the terminals just as they were when Cordero last visited. When Manuel laid eyes on Carter, her face, her figure, he spilled his coffee on his trousers as he sat up straight while Lucas remained where he was staring with his mouth open.

"Officer Lucas Rama Savoy and Officer Manuel Fonseca," Cordero said flicking a hand in the direction of the two officers by way of a hasty introduction. "FBI Special Agent Carter."

The two officers seemed dumbstruck. Then Manuel managed to utter: "*Bondia Mana Candy.*"

"*Bondia,*" Carter answered and smiled at the two officers. Cordero dropped off the reports, took her gently by the arm and led her out of the room.

"*Mana Candy*?" Carter asked Cordero as they walked down the corridor.

"Um...it's a Tetun expression for 'respected one,'" Cordero explained. Carter stopped to challenge that translation but he kept walking toward Jacobsen's office.

• • •

The INTERPOL director greeted them warmly. "Your report was very thorough, Agent Carter," Danique Jacobsen said. "Although you may have given Tino too much credit." Jacobsen looked across at Cordero. "And we—that is, the Prime Minister and I—are very grateful for your assistance. INTERPOL has issued a red notice for the arrest and extradition of Tengassi," she continued. "But as you probably know that means little unless the Indonesian authorities cooperate." Cordero and Carter were seated uncomfortably on the plastic chairs in Jacobsen's office enduring her debrief as best they could. "And he has people in Jakarta who will frustrate that. So I don't expect any further action to be taken against him. But at least his baby trafficking racket has been closed down and little by little—" she said and let the comment trail off.

"And Izzy?" asked Carter.

"Well that's up to Tino's people, not INTERPOL," said Jacobsen.

"He'll spend quite a bit of time in prison," Cordero explained. "Probably do him the world of good."

"But I have some more good news," said Jacobsen reaching for a file on her desk. "Another baby has been located in California." She opened the file and consulted the first sheet. "A doctor treating a couple became suspicious that their adoption could occur as quickly as it had. He ordered tests done, did some checking. Reported a series of anomalies that are being investigated and we're waiting for the full results. But it seems reasonably certain that this is another baby who's been taken from East Timor. A boy." She replaced the file on her desk. "With two babies recovered, including—thanks to you—the village chief's, local concerns should lessen considerably. And with Buzzi gone the way he has, those people upset by the death of the crocodile will feel things have been set right as well."

"Maybe it's true what they say about crocodiles only eating bad people," said Carter.

They finished the coffees Officer Furaha Oodanta had been sent to get them. "Well I guess that's mission accomplished, Danique," said Cordero and rose to leave.

"Not so fast," the INTERPOL director said. "Special Agent Carter has ten weeks to go on her secondment with us. We need to talk about what she will do."

Cordero looked at Carter, who appeared amused. "The next case on your agenda?" she suggested.

"We have a huge backlog of alleged war crimes to investigate," said Jacobsen. "After a softly, softly approach for many years, the government is coming under a good deal of pressure to hold people to account for what happened in this country. We don't expect charges to be laid, mind, and we certainly don't expect prosecutions. That is far too politically and diplomatically sensitive. But we do need to produce a report—a kind of truth and justice report—in order that something at least is on record."

"I haven't had experience in that field but I'm willing to give it a go," said Carter. "On one condition."

"And what's that my dear?" asked Jacobsen. "I'm sure we can accommodate any reasonable request."

"I'm sure Tino has other cases that will keep him busy. I don't speak Tetun," answered Carter. "I will need a translator. Could you arrange for Officer Estefana dos Carvalho to be transferred from Suai to this office in Dili to work alongside me?"

About the Author

Chris McClellan is a regular visitor to East Timor where he has been involved in media development initiatives and conducted research into the communication of agricultural science in remote mountain communities. He is a former journalist whose work has been published in Australia, the US and the United Kingdom and has taught politics, philosophy and communication skills at four universities in Australia. He has authored or co-authored a number of non-fiction books on subjects as diverse as US-Cuban relations, clerical sexual abuse and religious sociology. He lives in the Blue Mountains west of Sydney, Australia.

About the Author

Chris McGillion is a regular visitor to East Timor where he has been involved in media development initiatives and conducted research into the communication of agricultural science in remote mountain communities. He is a former journalist whose work has been published in Australia, the US and the United Kingdom and has taught politics, philosophy and communication skills at four universities in Australia. He has authored or co-authored a number of non-fiction books on subjects as diverse as US-Cuban relations, clerical sexual abuse, and religious sociology. He lives in the Blue Mountains west of Sydney, Australia.